Scrumptious

Amanda Usen

sourcebooks
casablanca

Published by Sourcebooks Casablanca, an imprint of Sourcebooks, Inc.
P.O. Box 4410, Naperville, Illinois 60567-4410
(630) 961-3900
Fax: (630) 961-2168
www.sourcebooks.com

Printed and bound in the United States of America.
QW 10 9 8 7 6 5 4 3 2 1

*For Ben, as always, my hero,
my inspiration, and my world.*

Chapter 1

MARLENE BENNET EASED THE WATER BATH OF CRÈME brûlées out of the oven and ignored the ominous sounds of all hell breaking loose on the hot line. Her palm ached to wrap around the handle of a sauté pan. Her fingers itched to grab a pair of tongs and take control of the grill, but that wasn't her job anymore. She ruled the bakeshop now, and really, it was better this way. She gritted her teeth and kept her hands steady on the steaming hotel pan, taking slow, measured steps toward the baker's rack to avoid sloshing hot water on top of her custards.

She slid the tray home, smiling a little. Even though the urge to take action on the line traveled through her veins like napalm and nearly made her head explode, it couldn't detract from the pleasure she felt at the sight of a dozen beautifully set custards.

"Marlene!" Olivia's harsh shout turned her small smile into a grin.

She checked the croutons in the other oven and set five more minutes on the bakeshop timer. Croutons were sneaky. It was dangerous to leave them alone for too long.

"Marly! Get up here! I'm in the weeds!"

Marlene dodged around her rack and the stainless steel prep table, hung a sharp right, and scooted through the narrow hall. The dry heat smacked her in the face as she stepped behind the line, and she took a deep breath, tasting the air to see if anything was burning. The heat of the grill brought a welcome looseness to her tight muscles and a happy flush to her cheeks. Olivia, her boss and best friend, stood staring at a long line of tickets.

Marlene reached across her line of vision to set the timer in the hot-line window.

"What's cooking?" Olivia asked, olive-green eyes curious behind too-long, stick-straight bangs. She had the rest of her blond hair confined in a neat braid down her back. She was a straight-up kind of girl in most ways, actually. Her body was lean, her posture excellent. Even her earnest expression gave the impression of candor and linear thinking. The only thing to escape rigid control were her bangs, and Olivia did everything she could to contain them.

Marlene pulled a pair of tongs off the oven door, soothed by the feel of the familiar tool in her hand. "Croutons. Where's Keith?" She asked the obvious question. The board was full of tickets, but Olivia's husband was nowhere in sight. She kicked a pile of slick grilled vegetables, compliments of Keith no doubt, under the floor mat for later sweeping.

"Don't know, don't care."

"Yeah, right." Marly stuffed her craze of multi-colored brown curls beneath her toque. Her hair corkscrewed in five different directions on a tame day, and it was safe to say one or two pieces of cheesecake weren't going to help or hurt her figure. Luckily, lush was coming back in.

Olivia threw onions and peppers into her sizzling pans. "I'm not dragging Keith's sorry ass back up here today. He's working tonight. I only asked him to come in for lunch because Danny called in sick." She ducked to check the lone steak sizzling in the oven, and Marly hoped it was sweat, not tears, she wiped out of her eyes.

Her crouton timer buzzed, and a second later the one in the bakeshop went off too. "Hang on."

When she returned, Olivia picked up their conversation. "What are you doing tonight? Can you meet me at the bar after service?"

"At this pace, we can walk over together." Marlene flipped three chicken breasts on the grill, checked the board, pulled two pieces of salmon out of the cold drawer, seasoned and oiled them, then laid them on the hot side. The flames rose up, but she was already pulling down hot plates for the next table.

"Nah. We've only got sixty on the books tonight. I'll leave as soon as we plate the last reservation. Keith can close."

"If you can find him," Marlene said dryly, but not without sympathy. Not entirely.

Olivia pushed a plate into the window with a little more force than necessary and had to wipe the rim.

"You can't work double shifts forever, Olivia."

"I know. Neither can you. Just meet me at Johnny's around ten. I have a surprise for you." A smirk replaced her frown.

"I hate surprises," Marlene reminded her.

"You'll like this one."

Marlene narrowed her eyes and crossed her arms, leaning against the counter. She glanced meaningfully at the smoking grill and began to count backward from ten.

Olivia caved in time to save the salmon. "Joe Rafferty is coming through town tonight."

Marly laughed in delight as she flipped the fish. She had only seen Joe in person once, at Olivia's wedding, but she had paged through the wedding album countless times just to imagine him naked. Tall, dark, and delicious—even in two dimensions—Joe Rafferty had the kind of lethal sex appeal that made her think dirty thoughts, apparently not an uncommon reaction among women. According to Olivia's culinary school stories, he had slept with every available female, a few unavailable ones, three mail clerks, and at least one chef instructor during their two years at the Culinary Arts College. With rolling admissions twelve times a year, the number had been getting up there by the time he graduated. She imagined a night with Joe would be an experience to remember. Fondly.

Olivia brought her back to the present by sliding four hot plates in front of her. "He's on his way to California, but he's going to visit his dad in Kentucky first. Since New York's on the way, he's stopping in Norton. Think of it as a gift."

"I don't mean to sound ungrateful, but it took you long enough."

"The opportunity didn't present itself. I don't know why you're complaining. You have plenty of local guys to torture. You know Danny hasn't dated another woman since you slept with him, right?"

"Not my fault. Strip poker. I lost. What could I do?"

"Marly, you only lose on purpose, and poor Danny just works here to be near you."

Marlene shrugged, unrepentant. "You shouldn't have hired him."

"I would have been stupid not to hire him. He's a

darn good grill cook. Do me a favor and stop having sex with him, though." Olivia gave her a censorious look. "That's what people usually do when they break up with someone. It's considered humane."

"Aw, but he looks so sad, and he asks so nicely."

"Hence Joe. Joe is not nice. You can't break his heart, and since you don't seem to have one, I don't have to worry about him breaking yours either. You guys are two sides of the same coin."

"How do you mean?" Marly put the plates in the window and buzzed the waiter for pick-up.

"Joe moves around the country like you move around Chameleon. He gets bored easily too."

Marly laughed, then realized Olivia was serious. "Are you kidding me?"

"What?" Olivia asked. "You aren't going to tell me you're sick of the bakeshop now too, are you?"

Marlene stared at her friend, deeply regretting that she had made up that lame excuse for quitting the hot line. How could Olivia not realize what was going on? They'd known each other for almost half their lives. No matter what Marly had said six months ago, Olivia should know better. Cooking was her life, and Keith Watson was a no-talent hack. Marly shook her head. "You know I love the bakeshop." And the restaurant. And her friend, although at the moment she wanted to strangle her.

"Good." Olivia stretched until her spine popped. "I've got to get prepped for tonight."

"Keith's coming back for his shift, right?"

Olivia nodded uncertainly. "You don't have to stay. Like I said, there's only sixty on the books."

"Sixty will turn into a hundred, and you know it," Marlene warned.

"Anthony can help."

"The salad boy? Yeah right. He's been working here, what? A week? Admit it. You need me."

Olivia sighed. "I'll get you out as soon as I can. Thanks, Marly. I know you don't want to be on the line, and I appreciate your help."

I don't want to be on the line with Keith. Marlene forced a smile to her lips but didn't say what she was thinking because her salmons were done and it was time to fire the next table. She was afraid she'd lose if she forced Olivia to choose between her and Keith. Wasn't that the way it always worked? Staying out of the fray in the bakeshop was getting more difficult by the day, but sharing the line with Keith was not an option. Despite his culinary degree, the man could not cook, and Olivia stood by her husband, seemingly oblivious. Marlene stopped that line of thought before it could hurt and concentrated on the orders.

Right here, right now, for this table, she could make it right. Her world would steady itself for the moment too, thanks to the satisfying lunch rush. She'd get her fix.

"Fire table six," Marlene said, taking control of the board as another flurry of tickets hit the spike.

When the rush died down, Marlene returned to the bakeshop with a happy buzz of anticipation rolling around her brain. Joe Rafferty was coming through town tonight. How perfect was that? No fuss, no muss—just a good time with no expectations of commitment. Some might call that shallow, but her absentee dad and three stepfathers had taught her that low expectations were rarely disappointed. She brushed crouton crumbs into the trash can and wiped down the butcher-block table with hot, sudsy water, scrubbing at hardened chocolate residue as she tuned in to the late-afternoon waiter chatter.

"Better hope Olivia cooks it," she heard Shane, her favorite server, declare as he breezed into the back room, closely followed by Beth, his new trainee.

"Cooks what?" Marlene automatically asked.

Shane dropped his tray in the adjacent wait station and began pulling lunch salads from the reach-in while Beth filled two sidecars with the house dressing. Beth was eager and very young, dewy even, but Marlene liked her anyway.

Shane lounged against the table while Beth began to slice bread for the baskets. "Keith is out front chatting up the tables again. I was telling young Beth here that if the customer wants *the best paella this side of Spain*, she better hope Olivia cooks it." He paused. "Tuck your thumb in. I don't have time to take you to the emergency room." Beth moved her thumb out of the path of the serrated blade and blushed.

"Be nice," Marlene chastised him.

"I'll be nice as long as I don't have to wait for my plates. But that ain't gonna happen. 'Cause Keith is off again, and this time I don't think he's in the dining room, if you know what I mean." Shane gave Marlene a loaded look. "Oh well, at least my paella won't taste like a shoe on fire, even if I do have to make my own drinks."

"What do you mean, Shane?" Marlene gave him her

own meaningful look, an evil dominatrix glare no gay man could resist.

"Let's just say I'd stay out of the dry storage room if I were you. Wouldn't want to catch something nasty." Shane swept toward the dining room, enjoying his exit line, carrying salads, bread, and a confused Beth along with him.

Shit. Shit. *Shit*.

That floozy bartender had been trouble from the minute she walked in the door wearing fake eyelashes and bright pink lipstick. Every time Nikki walked by, Marlene expected her platform heels to light up like stripper shoes. Keith wouldn't dare fool around while his wife was on the premises, would he?

Marlene wiped her hands on her rag and slipped out of the bakeshop.

She could hear Olivia safely calling back orders from behind the line, and the late servers were busy watering tables. No one witnessed her slick, Pink Panther–esque tiptoe down the back hall. She stepped around the dry goods delivery and silently opened the door to dry storage.

Spices, garlic, and just the faintest hint of damp, earthy potatoes perfumed the air. The small room was divided into three sections by tall, stainless steel, commercial shelving. Above the onions and potatoes on the bottom shelf, large cans of tomato puree, clam juice, and just about everything else under the sun blocked Marlene's line of sight. She edged forward. In the split second before she stepped around the last bank of shelving, she hoped the rhythmic bumping sound she heard was the dish machine echoing down the short hallway.

No such luck.

Keith was hip deep all right, boning away, his checked pants around his ankles. Nikki was braced on the broken ice machine with her eyes shut and her mouth open, holding on for dear life as her high heels clacked together behind Keith's back.

Marlene couldn't stifle a snort. He still had his chef coat on, for God's sake. Now *that* was lazy. "Zip it up, buddy. You are so busted."

Nikki's eyes snapped open, and Keith's butt tensed. They froze, mid-bump, which made Marlene laugh until she heard a sharp intake of breath behind her left shoulder. Her heart dropped into free fall as Olivia's quiet voice cut the sudden silence.

"You're fired too, Keith. And homeless. Get out of my restaurant. Get out of my house. I'm so finished with all of *this*." Her disgusted wave encompassed the sweaty pair, the dry storage room, the restaurant, the whole damn state of New York. Marlene swallowed the sudden lump in her throat and blinked away the flash of hot tears. She felt guilty for being fiercely glad Keith had finally done something Olivia couldn't ignore. Without Keith, things would get back to normal around Chameleon. The restaurant had suffered enough under his hands and, damn it, so had Olivia, whether she knew it or not.

Keith scrambled to yank up his pants, eyes wide over his shoulder. "Livy, you've got it all wrong—" he began.

Olivia shook her head slowly. "Don't even start. I'm not stupid, and I know this isn't the first time. But I am done. Just get out. I'd rather do every goddamn job in this place by myself than pretend you're not a waste of space for one more minute. I mean, you couldn't even wait until service was over?" She checked her wristwatch. "You couldn't keep your dick in your pants for another hour, give or take your smoke breaks? It's asking a lot, I know. Well, don't let me stop you now. You two can finish in the parking lot"—her hard gaze swung to Nikki—"which is where I'm sure you've had most of your experience."

Nikki's dark eyes shot wide at the insult, but Olivia turned her back before she could respond. "Get them out of here, will you?" she threw over her shoulder as she walked swiftly back down the hall toward the line.

Marlene heard Shane call another late order, and Olivia answered back, way too calmly. "Do you think I'm fired too?" Nikki asked, bouncing her boobs back into her hot pink, front-clasp bra. Thank God she'd already pulled her skirt back down. Marlene had seen enough for one day.

"I think that's a safe assumption," she replied.

Nikki glared at Keith. "You are going to be in so much trouble." He flinched as her fake nail stabbed him in the shoulder. She gave him another quick shove before she flounced out the door, making good time despite her impractical shoes.

Marlene eyed Keith, who was still fumbling with his zipper.

Two years ago, when Olivia had brought him home, he had possessed a wiry, whipcord strength under his culinary school padding and a relentless charm that was hard to resist. Now, like many other night chefs, he was blurred around the edges from too much rich food and too many late nights at the bar. His charm had dissipated too.

"She can't fire me! I own half this restaurant!" Saliva flew from his wet lips.

"Are you sure?" Chameleon had been a graduation present, not a wedding present, and she wondered gleefully what the courts would have to say about that.

"You have to talk to Olivia for me. She listens to you." A fact Keith had never been happy about before this day. "It will never happen again. This was the last time."

Unbelievable. She shook her head. "Are you kidding me? I'd never take your side in this." He hadn't even apologized, for God's sake. "We've been covering your ass for way too long."

"You're just jealous because I went to culinary school, and you didn't. Chameleon is the only game you've got," he shot back with a sneer.

"Hardly. Any restaurant in town would have me."

"You mean every chef in town *has* had you."

"At least I'm not married, asshole."

Keith finally got his pants fastened and brushed past her, all righteous indignation and bruised ego, still trying to bluff like a kid caught cheating on an exam instead of a grown man cheating on his wife. "I'll be back," he said.

"No worries." Marlene trailed him to the parking lot. "I'll cover your shifts."

He flipped her the bird, and she returned his sentiment with a double thumbs up before heading back into the restaurant to find Olivia.

Chapter 2

Joe Rafferty swung his long legs out of his Jeep Cherokee and slammed the door. The tiny parking lot behind Chameleon was nearly empty, but habit had made him park on the street to leave the lot free for paying customers. He approached the back door, breathing in the familiar restaurant smell of old, damp grease. The screen door swung open in his hand. He locked it behind him.

The kitchen was silent. The dishwasher's door was down, cycle finished, and the stainless steel table in front of the industrial-size machine was stacked with the dark-red, perforated floor mats used to cushion tired legs and provide a less slippery surface for spills. Wet pans, plastic containers, metal and wooden spoons and spatulas were neatly stacked beside the machine, so he assumed the dishwasher was busy distributing clean dishes around the kitchen.

He picked his way through the debris on the floor and grabbed a stack of six pans, the size he figured Olivia would use in the sauté station. He carried them through the tiny dish room to the hot line, set them down in the serving window, and looked around, nodding to himself. She had a nice set-up.

Walking past the hot line, he turned left and passed through a narrow hall into a large room. In front of him, he saw the door to a walk-in refrigerator, held open by plastic trailers tossed over the top of the door. A stainless steel table and two full-size racks formed an island in the middle of the room. Along the wall to his left were two stacked deck ovens, a small electric stove, and a closed door, presumably the business office. On the other side of the racks was a small bakeshop.

Unable to resist, he walked over to take a look in the glass-front reach-in refrigerator. His eyes skated over the dessert menu taped to the glass. Just as he tugged the seal loose on the refrigerator, he heard the walk-in door swoosh shut behind him.

"Hold it right there, cowboy!" Olivia's welcoming drawl brought a smile to his face.

"You left the back door unlocked, kiddo. No telling who's gonna walk in." He tried to frown, but he was too damn glad to see her. He held out his arms instead, and she slid into them, giving him a tight squeeze.

"With your sweet tooth, I thought you might have put on a few pounds over the years," Olivia said as she laughed up at him.

"I move around too much to gain weight." Joe turned her around to face the dessert cooler. "In fact, I'm starving. Can I do some quality control for you?"

Olivia snagged a dessert plate from the cart of clean dishes parked in the bakeshop. She looked inquiringly at Joe, and he pointed at the chocolate cheesecake.

"Good choice." She slid a piece onto the plate but held it just out of reach. "Ah, ah, ah! We can't forget the garnish!" She piped whipped cream onto his plate from the bag in the cooler and then added a few raspberries, chocolate-covered espresso beans, and a fork.

Joe ignored the utensil and picked up the whole piece of cake with his fingers. He dragged it through the pile of whipped cream and took a large bite. Cool, rich flavors exploded in his mouth, exciting and comforting at the same time. This was no dessert for amateurs.

"Heavy duty," he said, swallowing, enjoying the nutty aftertaste of the chocolate and hazelnut crust.

"Over a pound of bittersweet, four shots of espresso, and enough dark rum to knock you on your ass."

"Your recipe?" he asked.

"Nope. My friend Marlene does all the desserts."

Her expectant smile begged him to ask, "Is she good-looking?" The role of lady-killer was so easy for him to play that he slipped into it without any effort at all. That was the problem.

"Don't you remember? You saw her at the wedding. She was my maid of honor," Olivia said.

"Redhead?"

"Not this week, but yeah, that was her. You can refresh your memory in a few minutes. She went over to Johnny's to grab us a spot at the bar."

He definitely remembered the redhead. Great rack. Nice ass. She'd had curves that made him want to strip off her blue satin bridesmaid's dress and explore how her body came together. He probably would have too, if he hadn't gotten called home to the hospital. That had been the beginning, his mother's first surgery.

Joe redirected his thoughts to the redhead. His cock stirred. She was hot all right. Or else this cheesecake was even better than he thought.

Olivia untied her apron and folded it into a neat square. "Joe, I need your help," she said.

"Anything, kiddo."

She boosted herself up onto the prep table and stared

at her lap. Then she blew out a deep breath and met his eyes, but she didn't say anything. He stopped chewing for a moment to examine her. Her eyes were clouded, not their usual keen green, and she was stalling. Very unlike Olivia. She was a straight shooter, a bottom line, no bullshit, get-it-done kind of girl, which was why they had become such fast friends in culinary school.

Joe set his plate down and leaned against the table, waiting.

She finally spoke. "I need a chef."

"What happened to Wonder Boy?" Joe tried to look surprised.

She stared at the ovens behind his head. "He couldn't keep it in his pants."

He said nothing. It was the kindest thing he could do. He had never hidden his opinion of Keith Watson.

"It won't change things too much around here to have him gone, really," Olivia admitted. "He's been a lazy pain in the ass for at least a year. Marly and I have been working doubles for weeks. I'm exhausted and bitchy and strung out, and if I have to break down one more stupid chicken or peel one more potato, I'm going to lose it. Just freakin' lose it, I swear!" Olivia's voice, which had been gaining steam, trailed off. "I don't want to give him the satisfaction of seeing this place go under without him. And I can't do it alone."

Admission of weakness from Olivia was the equivalent of a nervous breakdown from anyone else. That fact alone told him she must really be up against a wall. He frowned.

His plans had been set for months. He had to be in Kentucky by the Fourth, then in California by the second week in July to audition for a resort job with killer benefits, two of the three things he'd promised his mother before she died. Joe shook his head, thinking hard, trying to rearrange the details.

"Don't say no, Joe. Just think about it," she begged.

"I'm on a tight schedule, kiddo. Give me a minute. How'd it get so bad?"

"Heck, I don't even know." She brushed her hair out of her eyes. "One little thing at a time. Partying with the waiters. Then a few other women. I ignored it. If Keith had just been able to pull his weight in the kitchen, I could have made it work, but I can't do my job, his job, and run the business too. Not if he's going to start screwing around with the staff." Olivia paused. "It doesn't help either that Marlene hates his guts."

"She's good-looking and smart? I like her already. Can she cook?"

"Anything that doesn't cook her first." Olivia sighed. "My parents would have sent her to culinary school with me, but she refused to go. She said someone needed to be here to cook while I was gone."

"Can Marlene be your chef?" he asked.

Olivia shook her head. "She flat out told me she couldn't stand to be on the line another minute. Can't blame her. We both know it's a bitch of a job."

Joe nodded. "Only an idiot would want to cook for a living."

She smacked his arm. "Oh, shut up. You know you love it." Her lips twisted. "Please stay, Joe. Just for a little while. It won't take me long to figure this out, I promise."

Her green eyes were soft and pleading, but it was the desperation in her voice that got to him. If it had been any other woman, Joe would have thought she was hitting on him, but he and Olivia had veered off that road a long time ago. Way off.

Gently, he grasped her by the arms and made his decision. "Kiddo, it's not that I don't sympathize, because I do, but if you really want my help, then you're going to have to suffer a little first. There's something I need to say to you."

His grin must have tipped her off because she bared her teeth and snarled at him. "Don't you dare."

Joe chuckled and ignored her. "I told you so." He said it again, slowly, deliberately shaking her shoulders to punctuate each word.

Olivia covered her ears and closed her eyes. "Shut up! I'm going to impale you with Marly's dough hook."

Joe crowed the words one last time. Nothing he had said two years ago could talk Olivia out of marrying that useless son-of-a-bitch pretty boy, and he had said plenty. Damn, but he was glad she'd given Keith the boot.

Olivia gave him a shove. "You are *such* a jerk. Why does everyone blame the victim? Has it even occurred to you that I might have a broken heart here? I was married to the guy for two years!"

"Yeah, but you didn't like him either. You just liked him liking you. C'mon." Joe slung his arm companionably around her shoulders. "Let's go find that pretty pastry chef of yours. You need a drink."

"Want a drink," Olivia corrected him. "The day I need one is the day I'll quit drinking. Way too many alcoholics in this business."

"Hey, I resemble that remark!" Joe grinned.

"Speaking of which"—she squeezed his arm—"how's your dad?"

"The same."

"Sober?"

"Hardly ever."

"I'm sorry, Joe." Olivia flipped off the lights, automatically grabbing his dessert plate and carrying it with them to the dish room.

He shrugged. "Not gonna stop me from having a beer."

"Good. Wait here. I want to double-check the front door."

"Where's your dishwasher?" he asked.

"Out early for good behavior."

While Olivia darted to the front of the house, Joe leaned against the screen door, breathing the dark, sulfurous breeze coming from the cooled-down blacktop parking lot. Across the street, the neon beer lights of the bar beckoned to him. For most of his adult life, a bitter brew and a sweet, willing woman were all he wanted out of a good night.

There hadn't been any good nights since his mother had died six months ago. She'd ruined his idea of paradise but good. Thirty-three years old and what did he have? Beer and women. No house. No wife. No kids. Nothing to call his own but a first-class résumé which didn't get him anything but more work.

Joe made a sound which might have been a sigh. From him, it was more of a half cough, half groan. Ignorance hadn't exactly been bliss, but at least he hadn't had this dull ache in his middle, this sick sense of guilt. He felt like he was strangling. Would it be any easier to breathe in California? It had to be.

He would help Olivia first. Then he'd keep his promises to his mother. He'd go to Kentucky and set his father straight. He would start over, settle down, find a woman who could mean more to him than just one night.

Easy, right?

Chapter 3

THE DOOR TO THE BAR OPENED, AND MARLENE'S PULSE kicked up a notch.

Perfect did not even *begin* to describe Joe Rafferty. The man was flawless, she decided, watching Joe and Olivia make their way across the bar. His wide shoulders were a revelation, broad and elegant, flowing into strong, well-muscled, but not freaky-big biceps. In the dim light, his eyes flashed the light—piercing blue she remembered from the wedding. If anything, his attraction had intensified over the past two years because there were intriguing shadows in those pale eyes now.

Joe held out his hand to her, and she took it, noticing that his tan forearm was crisscrossed with burns, old and new. She could actually see the raised, red splatter pattern of a grease burn on the inside of his right wrist. Was he careless or just plain tough? Either way, his wicked grin was a welcome sight, and his hand felt strong and solid. She slid her thumb across his palm to get a cheap thrill. The firm ridge of callous at the base of his index finger confirmed her guess: he was a working chef, not just a paper boss. Joe raised a dark eyebrow as Marlene caressed his finger, but he didn't pull away.

"Joe Rafferty."

"Marlene Bennet," she replied, one degree short of an obvious purr.

The knot of tension she had been holding between

her shoulders all day began to disentangle. Of course, the loosening could have something to do with booze on an empty stomach, but Marlene attributed it to the fact that she was going to get laid tonight. She swayed too close, caught by the warm, breezy scent of the road on his skin. She felt as if they'd done this dance before and were just waiting for the room to clear. Any second, she expected his arms to go around her, his lips to take hers in a hard kiss.

She cocked her head and gave herself a mental shake. Whoa, maybe she should have waited for Olivia and Joe to arrive before finishing her second martini.

Joe dropped her hand and turned his attention to the bar. Johnny responded to his signal immediately, unusual on a busy night.

"What'll it be?" the bartender asked.

"Guinness." Joe laid two twenties on the bar. "Ladies?"

"Gin and tonic," Olivia said.

Joe chuckled.

"Just one, I swear. I'm beat."

"The last time I saw you drink gin and tonic, you drank half a bottle," Joe reminded her.

"You drank the other half!" she protested.

"I'm a guy."

Their easy banter sparked a brief flash of jealousy in Marlene. She didn't want to feel like a third wheel tonight.

"Marlene? Can I buy you a drink?" Joe asked.

"Absolutely." Anticipation made her insides fizz.

"Marly special, coming up," the bartender said.

She hopped off her stool and linked her arm through Olivia's, then winked at Joe. Time for a little bathroom reconnaissance. "We'll be right back."

She could feel Joe's eyes on her as they walked away. She concentrated on putting one foot in front of the other. Tripping would be bad. She barely managed to acknowledge a greeting from Danny, who was sitting with some of his friends in the back. He was lucky Olivia was having too much fun to give him hell for showing up at the bar when he'd called in sick to work.

Out of the corner of her eye, Marlene could see Olivia's smug grin. They slipped into the rose-colored bathroom and dropped the hook and eye lock into place. It was a tiny space lit with a bare, pink bulb. Olivia sat in the rickety, wicker chair in the corner while Marlene collapsed against the sink.

"Olivia, honestly, you don't want some of that?" She gestured through the door in Joe's direction.

Olivia shook her head firmly. "Not interested."

"Not possible. I can't believe you two never hooked up."

"Only once." Olivia's smile was Mona Lisa annoying.

"You never told me!" She leveled an accusing glare at her friend.

"Total non-starter. It was before I met Keith." Olivia continued, "Joe goes through women like other guys go through socks. I'm not one of them."

"I want to be one of them," Marlene said fervently.

"Good for you." Olivia stood. "Are we done here?" she asked, her hand on the knob.

"Yeah, I just wanted to make sure. I'll be out in a minute." Marlene caught her arm. "Olivia? Are you sure you're all right?"

"Yes." Her voice was flat.

"Promise?" Marlene pressed.

"Yes."

Marlene waited for a couple seconds. "You did the right thing."

"I know."

She could see from the steady look in Olivia's eyes that she did. Really. Olivia sighed quietly.

"It's okay, Marly. I'm fine. I just feel like an idiot. It's not just Keith's girlfriends. It's all the other stuff. We met in *culinary* school. He got good grades, top of the class. I learned to cook. Why didn't he? How did Keith get around that one simple thing?"

Marlene had a few theories, but she kept them to herself. She was just glad Olivia had come to her senses. "You knew how to cook when you got there."

"I guess I did." Olivia bit her lip. Her eyes were doubtful. "He *was* charming, right? I mean, I'm not crazy. I'm not an idiot. I was head over heels for the guy. Keith had something, right? Something?"

Marlene wrapped her arms around her. "Yeah, he had something. He talked a good game. He really did. He had me going for a while too." She ended the hug with a hard squeeze. "Not as long as you, though. Seriously, are you sure you're okay?"

"I knew it was coming." Olivia brushed her bangs out of her eyes. Then she squared her shoulders, opened the door, and stepped out, shutting it behind her. Typical. No more discussion. Once Olivia made a decision, she moved on and shut the door behind her.

Marlene turned to the mirror and saw a frown on her face, so she blew a breath out through puffed cheeks to erase it. Her heart ached for her friend, even though she knew love was a loser's game. Anyone reckless enough to get married should expect disappointment.

Her own father had only stuck around long enough to leave at the worst possible time, and her mother still hadn't learned her lesson. She was about to marry number five. Other than celebrities looking for publicity, who actually did that? That kind of optimism was lethal. It was much safer to stay single and move on to the next guy before things got complicated. The world was full of next guys. In fact, there was one waiting for her in the bar.

Now that Keith was gone, she would happily resume her place on the line and work doubles until Olivia hired someone to make the desserts. Starting tomorrow, she would help Olivia put her life back together. Tonight, however, she was going to play with Joe.

"Go get him, girl." She practiced a smile in the scarred mirror over the bathroom sink, then opened the door and stepped out into the bar.

———

As the girls crossed the bar to the ladies room, Joe saw them catch a wave from three guys in the back. Marly dropped a kiss on a long-haired guy's cheek as they passed the table but didn't stop to chat. Joe's eyes narrowed.

"Marly is a force of nature," the bartender commented, snapping Joe's gaze from the low waistband of Marlene's jeans, where her pants dipped almost but not quite far enough to display the dimples he was imagining at the base of her spine.

"I can see that," Joe said, looking at him as he set the drinks on the bar. He took Joe's twenties, making change for his tip. Color tattoos wound all the way up the bartender's arms and down to his wrists. He had three piercings that Joe could see and a shaved head. "Is that a warning?" he asked.

"Hell no. I'd never warn anyone away from Marly. I like her too much. Everyone does." He glanced around the bar. "She's a heartbreaker, but totally worth it."

"Good to know." Joe didn't keep the sarcasm out of his voice.

The bartender shrugged and moved down the bar to take an order. Did he look like a chump? A sensitive, bleeding heart? If so, it would be the first time in his life. Usually guys warned him away from a girl because they didn't want him poaching on their territory or ruining a "good" girl with his two-night maximum policy. This was the first time someone had tried to cushion *his* fall.

For a second, Joe thought about calling the bartender over and telling him not to worry, that he didn't fall in love. Didn't want to, hadn't tried. Making a commitment just caused complications when you broke it. Even true love, the real stuff, couldn't put the brakes on a Rafferty. Joe's latest reminder in that vein was still so new that it hollowed out his chest and made him clench his teeth.

When he had visited his mother in the hospital that last time, she had reminded him of a pirate, with a bright head rag and a jolly expression in her hollow-eyed skull. Joe had hated seeing her like that, but at least the drugs kept her cheerful. Cancer had stripped his mother down to bare bones, removed both her breasts and all of the color from her cheeks, but it had not destroyed her spirit. Her shape was slight under the covers of the hospital bed, but her hand, grasping his, was strong.

"Joseph, we haven't set a very good example for you," his mother said without preamble. "Your father and I love each other very much, you know."

Joe stared at her. What the fuck?

"It's not easy. You can't judge a marriage unless you're in it. It never meant anything. He stayed, right? He never left us. Your father is a good man." Joe tried to interrupt. He didn't want to hear this, but his mother squeezed his hand even tighter, and he could see that it cost her to speak, not only physically but emotionally. She could have her say, then, if it mattered that much to her. It wouldn't make any difference to him.

"People talk, Joe. I hear about you. You don't bring any girls home, but I know you have them. A lot of them. Do these women make you happy, soothe your soul? You need to find someone who makes you a better person. I do that for your father. He does that for me. The rest doesn't matter." His mother shut her eyes and leaned back against the pillow, but she didn't let go of his fingers.

"You were a good boy, Joe, be a good man." His mother's voice was a whisper, as thin as the rise and fall of her chest under the flimsy blanket. The lines between her brows were pronounced, drawn with pain, but her lips tilted up at the corners. Slowly, her eyes opened again. They were clear—painfully clear.

"Find a real girl, Joe. Quit screwing around. If it hasn't made you happy by now, it isn't going to."

"That's not fair, Mom. The whole *do as I say, not as I do* thing just doesn't work for me. It never has."

Helen's smile was gentle and chiding. "Promise me you'll find a nice girl."

Joe said nothing. He wasn't going to argue with her today.

"Joseph."

Joe pulled his gaze from the floor and looked into his mother's bright eyes. She was his anchor, the one thing that pulled him through. The only one who was always on his side. He couldn't deny her.

Joe nodded slowly, once.

"You're just saying that because I'm dying, but I'm going to hold you to it, see if I don't." For a moment, the air in the hospital room felt charged. Helen Rafferty had never claimed her Irish roots, but she had ways. "I'm not done yet."

"Of course you're not," he said.

"That's not what I meant, love. I have one more thing to ask of you."

"All right."

"You'll have to take care of your father."

Joe stiffened. He glared at his mother and pulled his hand out of her grasp.

"Give him some time—not too much time—then you'll have to go to him. He's not going to take this very well."

Yeah, right. He would probably have to track his dad down on a Caribbean cruise and remind him he'd ever been married. "Sure, Mom, whatever you say."

"You don't believe me, but you'll see. He'll need you, and you'll have to forgive him. Now, get my lipstick, please. Your father will be here any minute." Joe stood up, found the tube, and held a mirror steady as she stroked it slowly over her dry lips. He kissed his mother's cheek.

"Joe?" He had inherited the color of his eyes from his father, but all the ice came from her. She used it to good effect as he paused at the door.

"No more sluts," his mother said softly.

Joe slid out of her room to avoid meeting his father in the hospital hall. The next day, Helen Rafferty suffered a massive stroke, and before he had a chance to tell her that his love life was none of her damn business, she left them.

Joe took a deep draw on his beer and let the thick, bitter brew pull him back into the bar.

He hadn't been celibate after his mother's death, her injunction notwithstanding, but sex hadn't brought him the satisfaction he was expecting. Getting a girl home and getting her naked used to be exciting. Getting laid had been fun. Now it felt like another job. He could do the work, but he didn't always feel like it.

This boredom was different than the restless itch that usually got him moving toward the next job, the next city, the next girl, and the next bar. It hadn't disappeared when he threw all his shit in the Jeep and hit the highway either. It was still there when he crossed the first state line. And the second.

By the time he hit New York, Joe had decided to honor his mother's last wishes. All of them.

Rafferty men didn't settle down. It wasn't in the blood. He didn't know if it was possible, but his decision to try had brought him peace for the rest of his journey to Norton.

Even so, the bartender's words intrigued him.

What kind of woman came with warnings attached? His favorite kind, no doubt. A no-strings woman, someone who wanted what he did—a good time and nothing more. That long-haired guy hadn't been the only one to look up when Marly walked across the room. A lot of guys had smiled—whether with pleasant memories or wishful thinking, Joe didn't know, but Marlene certainly had a lot of admirers in this room.

He glanced toward the bathroom and wondered, not for the first time in his life, why girls couldn't pee alone. Finally, the door opened and Olivia emerged. She crossed the room and slid onto the stool next to him. She drained her drink and set the glass firmly on the bar.

"Joe? You never gave me an answer."

Olivia was the closest thing to a little sister he'd ever had, and if she needed him, he wasn't going anywhere. He couldn't change his mind now just because the pastry chef gave him a hard-on, even if he was trying to turn over a new leaf.

"I'll stay."

Olivia's smile lit up the whole smoky bar. "Two weeks, Joe, that's all I need. Advertisement goes in the paper tomorrow, and I'm meeting with my lawyer this weekend. Thank you."

"No problem, kiddo. It'll be like old times."

Her lips tightened. "Keep an eye on me, cowboy. I'm a little afraid of what I might do if Keith tries to come back to work. Lorena Bobbitt did not have my knife skills."

"You sound really pissed," he observed.

"Watching your husband screw the hired help has that effect on a girl."

"Really? You saw them?"

Olivia nodded.

"Then I'll help you carve," he said grimly.

Olivia hopped off the bar stool and gave him a brief hug. "I'm going home. Rough day. You need a place to stay?"

Joe shook his head and pointed at his almost empty glass. "I want another beer." And more information.

"Right. I'm sure that's what you want."

Olivia's mocking green eyes said he also wanted Marly, and Joe didn't correct her. "Get some sleep, kiddo. Leave the late nights to the professionals."

He walked her to the door and watched until she climbed into a blue Honda parked across the street. She started it up and waved.

Joe turned back to the bar and locked eyes with Marlene, who was now waiting for him. No doubt, he was headed for trouble.

Chapter 4

MARLENE TOOK A SIP OF HER FRESH DRINK, FEELING THE bottom drop out of her important parts when Joe claimed the bar stool next to her and downed his beer. The flickering light of the votive candles played across the hollows in his cheeks, throwing his cheekbones into sharp relief. He had at least a day's growth of beard on his face, and she was finding it increasingly difficult not to rasp her fingers across his cheek, just to see if it would make a sound. Joe gestured for another beer, then turned back to her.

"What's really going on around here?" he asked, giving her that wicked smile again. This time, Marlene managed to still her beating heart.

"Do you mean with Olivia and Keith or are you talking about in the larger sense of the word?" Marlene lounged against the bar, feeling expansive.

"Start with today," he said.

"Olivia didn't give you the dirty details?"

"Nope."

She grimaced. "I found Keith in dry storage putting it to sweet Nikki, the bartender. Olivia walked in right behind me. It was ugly, but I think she's finally done with that jerk."

Joe snorted and shook his head. "You wish."

"She means it. Trust me. I've seen her in denial for, like, the last year at least. This was different. She called her lawyer. Things are going to change around here."

"Things never change," he stated.

"Cynical much?"

"More like honest. And realistic."

"Or jaded?" Marlene suggested.

He shrugged.

Marlene sipped her martini. She didn't want to get into all this right now. She and Olivia would handle Keith together, just as they handled almost everything else. Olivia had gone to culinary school alone, and she had certainly decided to marry Keith all by herself, but other than that, they had been a team since they were fifteen and Olivia had found her sobbing after school. She changed the subject. "You know, I've heard more than a few stories about *you* and women over the years."

Joe frowned. "How about I buy you another drink and we talk about something else?"

"What fun is that? I've got burning questions about the logistics involved with you and all those cheerleaders in high school."

"Huh? Oh." Recognition dawned, chasing the distant look from Joe's eyes. "I never should have told Olivia about that."

For the first time in Marlene's entire life, she envied a cheerleader. All of them, in fact. Joe was hot in the first place, but when his eyes lit up with sexy memories, he was positively volcanic. She began to tingle. If he could do that to her with a simple look, she couldn't imagine what he could do with the rest of his body. Thank God she had something all those skinny, perky, blond eighteen-year-old cheerleaders hadn't had.

Experience.

She grinned. "C'mon, quarterback, it's halftime, and I'm hungry. Want to get something to eat?"

"Sure, sugar, what's your pleasure?" he asked.

Marly drained her martini and set the top-heavy glass carefully on the bar. "My place. I've got a full fridge, and it's just around the corner," she answered, looking him squarely in the eyes.

He looked at her silently.

"Scared?" she asked, raising an eyebrow.

"Of a little thing like you? Hardly." He stood and stretched. "I'm beat, though. Long day."

Marlene followed him up, standing so close that she could smell the beer on his breath and feel the heat of his body through his clothes. Her eyes drifted shut, but a wave of dizziness snapped them open again. She staggered, and Joe caught her around the waist, steadying her with his body. She looked up at him. "If you need a more noble reason to take me home, I could use a ride."

"You don't have a car here?" He scowled.

"Nope. I walked."

"At night? In the dark?"

She shook her head. "I walked in to work this morning. I wasn't expecting it to be such a late night—not that I'm complaining."

"I'll take you home then," he said slowly, more slowly than she would have expected from a guy who was about to get lucky. He urged her toward the door with a broad hand on her lower back.

Joe pulled the door of the bar open for her, and she stepped out onto the sidewalk. The cool night air made her shiver. Western New York nights were never really warm until mid July, and tonight was no exception. He opened the door of a black Jeep parked on the street. "This is it."

She grinned as she stepped up into the Jeep. It was a pity she wasn't the type to pretend she needed a boost. Joe crossed to his side and climbed in, automatically fastening his seat belt and glancing down at hers.

"You wouldn't really walk home alone, would you?" he asked.

His protective streak was cute. Predictable but cute. "I had no intention of going home alone." She let the innuendo hang in the air for a minute as Joe pulled away from the curb, then she giggled. "Olivia was going to drop me off. Guess she decided you'd do a better job, huh?"

"She was tired."

Marlene grinned. "How unfortunate." She pointed down the road. "Turn right at the light. Then second house on the left past the stop sign."

He followed her directions and pulled into her driveway two minutes later.

"Back entrance. The top floor is mine." The bottom half of the two-story house was rented by Thomas and Bill, who were devoted to each other and to their beagle, Samson. Marlene met Joe on the other side of the Jeep and led him up the wooden decking staircase. When he paused at the top, she took his arm and pulled him into her kitchen.

"Come on, I'm starving," she said.

She snapped on the kitchen light. Warm track lighting lit the butcher-block island in the center of the room. The island was ringed with shelves that held her favorite and most useful kitchen appliances—KitchenAid mixer, food processor, cappuccino machine. Wide drawers held the smaller stuff like a mandolin, all manner of peelers and zesters, scoops and spatulas. On top of the island, a sturdy, wooden knife rack and a sink put everything she might need close at hand.

Marlene flipped another switch to light up the wide gas range on the left-hand wall next to the fridge and kicked her clogs into the pile of shoes at the door. The tile was cold on her bare feet. She pulled two beers out of the fridge and handed one to Joe.

He shook his head. "I should get going."

"Can I make you an omelet first?" she suggested, gazing into the fridge. Yellow peppers, ham off the bone…hmmm, cherry tomatoes, did she still have mushrooms? She dumped an armload of ingredients onto the counter next to the stove. Without turning around, she asked, "Am I making one or two?"

She got her answer in the form of a hiss as Joe twisted the cap off his beer. Hiding her triumph, she pulled a loaf of sourdough bread from the top of the fridge. "You can make the toast." She tossed the loaf onto the island and pointed at the knife rack and the bright orange toaster.

Show time.

She pulled a ten-inch All-Clad sauté pan from the cupboard and set it on the flame. Her knife flew through vegetables and herbs. She whisked three eggs in a metal bowl with a splash of milk and tossed the onions in the hot pan, followed by the mushrooms. They hissed and screamed as she flipped them in the pan. Next, she added the tomatoes and ham to warm them, then the spinach, reaching over to the sink to add a few drops of water. She tossed everything once more and reserved the vegetables on a plate while she wiped out her non-stick pan and returned it to the fire, hyper aware of Joe watching her from the island.

Marlene tended the eggs carefully, moving them around the pan until they set. She spread the vegetables in a line down the top third of her perfect yellow circle.

"Feta or goat?" she asked.

"Feta." Joe's voice was rough.

Marlene added the cheese, flipped one side over, and rolled a perfect omelet out of the pan.

Then she wiped out the pan and did it again. Take that, cheffie boy.

"Want to eat on the roof?" she asked, as Joe piled buttered toast on the plates.

At his nod, Marly put everything on a tray and led him to her small balcony. She set the tray on a small table just outside the French doors and clambered, barefoot, over her balcony railing. "Up we go." Reclaiming the tray of food, she scaled the gentle slope of her dining room roof. Joe followed, carrying their beers.

They reached the top and stepped down over the wooden railing.

She was proud of her rooftop garden patio, complete with tomato plants, herb garden, and two padded lounge chairs stretched out on either side of a low, wicker table. She set their plates on the table and beckoned to Joe, patting the spot next to her, trying to read his expression.

The heat was still there, but she didn't feel the pull, the opening she needed to draw him closer to her. Instead of sitting down beside her, he took the opposite chair. Marlene swallowed a bite of her eggs, washed it down with a long swig of cold beer, and wondered how she was going to get him to kiss her.

—~w—

Joe watched Marly eat. She wasn't at all self-conscious about enjoying her food. In fact, she smiled slightly to herself in anticipation of each bite, as if she knew it was going to be good. She glanced up and caught him looking at her.

"Something wrong with the food?" she asked.

"No, it's good. Thanks."

"Only good?" She made a face.

"It's fantastic, sugar. Beats the hell out of IHOP."

A slow smile spread across her lips, and Joe watched that too. She looked as if one sudden move would unravel her. One button undone, one more strand of hair slipping down, if she shrugged out of her sweater all else would move toward entropy and she would sprawl, naked and unhinged, on her chair. She was trouble, all right, serious trouble. The kind he usually welcomed, sought out, and definitely enjoyed. His gut twisted.

"Penny for your thoughts," she said.

Joe placed his empty plate on the wicker table and stood to look out over the edge of the roof. "Just admiring the view."

Marlene joined him and pointed out over the street. "You can see the restaurant from here." Just over the trees, Joe could make out the roof of the bar. He leaned down to sight along her arm. It wobbled, just a bit. Beyond the bar, Joe recognized the dark front window of Chameleon and its adjacent parking lot. As her arm dropped back down to her side, he caught her scent: onions faintly, a damp smell of flowers from her hair, and then something sweet like vanilla.

He shouldn't have let it get this far. He was a lot of bad things when it came to women, but a tease was not one of them. Selfish, now that Joe could cop to. He was trying to reform, but he was a guy after all. It was hard to work against his instincts. He had recovered his restraint on the way up the stairs, but then he'd caught a glimpse of her tricked-out kitchen from the doorway and wanted to see more.

Of her kitchen. Right. He could tell himself whatever he wanted, but all bullshit aside, he'd left the bar with her, walked into her house with her, and now he was alone on the roof with her. If he wasn't stupid and he wasn't a tease, what the hell was he doing here?

Exactly what he'd been doing for half his life, he decided disgustedly: taking the easy road with a beautiful and willing woman. It was as if the moment he made his decision to be good, the devil had tossed a woman up onto Earth who was everything he couldn't resist. He swallowed hard against the urge to lean in to get a better whiff of her sweet scent. He clenched his hands into fists against the desire to touch her glorious curly hair, her sexy body, full of the curves of a woman who liked to cook. Her skin looked so soft he was already imagining how it would feel under his hands, against his bare chest, pressed against his groin as he shaped her body to fit his.

He should leave. Right now. He wasn't that guy anymore; he was going to settle down, find some peace.

He didn't move.

The selfishness that had led him out of the bar and into Marlene's home demanded satisfaction. He looked down at her standing next to him, just the tiniest bit too close for politeness. He met her eyes. She didn't look away. Instead, she smiled and turned toward him, tilting her head just a hair to the right. They both knew how to play this game. One kiss then. Clearly, she was waiting for it. Then he would go.

Abruptly, he leaned down to take her mouth.

Their lips touched and he welcomed the instant lust, the harsh need, the promise of forgetting that she offered to him. He had half expected a sloppy kiss, full of drunken enthusiasm. Instead, her lips were tentative, responsive to the slightest pressure of his questing mouth. When he deepened the kiss, she opened to him. When he pulled away, her lips danced lightly over his. He pressed her into the rail and she gave beneath him, arching, thrusting her full breasts toward him. She tilted her hips in blatant invitation as their tongues asked and answered questions in a rapid exchange of straightforward desire.

He pulled her closer, until they were joined at chest, hip, and thigh. They moved as one, with communication hardwired between them, bypassing speech, relying on touch. Her body screamed *Take me!* and his body answered with a clear, violent affirmation. It felt comfortable, familiar. He was harder than he'd ever been in his life. Dimly, he knew his brain was telling him to hightail it out of there, but he was operating on instinct, and any rational thoughts were much less compelling than the woman slowly grinding herself on his left thigh.

Yes, he would take her. He'd been thinking about it from the minute Olivia had recalled Marlene's existence to him in the bakeshop. Been pretty sure of it when her eyes met his with no-bullshit heat in the bar. He was dead certain of it now.

He bent to lift her into his arms, so intent on getting

her to the chair without losing contact with her mouth—a mouth that promised oblivion with every slow, gliding movement of her tongue—that he didn't pay attention to the banging noise coming from the vicinity of her front porch. Instead, he pulled her shirt above her breasts and cupped each warm curve in his hands. He flipped her black, lacy excuse for a bra below her breasts, so he could suck a pink nipple into his mouth and draw a long, low moan from her throat.

Joe reached between them to press his palm firmly against the denim between her thighs. She pressed back.

"Marlene?" a deep voice called out from the dark beneath them.

She stiffened, hissed, said nothing.

"Marlene? Are you up there?" the man called again, louder this time.

"Shit," she panted and slid out from underneath him to weave across the roof, pulling her shirt down as she went. Joe followed and recognized the long-haired guy from the bar standing on her porch.

"I saw your lights," the guy said.

A booty call for sure.

Reality reasserted itself in the cool, midnight breeze. *No more sluts.*

"You said you wouldn't do this, Danny." Marlene sounded admirably patient for a woman who had been half naked five seconds ago. "We talked about it, re-member? Go home. I'll see you tomorrow."

She turned from the rail. They both listened as his footsteps thumped slowly down the staircase.

"That was Danny. The grill cook. Keith's right-hand man."

Fantastic.

"We're friends," she added.

"Uh-huh," he said.

Marlene shrugged and sat beside him on the chair. Her hair was slipping out of its clasp, and she reached up to release it. It fell in a thick, bright mass around her shoulders, and Joe wanted to touch it. Instead, he stood. He wasn't going to have a second chance at redemption tonight.

"Thanks for the food. I need to get some sleep," he said.

She stood with him, leaning into his chest. "Sleep here."

Even with the bizarre interruption, his body responded. She was exactly his kind of girl. He was still plenty hard, plenty ready, but he'd lost the recklessness he'd had before her friend showed up. If he took what Marlene was offering, this night would end like every other hookup he'd had since his mother died. Empty. Guilty. Forgotten.

He had no doubt whatsoever that they would enjoy each other. Hell, they fit together like two pieces of the same twisted puzzle, but any joy they found tonight would be temporary. He wanted a return of the easy peace he'd felt driving into town tonight, and he wasn't going to find it with Marlene, that was for sure. He couldn't believe he felt this way, but it wasn't worth it, especially since they were going to be working together at Chameleon. And she had been drinking. A woman who could whip out first-class omelets after several martinis and leave the kitchen spotless deserved more than that, even from him.

"I can't stay," Joe said.

"So don't. You can leave. After." She reached up to pull him back down to her mouth.

He caught her arms and twisted them behind her back

to keep her still. "I don't want you to be accused of beer goggling, sugar."

"My reputation can take it." She took advantage of her position to press even closer to him, forcing him to embrace her or fall over. Her breasts pressed firmly against his chest. His cock twitched. "I only had one beer," she whispered.

"And a few martinis. Let's pick this up tomorrow and see where we are."

Marlene froze.

"You've got to be kidding me." She shook off his arms and stepped back, hands on her hips. Her gold-flecked eyes shot hellfire and her voice was sharp as disbelief turned into visible fury at his rejection. "There is no tomorrow. I'm a *Top Gun* kind of girl," Marlene said.

"I'm trying to do the right thing here," he protested, stifling a chuckle. He knew exactly what she meant: he'd get one chance and one chance only. They were birds of a feather all right.

Marlene raised her chin. "I wasn't expecting an attack of scruples from you, Rafferty. I could swear Olivia told me you seduced a chef instructor in her own kitchen."

"She seduced me," he answered automatically.

"And her husband?"

"Watched." He crossed his arms, getting annoyed.

"Yeah, well, where's that Joe Rafferty? I was looking for him."

He stared at her for a long minute. She'd certainly nailed that one. Good fucking question. At last, he said, "He's gone."

"You could have mentioned that earlier," she said through gritted teeth.

"Yeah, probably. I'll see you in the morning."

"Not if I can help it."

Joe paused. "This probably isn't the best time to tell you this either, but Olivia hired me to help out at Chameleon for a few weeks. Is that going to be a problem?"

The only outward sign of whatever emotion she might be feeling was the slight dip of her chin and the way her eyes sharpened and glowed gold in a glare worthy of a deadly jungle cat. She shook her head slowly. "Not for me."

Joe stepped over the balcony railing and made his way back down the roof.

Since he'd pretty much ruined any chance of being invited back, he paused to enjoy her kitchen again. It was small, cozy, with no wasted space. She had all the right equipment, with plenty of counter space and good lighting too. He almost regretted that he'd never have the chance to eat a meal at her weathered cherrywood table with the Mason jar of daisies, never have a chance to fire up that sweet looking stove.

He should have just had sex with her. Then he could have made pancakes in the morning in her perfect kitchen. Blueberry. Or maybe banana–chocolate chip. Joe cursed the changes that had come over him. Since when did he turn down a willing woman? Since when did working together make any kind of difference to two people out for a quick, convenient lay? Sex was simple, almost involuntary, like breathing.

And since when did he want to make pancakes?

Joe forced his brain to a swirling halt. He had to be at work in—he checked his cell phone—six hours. Driving all day had taken its toll. He was toast. His head ached, his balls were killing him, and he still had to find a decent motel.

Joe opened the kitchen door and descended the stairs.

She was just a girl. Enough.

It was time to focus on the next relevant task, like finding a place to get some sleep, not that it was going to help very much. Yup, should have just slept with her. Tangling with Marlene had probably guaranteed his next two weeks at Chameleon would be hell.

Joe slid into the Jeep and turned the key. As he put the truck in reverse and glanced up into the rearview mirror, he was surprised to discover a smile on his face.

Chapter 5

MARLENE'S HEAD POUNDED IN TIME WITH HER BLARING alarm clock. She smacked the top of the clock until it shut off, but her head still ached to the beat. Boom. Boom. Boom.

Her blood froze.

She burrowed deeper into the covers trying to find a safe place to hide before her memory caught up with her. Maybe it wasn't as bad as she thought it was. Boom. Boom.

Oh God.

It was. It totally was. She tried to pinpoint the exact moment that the beer had kicked in and she had gone from cheerfully buzzed to shit-faced without pride. She groaned aloud.

The only thing that made her feel marginally better was that Joe had made the first move to kiss her. Of course, he probably would have had to jump off the roof to avoid her. She carefully drew back the covers and sat up, assessing the damage. Throbbing head, unstable stomach, but not going to throw up. Not yet at least.

She walked slowly into the bathroom, trying to keep her head on a level plane. After popping two ibuprofen, she reversed course to the kitchen to get a large glass of water and a couple of crackers.

The dirty omelet pan mocked her from the sink. She ignored it and programmed the coffee maker to begin brewing in an hour. Hopefully, she'd feel alive by then.

Safely back in bed and under the covers, with her pillow over her head, Marlene permitted herself to think about Joe's kiss without remembering its disastrous aftermath.

Kissing him had been like having a conversation—a really hot, unexpected conversation with a stranger. Holy shit, that man could think with his lips. Heat stole through her arms and legs. Even in her weakened, half-dead state, Marly wanted to finish that conversation. She wanted it bad enough to consider finishing it by herself.

No, taking care of things herself in this condition would probably make her head explode.

Oh God, she should have hit the road when she started talking to herself in the ladies room. Every girl knows that's a bad sign. She remembered ignoring a number of dangerous signs last night. Drinking on an empty stomach, having more than one drink in an hour, ignoring the word no, begging, for heaven's sake—

The full effect of her crash and burn touched down in her tender brain, and she groaned into the pillow. She had failed to seduce the man who slept with everyone. And she'd referenced *Top Gun* in the attempt. She wasn't sure which was worse.

Olivia was going to laugh her ass off.

—∾—

"We need butters piped," Shane greeted Marlene just inside the back door of Chameleon. "Who's the new guy?"

"Huh?" Marlene needed more coffee.

"He's in whites, and he's talking to Olivia in the office. He's hot. Do you know anything?"

"Nope." Deny, deny, deny.

Joe's beat-up black toolbox was sitting on the dish rack, locked with a heavy padlock. *Rafferty* was scrawled across the top in indelible marker.

Marly's mouth watered. She closed her eyes and swallowed the bile rising in her throat. She would not puke. Aside from matters of pride, no one ever cleaned the employee bathroom. She took a shallow breath to conquer the nausea just as Joe and Olivia came around the corner from the back room.

"Good morning," she said, clearing her throat. "I think. Sorry I'm late. I'm considering the hair of the dog."

"Doesn't work. I've tried it," Joe said.

Naturally.

He was clean-shaven and wearing a blindingly white, double-breasted chef coat with his name on the pocket and traditional checked pants. He looked good, damn it. His baseball cap was on backward, and his apron was folded down and looped twice around his hips. The bastard looked Downy fresh.

"Danny's late again," Olivia said. "I'm gonna have to talk to him. He didn't look sick at Johnny's last night."

"No, he didn't," Marly agreed. He also didn't look sick when he was standing on her porch, ruining her damn night.

Joe raised an eyebrow but said nothing as Olivia followed Marlene toward the bakeshop. Joe, mercifully, headed toward the line.

Olivia followed her into the back and handed her a glass of water straight from the tap. "Here, drink this and give me all the dirty details."

"Joe didn't tell you?" Marlene asked.

"He said you make a great omelet, which I already know. He stayed for breakfast? He's not usually into that."

"Oh, right." Marlene sagged against the cold glass of the dessert reach-in cooler, head back, eyes shut, feeling Olivia's scrutiny.

"You are the exact shade of a pistachio crème brûlée."

"Thanks. Every girl should hear that the morning after," Marlene said, opening her eyes.

Olivia's expression was expectant.

Marlene didn't say anything. Hurt and surprise warred across her friend's face. "You really aren't going to tell me anything?" Olivia asked.

She always dished the details of her sex life to her poor, married friend. There was no way she could freeze her out, especially now. Olivia claimed a vicarious thrill or two kept her honest. Not that it was really an issue anymore. Marlene sighed. Deeply. "It seems your friend Joe is not interested," she confessed.

"Huh? Not possible."

"He took me home. I made omelets. Everything was going great. Then Danny showed up." Olivia's eyes widened. "I sent him packing, but by the time I turned around, Joe had changed his mind. I made an ass of myself and he left. Then I passed out."

"Oh, honey, I'm so sorry!" Olivia gave her a hug.

"Plenty of other fish in the sea." She could be philosophical, right?

"I never would have asked him to help out around here if I thought there was going to be a problem," Olivia said, releasing her.

"How could you know? A heads-up would have been greatly appreciated, though. I might have been able to control myself if I'd known he was going to be working here," she said sourly.

"He hadn't said yes yet," Olivia explained with an apologetic frown.

"Any chance he'll change his mind?"

Olivia shook her head.

Marlene exhaled. "I'll live. Leave me to my misery, but get me the prep list soon, okay?" It was going to be a long day and an even longer night, but even with her hangover and Joe in the house, she couldn't wait to step back into her old job on the line. Anticipation and adrenaline began to chase away her headache.

Olivia grimaced. "Ummm, I told Joe you'd show him how things work prep-wise after lunch. Want me to do it instead?"

Marlene swallowed the returning flood of salt water in her mouth and shook her head. "I can handle it. What's he going to be doing around here, anyway? Prep?"

Olivia gave her a bewildered look. "No—I thought you understood. He'll do Keith's job on the line until I can hire somebody. You're absolutely right: we can't work doubles forever. It's not fair of me to expect you to cover for Keith anymore. We need another chef in here."

"Right. Silly me," Marlene said faintly, swallowing convulsively.

Olivia was already heading back to the line.

Of course Olivia would want to get a chef, a real chef, into the kitchen. Alcohol must have dissolved her brain cells or Marlene would have immediately realized where Joe fit in around here. After all, someone had to fix all the damage Keith had done over the past two years, and it couldn't be her, not really. Who would make the desserts on such short notice? She couldn't do justice to both jobs, and Olivia spent a good twelve hours of the day at Chameleon already. She couldn't start spending every night on the line too. They'd have to put a cot in the office.

Resentment flared inside her, a brief flash of bitterness that left her exhausted. They definitely needed another cook at Chameleon, but she hadn't expected Olivia to replace her completely. Part of her wanted to chase after Olivia and tell her she wanted to work on the line again, but just like with cooking, timing was everything. She didn't want to have that discussion when she was so hungover she could barely see straight. Plus, what good would it do? Joe was already here.

Marlene leaned over her prep table, resting her head on her forearms. Sudden, debilitating depression made her want to lie down on the floor mats. The day's work loomed in front of her, seemingly impossible. Self-loathing brought on by last night's miscalculation was acute and agonizing, and that wasn't even the worst part. The real kicker was that she was going to have to answer to Joe now. He was going to be giving her his prep lists, and she was going to be explaining her dessert specials to him before she left every night. For the next two weeks, Joe Rafferty was going to be all over her world, and she couldn't do a damn thing about it except suck it up—and pretend like she didn't care.

She took a deep breath and blew it out slowly. It wasn't the end of the world. She recognized the symptoms of the hangover blues, and she only knew one cure: time. Since she couldn't do anything to make the day pass faster, she'd have to go for the second best remedy: work. She forced herself to get moving.

By the time service started, she had lemon tarts and more crème brûlées in the deck oven and garlic marinara at a bare simmer on the back of the stove. Veal demi-glace was reducing on the front burner, sending up thick, rosemary-scented steam. Her headache had receded to a dull buzz, and her stomach was behaving nicely after a pile of extra crispy hot wings, thoughtfully provided by Olivia, who kept a gallon of Anchor Bar wing sauce on hand for hangover emergencies.

Marlene filled a bain-marie with marinara, another with demi, and carried them both up to the line where Olivia was explaining the lunch menu to Joe. Danny had finally called in sick again, so Joe was going to jump in on the line. On any other day, it would have been Marly. She ignored the stab of jealousy and plunked the tall, round pots of sauce into his steaming water bath.

"Thanks," he said, taping the grill menu above his workspace. Hotshot. The sauté station was easier on the lunch menu. He should be starting there. She turned her back.

On her way to the bakeshop, she was struck by sudden inspiration and veered into the waiters' station, where Eric and Shane were doing last minute side work before the lunch rush hit.

"Hey, guys, do me a favor? I really don't want to get into a long explanation, but could you slam the new guy for me?" She nodded in Joe's direction. "Please? Really bury him, okay?"

She didn't have to explain what she meant. Waiters held a lot of power over timing in the kitchen. They could steer all their customers toward grilled entrees or, if that didn't work, they could simply turn all their tickets in at the same time. A few pissed-off servers could wreak havoc on a busy lunch.

Shane scowled. "Hell no. I need forty bucks to make rent this week, and I'm not gonna get it if the food is slow."

Eric nodded in agreement.

"Come on, guys. I'll make sure it doesn't affect your tips," Marly promised.

Shane arched one eyebrow. "If I get a single complaint, you're sending out free desserts."

"Done." She nodded.

Eric shrugged his assent, and Shane tucked his order pad into his apron. "I hope it's worth it."

She grinned. "Oh, it will be."

Marlene felt bad for Joe for about five seconds. They had fifty on the books, not counting walk-ins, and lunch was fast. Joe was really going to get it.

Twenty minutes later, the orders came in.

All for the grill. All at the same time. It was beautiful.

And the perfect cure for a hangover.

—⁓—

Marlene heard Olivia bellow her name just as she pulled her lemon tarts out of the oven. Olivia rushed into the bakeshop with Joe close behind her. "Could you break these down into lunch steaks?" She flipped two bloody beef tenderloins onto Marlene's prep table and didn't wait for an answer. "Joe, you want to switch stations? I told those idiots to go easy on the grill."

"Hell no."

Marlene hummed as she stripped the chain off the

first tenderloin and began trimming silver skin. Perfect six-ounce steaks fell away from her blade.

"Quit showing off." Olivia pulled the digital scale off the shelf and set it next to Marly's cutting board. Marlene rolled her eyes but began checking every other steak as Olivia herded Joe back toward the line.

When the last steak was cut, she arranged them in a shallow third pan and added whole cloves of garlic and a handful of rosemary stems. She poured olive oil over the meat to preserve it and carried it up to the line.

Ten tickets were hanging. Olivia worked in silence, her face stern as she pulled pans down to heat side vegetables. Joe, on the other hand, was whistling. Marlene counted eight steaks, six chicken breasts, and three pieces of salmon on the grill. He probably had more in the oven too. Her lips twitched. He crossed two perfectly charred Cajun shrimp skewers on each of the three salads that Anthony, their newbie garde-manger cook, had placed in the cold window.

Eric reached into the window.

"Don't even think about it." The waiter jerked his hand away from the salad plate. "That's not your table." Joe nodded at the long line of tickets. "If you boys are going to pull this shit, then you'll have to wait your turn." His voice was a silky snarl. "Your tips are in my hands now."

Eric backed away from the line.

"You guys need anything else?" Marlene asked quickly.

"Not a thing, sugar," Joe replied.

She fled to the bakeshop.

Joe appeared by Marlene's side when lunch died down to a trickle of deuces. He didn't look like he'd been in grill hell for two hours straight, she thought. The heat should have made him sweat a little at least.

She turned off the mixer and heaved the twenty-quart bowl of tart dough onto her table. "How was lunch?"

"It was all right."

That was an understatement. Joe had cooked himself out of that pile-up in fifteen minutes flat, and Eric and Shane were still sucking up to him. She hadn't had to comp a single dessert.

"Did you have a good time?" Joe asked, leaning against her reach-in.

"Huh?" Marlene widened her eyes.

"Your little boyfriends squealed on you. You can't trust waiters, you know."

"Trust has nothing to do with it." She'd left three desserts in the wait station, but Eric and Shane still weren't speaking to her.

"Maybe not, but Olivia asked for my help, Marlene. This place needs another chef, and I'm here, ready, and able to work. What happened between us last night has nothing to do with Chameleon. Can we call it even and get on with the job, for Olivia's sake?" he asked.

She faced the table, taking deep breaths to control her fury. How dare he speak to her in that reasonable tone of voice and suggest she didn't have her best friend's back? That's why she was here, wasn't it? To help Olivia run the restaurant? She had put up with a lot to repay the debt she owed Olivia and her family.

She began to wrap her double batch of tart dough into neat, flat disks while he watched, making the bakeshop feel even smaller than usual. When she was finished, she put the dough in the freezer, then wiped her hands on a damp side towel. She folded it into a perfect square and placed it on the table. "Shall we get started on the prep list?"

Joe stood to his full height, towering over her, no longer affecting his indolent pose against the refrigerator. "Not until you answer me." His voice was stern.

She shrugged. "We don't need your help, Joe."

"Olivia says you do. No offense, but if you're the only one in her corner, I can see why. I'd be pretty damn pissed at someone who encouraged the waiters to screw up service—for any reason. Count yourself lucky I didn't squeal on *you*, little girl. I'm very good at what I do, and I think you know it now, since you got yourself such an excellent demonstration of my abilities this afternoon. You can't scare me away with a grill pile-up. Why don't you just relax and let me help out around here until Olivia can find another chef?"

She ignored him and reached under the table for a cutting board.

When she straightened, Joe put his hand on her arm and turned her around to face him. His lazy smile pulled her in for a sucker punch. "Admit it, sugar, you don't have a problem with me in a professional capacity. You're just mad because I didn't spend the night with you."

For a brief second, Marly imagined grabbing her French knife from the table and whipping it into the center of his forehead. It gave her satisfaction while she considered his words, which hit too close to home. She already regretted her impulsive action, but she didn't want to admit it yet. At least not to him. She closed her eyes briefly. "Shit," she sighed.

"Yep." She could hear the smug grin in his voice.

"I'm not apologizing," she warned, addressing his chest.

"You don't have to. I'm not apologizing either," he said. "We've both got our reasons, but we have to be able to work together. Let's keep the personal stuff out of it. I've heard a lot of nice things about you, and I'd like to believe they're true." He held out a hand, palm up. "Friends?"

The fact that he was handling her made the situation even more annoying, but he had a point. She'd behaved like a twit. She took his hand, stifling a sigh as his rough palm slid over hers. Lust zinged through her. His other hand reached out to clasp her forearm, raising goose bumps she hoped he couldn't feel. Not fair, just not fair. Her libido didn't seem to register the fact that he wasn't interested, which was going to make the next two weeks challenging.

She shook her hand free of his, deciding to at least try to save face. If she couldn't control her inconvenient physical response to his hot body, maybe she could disguise it a little, set up a smoke screen. She raised her eyes to meet his. "Since we're getting things off our chests, I may have given you the wrong impression last night. I don't usually come on so strong," she lied. "Martini madness I guess. It won't happen again, especially since we'll be working together. As friends," she added. "Your virtue will be safe from me, I promise."

"Yeah?" He raised his eyebrows.

"Absolutely."

Joe flashed that wicked grin and chuckled. "For the record, I don't believe you."

Her jaw dropped and she sagged against the table, pretending to be crushed by his lack of faith, but really giving herself a moment to recover. She clapped a hand to her forehead in mock disbelief. "Now you're flirting with me? Jesus, your timing sucks."

He laughed again and dropped a cutting board next to hers on the table. "What's on the prep list?" he asked.

"Mirepoix for more veal stock, sliced onions and peppers, mashed potatoes, polenta, and rosemary red sauce." She grinned. "Oh, and you need more steaks."

"This place needs a prep cook."

"You're looking at her." And he was, damn it, looking at her in a way that made her remember how his lips had felt speaking to hers last night. Her mouth watered, but it had nothing to do with her hangover this time. She had to force herself to breathe slowly. She could feel her heart hammering in her chest, and her cheeks felt hot. She was never going to make it through two weeks with him if she went up in flames every time he smiled and his eyes got all crinkly.

For whatever reason, he wasn't interested in her. She wasn't interested either. Okay, so that was a lie. She was definitely interested, but Joe was, by her own declaration, totally off limits now. Even if she wanted him. Which she didn't.

Right.

The hubbub of the kitchen swirled around them. The dish machine roared faintly in the background. Waiters traded insults. Dishes clanked into bus tubs. Her sauces bubbled slowly, like her thoughts. Time to get back to work. If Joe could prep as well as he could cook, then she might even get out of here early today.

She turned and saw he was smiling at her. "Do you really want to know why I left your apartment last night?" he asked with a teasing grin that almost took her out at the knees.

"Nope." She left him at the table and headed for the walk-in. No way was she continuing this "about last night" conversation. She was pretty good at denial, but she wasn't a masochist. If he was just joking around, she wasn't interested in hearing what he had to say. If he was serious, then she really didn't want to hear it. The subject was closed.

He followed her. The walk-in refrigerator door swung shut behind them, making the forty-degree air feel like a sauna to her.

Joe stretched to hand her the bin she couldn't quite reach and told her anyway. "I'm reforming, and I didn't want you to take advantage of me."

She thrust the bin of carrots and celery back into his arms. She batted her eyelashes at him. He wanted to play? Fine, she'd play. "Thanks, I really appreciated that. I'll have you know I've never taken advantage of an unwilling man."

"Really? That's not what I hear. The bartender last night said you're a real heartbreaker."

"Johnny? He should talk. You should see what he gets up to in *his* spare time. Anyway, who cares? Olivia said you've left a trail of broken hearts across the lower half of this country," she retorted. "You good old boys invented the double standard, buddy."

Joe raised his eyebrows, so she continued. "You want every woman you meet to be a virgin, right up to the minute you get her to bed. Then you want her to work your pole like a professional. I don't play those games. I know what I want, and nine times out of ten I get it. You just happened to be number ten."

The walk-in was definitely too small and too hot. She kicked the steel door open and walked back to the prep table, grabbing a bin of onions on the way.

Joe followed her, seemingly oblivious to her growing irritation. "Number ten, huh? There were more than nine other guys staring at your ass in the bar last night. Don't sell yourself short, sugar."

Her hackles rose again. What was he trying to imply? She decided to ignore the bait. "Large dice, please," she said, pointing at the carrots and celery.

He nodded and began to chop. "How'd you get started at Chameleon, anyway?"

The change of subject caught her off guard. Marlene took a deep breath. Calm, calm. That was a fair question. "Olivia and I went to high school together. She brought me home, and her mom gave me a job." That was the short version.

The long version was more complicated.

She had been sobbing in the chemistry lab after school when Olivia had found her. It was her fourteenth birthday, the day her father had left for good. When Olivia heard that, she had insisted Marlene come to her parents' restaurant with her. The minute the screen door had slammed behind her, she was hooked. The kitchen was noisy. People were swearing. It smelled like wet noodles, garlic, and hot grease. She had never been in such a wild place.

That first day, Mr. Marconi had shoved a huge bowl of spaghetti and meatballs at her. He had a sharp face.

His cheekbones were stark slashes above his hollow cheeks. His chin was pointy, and his nose was hooked, but under his heavy, dark brows, his eyes flashed a warm green, like Olivia's.

She had tried to play it cool, but her mouth was watering. That spaghetti had never been anywhere near a can. "It's okay. I'll get something at home," she had mumbled.

Mr. Marconi winked at her and took a big bite out of the enormous sandwich sitting on his cutting board. A piece of steak fell out onto the mats at his feet. He frowned and nudged the meat under the table with the toe of his black boot.

"Eat."

She ate. The sauce had a woodsy flavor and sweet, brown bits she would later learn were currants. It was the best thing she had ever tasted. After that first night, she didn't resist, and the entire Marconi family had swept her under its generous, Old World wing. She learned the secret of that rosemary sauce and all the other sauces from Mr. Marconi. She learned the rhythm of the kitchen from him too: how long to leave a steak on the fire for a perfect medium rare, how to get a twelve-top into the window, hot and on time. At his elbow, Marlene learned how to get prepped for a busy dinner service, specials and all, and still have time to meet with the servers and feed her own body before the doors opened for service.

Grandma Marconi had welcomed her in the bakeshop too. When Nonna got too tired to spend so much time on her feet, Marlene had learned the secrets of butter, sugar, eggs, and flour from her, while Olivia stayed on the line to help her father. When the mixers whirled,

Marlene could still hear a soft, Italian accent in her ear. She could still feel Nonna's hand, knuckles swollen with arthritis, guide her own when she folded stiff egg whites into cake batter. Every time she smelled chocolate, she thanked Nonna for teaching her its pleasures. Her heart was on the hot line, but she had a gift for the sweet stuff too, and that gift allowed her to stay at Chameleon when Olivia brought Keith home.

Marlene realized Joe was waiting for her to go on. "I like cooking," she said finally. "It isn't rocket science, and I'm good at it."

"You've worked on the line, right?" His knife moved quickly but with absolute control through the pile of peeled carrots, reducing them to equally-sized pieces, hands so sure of his knife, he barely even glanced down at them. He kept his eyes on her.

"Of course." She kept pace with him, evenly dicing onions to complete the mirepoix.

"How come you aren't up there now?"

"There's plenty for me to do back here." She paused to pour oil into a large roasting pan.

"I'll do that." He took the pan from her and tucked it into the oven.

"If I need help, I'll ask for it," she growled.

"I doubt that." Her disgusted look was lost on him as he began dismantling celery. "In fact, you seem like a lone ranger around here, baking, prepping, messing around with service. Chameleon needs teamwork, sugar." She couldn't even begin to imagine where he was going with this. "I'm not a bad guy to work for—"

Her knife hand froze halfway through an onion. She left it sticking there and spun to face Joe, her hands on her hips. "Hold it right there, cheffie boy. I don't work for you. I work for Olivia. I do a lot of things around here because there isn't anybody else who can do the job right." She ignored the gibe about this afternoon's mischief because he had a valid point. "I can't deny we need more working bodies around here, and if one of them has to be you, so be it, but you are not my boss. You keep that straight, and we'll get along just fine." She turned back to the vegetables.

Why was it every guy who walked into a professional kitchen thought he could do a better job than the women? Joe was just like every other hot shit Culinary Arts chef who liked to strut down the line. Just like Keith. There was no way she was going to take orders from Joe, even for a minute, never mind for two weeks. She was damn good at her job, and she didn't need him telling her how to do it. Teamwork her ass.

Joe stepped aside as Marlene pulled the hot pan out of the oven and swept the onions, carrots, and celery into the pan. He didn't blink as she shook the vegetables around in the sizzling oil and shoved the pan back into the oven, wisely staying out of her way.

She shut the oven door and looked at him. "By the way, I set Olivia straight about what happened last night. You didn't have to lie for my sake."

"Oh, right." He glanced away from her. "I didn't do that for you."

She shrugged. "No worries. I'm delighted to forget everything that happened after I popped the cap off that last beer, trust me."

He looked disappointed. "Does that mean you won't be quoting any *Top Gun* for me?"

"I'll peel the potatoes if you promise not to mention that again."

He shook his head. "No way. I have some particular favorites from that movie. In fact, if we don't get a move on, we won't be ready for dinner. You could say, 'We have a need, a need for—'"

"Stop it!" She laughed in spite of herself. He was an arrogant prick, but at least he had a sense of humor. She picked up a red pepper and began to chop. Joe started on the green ones. If he were a woman, she would probably like him in spite of his gigantic ego. Her grin slipped off her face.

Oh hell. No way. She did.

Maybe she *was* a masochist.

Chapter 6

JOE LEFT THE BAKESHOP AND RETURNED TO THE LINE after the peppers were sliced. Chameleon was slamming busy that night, and he had a ton of station prep to knock out before dinner service. Lunch had wiped out his backups, even though the grill station had been stocked at the beginning of service. He made a mental note to ask Olivia who had been working the grill. He wanted to thank whoever it was for setting him up so well.

He and Olivia had hauled ass through lunch service. Well, Joe had hauled ass, thanks to Marlene's little joke. After the initial crazy rush, Olivia had relaxed and begun to trust him. He had caught her openly grinning as he sweated over the grill. What kind of a Svengali waiter could talk an entire table into ordering steaks at lunch? Joe set up a cutting board and began to clean monkfish for his special.

He had noticed a curious dynamic in the kitchen. Chameleon was majorly understaffed, but everyone worked together to get the job done, a very unusual phenomenon in a professional kitchen. Usually, the front of the house and the back of the house fought like cats and dogs. The waiters complained that their food was slow, and the cooks were always pissed off because the waiters were raking in the tips while they did all the work.

Within the kitchen itself, there was a hierarchy too, with the prep cook being lowest on the totem pole and the sauté chef the highest. Joe hadn't ever worked in a kitchen where the first waiter off the floor was put to work picking chicken carcasses and the pastry chef made the veal demi. Now that he had given it some thought, he had really put his foot in his mouth about that whole teamwork thing. This kitchen ran like a clock.

After watching Marlene cook all afternoon in spite of her hangover, he probably owed her an apology too. What the hell had gotten into him this afternoon? He had intended to clear the air between them so that he could do the job he had promised to do. He wasn't sure how he had ended up alternately flirting with her and fighting with her for two hours when he should have been up here filling six pans with all the ingredients he'd need for dinner service.

She clearly had the prep under control, and the cooler was full of the amazing desserts he'd seen sailing out into the dining room during lunch. She was right: she hadn't needed his help with the prep list, but he'd stuck around to enjoy the economy of her motions as she banged out the work. Each task rolled into the next in a seamless progression until everything was cut, then cooked, cooled, labeled, and stored. He had a bad feeling he knew who to thank for the well-prepped grill station today.

Joe heard the screen door open and looked up from the monkfish tail. Every time he had heard the back door open today, he'd expected it to be Keith, arriving for work as scheduled. Evidence of his half-assed work ethic was obvious all over the kitchen: waxy, black grime mopped into the corners of the hot line; unlabeled, undated containers in the walk-in. From the dust on top of some of the number ten cans in dry storage, Keith hadn't been real interested in proper rotation either. Joe couldn't wait to rub his face in the fact that he'd been replaced.

The back door opened again. Closed. This time, he was not disappointed. He heard Keith greet Kevin, the dishwasher, and he tensed.

"What the hell are you doing here?" Keith stepped out of the dish room and strode down the front of line.

"Working." He smiled tightly, enjoying Keith's instant rage.

"That's my fish, Rafferty. Get your hands off it."

"You ordered monkfish? I'm surprised you could even identify it. A man who can't tell his wife's pussy from a bit of strange can't be trusted to identify decent fish, that's for sure."

"You're not the only expert on pussy around here."

"Guess not." Joe put his knife down and wiped his hands on a side towel. "You better scram before Olivia sees you. She's been making some pretty interesting suggestions about how to amputate your nuts."

Keith recoiled. "This is my restaurant too. I'm working tonight. I'm not going anywhere," he retorted.

Joe stepped out from behind the line. "Yeah, you are. It seems Chameleon is in the market for a new chef. This time, Olivia's looking for someone who can actually do the job, not just the female employees." He blocked the hallway to the office and the bakeshop.

"Move it, Rafferty. As soon as I find Olivia, you're out of here. She'll forgive me. She always does."

"Not this time." Olivia spoke from the hall behind Joe. "Hey, baby! Don't tell me you actually hired this joker?" Keith's abrupt switch to charm made Joe grit his teeth. Chicks actually fell for that shit? Olivia stepped forward until she stood next to him. Just for kicks, he slung a tight arm around her waist. Her face was drawn, and her eyes were hard as she spoke. Her body was rigid against his side. "Joe's done more work in one day, than you've done all month. Get out, Keith. You've already used every second chance you had here."

Keith glared at them, giving up the act. "I see how things are. I should have figured you'd show up sooner or later, Rafferty. Sloppy seconds the best you can do these days?" he sneered.

"Don't give me an excuse to fuck up that pretty-boy face, Watson. It's the only thing you've got going for you now."

Keith's cheeks flushed. He took a step forward.

Come on, come on, hit me, Joe thought, getting ready. He'd let Keith get in one good punch, and then he'd take him out back and work him over against the brick wall.

Keith turned toward Olivia instead. "Don't expect much from her, Rafferty. She's like ice in the sack."

"You can't melt ice with a limp torch, Keith," Olivia pointed out.

The mulish expression on Keith's face reminded Joe of the way his cousin's kids looked when they were seeing just how far they could push their mother before she lost her temper and applied a smackdown. He lifted his chin. "I want to get my knives out of the office."

"Be my guest," Olivia said. "You want a towel to get the dust off of them? Don't take too long. If you aren't out of here in five minutes, I'm calling the police."

Keith shouldered past them. Joe gave him a healthy

shove in the direction he was going, hoping Keith would turn around and give him another chance. "You want me to go with him?" he asked.

She shook her head. "Just tell me when he leaves, okay? I'll be up front."

Joe returned to the monkfish tails and picked up his blade.

"And Joe?" Olivia's voice was quiet.

He looked up.

"Don't ever refer to fish and my pussy in the same sentence. Got it?"

He nodded, chuckling. He had wondered if she'd heard that.

She rolled her eyes and went through the swinging door into the dining room. "Get him out of here, cowboy."

―⁓―

Marlene heard a noise behind her. She glanced up from the potatoes in time to see Keith duck into the office. She nicked her little finger with the swivel-headed peeler. "Damn." She dropped the potato and the peeler into the five gallon bucket of water and raced to the office door.

Locked.

She found Joe on the line, wrist-deep in monkfish, the nastiest bottom-dweller ever to hit the restaurants. "Does Olivia know Keith just locked himself in the office?"

"Locked, huh? He's got about two minutes before I haul his ass out of there."

"Can I watch?" she asked.

"Let's go, sugar."

The office door was wide open and the back room was empty and still when they reached the back.

"Maybe he went out the front," Joe said, heading in that direction.

"I'll check the back."

In the dish room, Marlene saw crusted-over sauté pans full of dried-out sauce and half-sheet pans piled every which way. Tea bags, sugar packets, and straws swirled in the clogged drain. The stainless steel sink was full of milky water, ice cubes, globs of swollen noodles, and sogged-out bread crusts. There were so many dishes piled up, there was no room to make room. But no sign of Keith.

"Holy shit, this place is a friggin' mess! Where's *Kevin?*" Marlene yelled to make herself heard in the wait station.

Shane came over to peer at the unscraped, unstacked dish mess, then ducked back down the hall as Joe and Olivia walked quickly through the narrow aisle between the reach-in cooler and the front of the line. When Shane got a safe distance away from the dish room, he called over his shoulder, "I just heard Keith tell Kevin he'd give him a hundred bucks to walk out."

"Fuck." Olivia said what Marlene was thinking.

Joe laughed. "You've got to give him credit for imagination. That's a good one."

"Where'd he get the hundred bucks?" Olivia wondered out loud.

"Probably out of your safe, kiddo. You really should have let me go with him," Joe said.

"That's it. I'm getting a restraining order." Olivia stomped out of the dish room.

"Hey, that doesn't get you out of KP!" Joe yelled after her.

Marlene and Joe locked eyes.

"I was pulling worms out of monkfish when Keith got here," Joe said. "Ladies choice: dish or fish?"

"I'll run the plates through," she said reluctantly.

"Sissy."

"There is no way in hell I'm cleaning up this whole mess though. Jacques is looking for overtime. He'll come in a little early. I'm going home to take a nice, hot bubble bath, and pretend this day never happened." She attacked the dishes with savage force.

"Uh-oh."

"What now?"

"Marly?"

"What?" This time with force and impatience. She had a lot of dishes to do and her headache was coming back.

"Have you lost that lovin' feeling?" Joe's light blue eyes danced above the barest curve of his full lips.

"Fuck off. I hope the worms bite you."

"They're dead."

"Too bad." Marlene didn't pause until she could hear that Joe was all the way back in his station on the line. Still, that was just on the other side of the dish room wall, and she could hear him humming the tune to "You've Lost That Lovin' Feeling," the bar pickup song from the *Top Gun* soundtrack.

Sense memory flooded her body and Marlene felt it again, his lips, their kiss. Perfect.

She must have imagined it, or better yet, it was an alcohol-induced hallucination. She put her palms on the raised rim of the stainless steel table to support her weak knees. When the heat waves didn't subside, she gritted her teeth and threw herself into scrubbing a stockpot.

She'd wash every pot in the kitchen if it would cleanse her traitorous memory of Joe's amazing lips.

She set the pot in a rack and pulled her cell phone out of her pocket to dial the night dishwasher. Jacques was happy to come in early, thank God, although it still took her forever to get out of the kitchen. It always did. There were so many details to be communicated, so many racks to check and things to label before she left for the day. Since Olivia was on the phone with her lawyer, Marlene had to answer Joe's questions and deal with the waiters too. Would this day never end? By the time she reached home, she was ready to collapse.

She dragged herself into the bathroom and poured a more than generous amount of bubble bath into the steaming torrent of hot water. "Ahhh," she sighed, easing into the water. Tears pricked her eyes as her muscles relaxed, telling her just how tightly she'd been wound all day.

Her telephone was ringing, but there was no way she was going to get out of the tub until her churning brain slowed down. The answering machine caught the call, and she heard her mother's bright voice. "Hi, baby, it's Mom. I'm home tonight. Give me a call if you want me to do your hair. I brought foil home from work. Love you."

Marlene's desperate desire to crawl into bed had dissolved in the bathwater. She was too wired to sleep, and it was only seven o'clock. A night with her mom and some new highlights sounded like the perfect antidote to her crappy day. She shifted to keep her hair dry, glad she had put it up before she climbed into the tub.

Just as she rose from the tub, someone started banging on her back door. No peace for the wicked, it seemed.

"Hang on," she yelled, toweling off and pulling on a robe. She was not surprised to see Danny on her back step, looking for all the world like a deer standing in the middle of the road staring at a semi-truck. "Oh, for God's sake, get that look off your face. Get in here." She opened the door and gestured at her fridge. "Have a beer if you want. I'm going to get dressed."

"Not on my account, I hope," he said, hopeful invitation shining in his glossy brown eyes. She looked at him for a moment and thought about it. He was really cute, with his long, dark blond hair loose around his face, and his beat-up jeans and worn T-shirt emphasizing the strength of his tight and toned body. Even though summer had just begun, he was tan, probably because he had skipped work and spent the day in the sun. God, he was such a puppy. The five-year difference in their ages yawned wide, and she didn't feel her usual desire to press herself against his warmth.

She shook her head in exasperation. "Do we have to go through this again?"

"Hey, hope springs eternal. I figure if I keep coming around, one of these days you'll decide to keep me."

"That's not the way I operate, Danny. You know that." He was fun and they were friends, but she'd never led him to expect more than that.

He ducked his head. "You mad at me about last night?"

"No, I'm not mad at you, Danny boy. Hang on. I'll be right back." He headed for the fridge, and she went into her bedroom to pull on jeans and a black tank top. She ignored his admiring gaze when she returned to the kitchen. No, she wasn't mad at him, but she wasn't going to encourage him either.

He lowered the beer bottle from his lips. "So, who was the guy on your roof last night? Weren't you at the bar with him too?" Jealousy and curiosity deepened his voice.

"It would serve you right if I said none of your business, but he's filling in at Chameleon until Olivia can find somebody to replace Keith. You'll meet him tomorrow." It wasn't the truth he was seeking, but it was pertinent information.

"Replace Keith?"

"Where have you been? Under a rock? Wait, don't answer that." She knew where he'd been last night at least. "We found Keith and Nikki getting it on in dry storage. Olivia kicked him out. Fired him too. Frankly, I'm not sure working with Joe is any better, but at least he can cook."

"Holy shit. I can't believe Keith didn't call me. Have you seen him today? Is he okay?" Danny raked his long hair away from his face. She noticed that his frown barely creased his unlined skin as he checked his cell phone for messages.

She scowled at him. "I saw his back after he paid Kevin to walk out today. Do not mention his name in my presence, Danny boy. He's a snake, and if you insist on calling him a friend, that's your problem."

Danny shoved his phone into his pocket and took a long pull on his beer. She knew he'd call Keith the minute he left, but he knew better than to push her. "Got a poker game tonight," he said, thankfully changing the subject. "You wanna play?"

She wasn't in the mood, but couldn't resist asking, "What's the buy-in?"

"Hundred bucks." He took another swig of beer.

"No thanks, too rich for my blood."

"The more that's in, the more you win. Especially you." His grin was full of mischief. "How 'bout you just come and play with my money? You can keep your winnings. I love watching you play poker."

"Sorry, I just made plans with my mom." Disappointment flashed in his wide brown eyes. She ignored it. "You better make it an early night, Danny. Don't even think about calling in sick again tomorrow. If you miss another shift, I'll fire you myself, even if we are short-handed." She took the empty beer bottle out of his hand and pointed at the door.

He stood up quickly, before she could step back, and locked his strong arms around her waist. "Would you miss me?" He dipped to brush his lips against the side of her neck. It didn't make her shiver like it usually did. She didn't pull away from him, but she didn't tilt her head to give him easier access either. They both sighed in disappointment.

Danny had a lot to learn, but he was sweet. She brought her arms up to rest on his shoulders. "Yeah, Danny, I'd miss you."

"Good." He dropped a fast kiss on her lips and released her before she could push him away. He grabbed another beer from her fridge and winked on his way to the door.

"That poker game in walking distance?" she asked, looking pointedly at the beer in his hand.

"Why? You wanna catch up with me later?" The look he was giving her now wasn't sweet at all, and it reminded her that although he might lack experience in some areas, he more than made up for it when he was naked. A few hours in bed with Danny might be just the thing to wash away the sting of Joe's rejection and the last dregs of her hangover.

Why not? She shook her head, more to herself than in answer to his question. "My mother is expecting me to walk in the door any minute." As soon as Marlene told her she was coming.

Danny shrugged and slipped out her back door, throwing one last smoldering glance over his shoulder. It was surprisingly effective, and she regretted kicking him out for a full minute as she stared at the sunset through the screen door. What on earth had made her turn him down?

A silhouette blocked the fading light, and she jumped, recognizing her downstairs neighbor as he knocked sharply on the door.

"C'mon in," she called. Good thing she hadn't decided to nap.

Thomas stepped into the kitchen and quirked one dark, winged eyebrow at her. "Were you standing there waiting for me?"

She shook her head. "Danny just left a second ago."

He stroked a long-fingered hand through his short goatee, which was starting to echo the thick, silver streaks at his temples. The man had a glorious head of salt and pepper hair, thick, coarse, and wild, and his unironed oxford, wrinkled khakis, and distracted expression completed the distracted English professor image. "Bill and I were thinking about heading out of town this weekend. Would you be willing to watch Samson?"

"I'd love it," she replied instantly. "When can I have him?"

His expression was sheepish. "Now? Bill's downstairs packing the car. We were going to take him if we had to, but if Aunt Marlene's available…"

She nodded eagerly, and he backed out the door, returning a few minutes later with the panting beagle, his leash, and a sack of dog food. Samson yipped and ran in excited circles while they exchanged the necessary details.

"Thanks, Marlene. We won't be home late on Sunday, I promise."

"He's no trouble. I love the company."

Thomas leaned down to give Samson a kiss. "Be good, monkey man."

Samson kissed him back and Thomas left, laughing and wiping his face on his sleeve.

"C'mon, Sam, let's go see Grandma." Marlene snapped the leash onto his collar, grabbed her purse, and led him out the door. The tip-tapping of his claws on the wooden stairs was a cheerful sound and she smiled, feeling optimistic about the turn her day had taken.

She'd been too hungover and shell-shocked this morning to talk to Olivia about working on the line again, but tomorrow was another day. It was probably better to wait and see what happened with Keith anyway. Joe was right about one thing: things rarely changed. If Olivia let Keith come back to work, Marly would be in the exact same situation as before.

She opened her car door. "Get up in there," she said to Sam, who leaped up into the driver's seat and clambered over the console. She started her car and pulled out of the driveway. Samson sat on the seat next to her during the drive, shedding like crazy.

Just as she turned into the driveway of her mom's

new house, she remembered she hadn't called to say she was coming. She put the car in park and pulled her cell out of her purse. She'd better make sure she was still welcome.

A man answered her mother's phone. Even though she should be used to it by now, Marlene stammered. "Oh, hey, um…is Kate there?"

"Sure thing." She heard him call, "Honey?"

A moment later, her mother answered, "Hello?"

"Hi, Mom, it's me."

"Baby! It's so good to hear from you—"

"Actually, I'm in your driveway." As soon as it was out of her mouth, she regretted not slowly backing out into the street and driving away from the house. The man's voice had killed her anticipation of an evening spent alone with her mother. She was almost certain her mom was going to marry this one too, and it was going to be painful to be nice to him. "I don't want to interrupt your night, Mom—"

Samson barked, and her mother squealed, "Have you got Sam with you? Get in here, silly, I can't wait to see him, and I want you to meet Richard!"

"Sure," Marlene sighed, staring at the brilliant orange-pink line on the horizon and wishing she had stayed home to watch the sun set from her roof. This was certainly turning out to be a full day, she thought wryly, as she pushed the car door open with her leg so Samson could scramble over her. He jumped to the ground, and she snatched his leash as it slid over her lap, letting him drag her up the steps and through the door her mom was holding open for them.

Marlene unhooked Sam's leash before she embraced

her mother. As usual, her mom looked like she had just stepped out of a beauty salon. She probably had, of course; she often worked late at the beauty shop. Her mother practiced her art as assiduously on herself as she did on her clients, and it showed. Her fair skin glowed. Her fashionably straight blond hair, cut with careful layers to frame her delicate features, fell in a smooth sheet to the tops of her shoulders, and she was wearing fresh lip gloss in a peachy shade that complimented her skin tone perfectly. Her blue eyes were accented by a bold slash of metallic green.

Marlene always felt a bit rough standing next to her, as if she could never quite remove the film of grease the restaurant left on her skin or repair the damage that working with her hands did to her nails. Automatically, she reached up to try to smooth her curls, which were even wilder than usual because of her recent soak in the bathtub. Her mother drew her into the kitchen for the meet and greet with the boyfriend, and Marly braced herself, preparing to be cordial but not too friendly to a man who didn't know that he wouldn't be around for very long.

The sight that met her eyes disarmed her completely. Her mother's new boyfriend was sitting on the kitchen floor, allowing Samson to lick his cheeks. "That's a good boy. You're a friendly little fellow, aren't you?" He grinned at the dog, almost caught a tongue in the mouth, and then laughed, noticing them in the doorway. He gave Sam a final pat and stood.

"I'm Richard Stone. You must be Marlene." She took the hand he offered and returned his smile. He was a few inches taller than she was, so that put him over six feet, and he was handsome, as all her mother's husbands had been. He was dressed in tan shorts and a sports shirt, and he looked smart and steady enough to hold down a job, which set him apart from her mother's ex-husbands. Well, excluding her father, who was a food broker, but his desertion put him in the same deadbeat category as the rest of them.

Richard slung an easy arm around her mother's shoulders and leaned down to kiss her cheek. "I'm off then. I don't need any highlights." He fluffed his receding hairline. "It might make the rest of my hair fall out. Have a good time, girls. Nice to meet you, Marlene." He gave her a friendly nod, her mother an even friendlier kiss, then left by the back door.

"He's…different," Marlene ventured when she heard his car start.

Her mom's laugh was a happy trill. "Yes, he certainly is. You know, I think he just might be—"

"The one?" Marlene suggested with a sigh, as her weariness returned. They were all the one.

"Don't look at me in that tone of voice, Marlene. At least I try. You gotta be in it to win it, babe."

"I know, I know." Her mom believed that happiness was a steady man, any steady man, and she was mercifully unaware of the ever-changing parade of men that circled her daughter. Occasionally, Marly would tell her about one random guy in order to pacify her. It was easier to recall exactly whom her mother thought she was dating than it was to tell her perpetually optimistic mother that she didn't believe in love. Actually, they shared the same dating philosophy. There was always a next guy on the horizon for them, but Marlene wasn't going to marry any of them.

She pulled her hair down from its twist. "Speaking of which, I turned down a poker game to take you up on your offer tonight."

"What was the buy-in?" her mom asked with a sly smile.

"Hundred bucks. We can probably still get in if you're interested," she offered. It would be fun to play with her mom, even if she lost her money. Her mother had taught her everything she knew about Texas hold 'em, the sole legacy of stepfather number two, who had left them for Las Vegas and the lure of a World Series of Poker bracelet.

Her mom reached up to catch a renegade curl. "I'd much rather play with your hair, babe. Would you like a glass of wine?"

Marlene blanched. "Hungover," she explained.

Her mother poured herself a glass of white zinfandel from the fridge and began assembling her tools. She ran her fingers through Marlene's hair. "Nice and dirty."

"Hey!"

"It's a good thing, baby. Now relax, and let your mama work her magic." She began to rub Marlene's neck in smooth, hard strokes, and Marly groaned, giving herself up to her mother's brand of tender, loving care.

Chapter 7

JOE GATHERED UP EMPTY PANS AND EXCHANGED THEM for clean ones in the dish room, stopping to grab a bucket of garlic mashed potatoes from the reach-in. In spite of the chaos Keith had left in his wake that afternoon, they had breezed through dinner service. It had been an easy night, as smooth as any he'd ever had, although he couldn't quite banish the image of Marly floating in a tubful of vanilla-scented bubbles. She'd left soon after Jacques arrived, thoughtfully leaving a diagram of the station and a prep list on his cutting board before she hit the door.

The warm air in the cooler registered just as he slammed the door shut. He checked the gauge. "Hey, kiddo, your cooler's going down," he called to Olivia. "Or up, actually. It's headed for sixty degrees."

"I'll call the repairman," she said, groaning.

He circled to the back of the unit and reached behind it. "Don't bother." He held up a length of electrical cord. "The plug fell out."

Her relief was visible. "Good eye. You just saved me a hundred bucks, at least."

"Excellent. You can buy me a beer." He filled all the slots in his workstation with fresh prep, then spread a length of plastic wrap over the top. He dropped the lid with a bang. "We all set up here?" he asked, looking around. The kid doing salads had left when the orders slowed down. The waiters were gone too.

"Just about." She was on her knees with her head stuck in the refrigerated bottom of her station reaching for something in the back.

"Mind if I go through the walk-in?"

"Be my guest. I'd love it," she replied.

Joe had been too busy watching Marly in the walk-in that afternoon to notice the refrigerator was a hellhole. He emerged to grab a rolling cart and began to fill it with half-empty, unlabeled containers lined with blue and green fur mold, red spotted dairy mold, and trailing sprouts of delicate, black spores. It was an impressive collection of death in plastic buckets.

He turned to the tall racks that lined the other wall of the cooler, trying not to judge. What the hell had been going on around here? For Christ's sake, somebody had put the chicken on top of the lettuce. He pulled the dripping box of raw chicken breasts from the middle of the rack and placed it on the bottom shelf, popping his head out of the walk-in just as Olivia entered the back room.

She surveyed the cart. "Looks like you found Keith's special shelf."

"Among other things." He pointed at the lettuce. "Do you guys always store chicken breasts above the lettuce?" he asked, unable to keep the "comma, stupid," out of his voice.

"Nope, bottom shelf, on the left," she answered.

"Yeah, well, this time it was parked above an entire case of romaine. Unless you want to cook it, that lettuce is garbage. Got a recipe for lettuce fritters? Veggie burgers?"

Olivia grimaced. "Trash it."

Joe nodded. Honestly, he wasn't that surprised by the mold—par for the course where Keith Watson was concerned—but after finding the dishwasher gone and the cooler unplugged, the misplaced chicken was one too many unhappy coincidences. "Hey, kiddo, did you check the safe in the office after Keith left this afternoon?"

She turned white. "No, I called my lawyer, and then the orders started coming in." She bolted toward the office.

"Son of a bitch!" He heard her say a minute later.

"How much?" Joe asked.

"Empty."

He whistled. "You keep much in there?"

"Five hundred bucks in petty cash and paperwork, but that's not the point, damn it. Hasn't he done enough? I mean, I married him and he ruined my restaurant. He made me look like an idiot by screwing around all the time. Now he's stealing from me? How am I going to get out of this? When is it going to end?"

"It's going to end right now, kiddo. Call your lawyer again. Tell him what happened. I'll finish up back here." He steered her into the office.

Since there wasn't anything left to do except pull the mats and give the line a quick sweep and a mop, which the dishwasher would do when they left, Joe laid his knives in his box and locked it. Then he gathered their aprons and towels and tossed them in the bin. He continued to tidy the back room until Olivia came around the corner.

"All set?"

"Yeah, Sean says not to worry. We'll sort it out in the courtroom. He's trying to get a court order to keep Keith out of here," she said.

"Good enough. Let's get a beer."

Olivia put her hand on his arm and shook her head. "You don't need me to go with you to Johnny's to see if Marlene's there, you know."

"Maybe I just want a beer," he countered.

"Right." She waved at the night dishwasher. "Night, Jacques, thanks."

Olivia gave him a pitying look, but she let him lead her out the back door and across the street. The bar was jammed, but Joe knew Marlene wasn't there as soon as he opened the door. No electric zing. No instant hard-on.

"Can we go now?" Olivia asked.

The same bartender from the other night, the nosy one, appeared just as they reached the bar. "You looking for Marly? She's not here."

"Give me a Guinness and an Amstel, Johnny." She jerked her thumb at Joe. "He's paying."

"Coming right up."

When the drinks arrived, he paid for them and led Olivia to a small booth just inside the door. He couldn't avoid her assessing gaze. "What on earth happened last night?" she asked.

"Nothing."

"That's what Marly said too, but I find it hard to believe since you two have been at each others' throats all day." She picked up her drink.

"She was plastered," he shrugged. "It didn't feel right."

Olivia choked on her beer. She wiped her chin with the back of her hand and looked at him as if he'd grown another head.

"Is that so hard to believe?" he asked.

"Yes!" She nodded hard.

"You women just don't appreciate a gentleman anymore."

"Joe! You aren't a gentleman! Bad-boy vibes come off you in waves, and women want that from you. I think you hurt her feelings." Her eyes held blame.

"She'll recover. She was just pissed," he said.

"Pissed enough to bury you with orders today," she pointed out.

"You knew about that?" He was getting a little tired of seeing her roll her eyes at him. "Look, we made up. It's over. We're buddies now. We shook hands and everything," he protested.

"You have truly lost your mind."

Joe shrugged again and took a deep, drowning drink of his beer.

"Fine, Joe, you can live in denial if you want. But I'm warning you: don't hurt Marly. She's really not all that tough. Her dad left when she was a kid, and her mom is on her fifth marriage, at least. She hasn't exactly had a good role model for relationships. If I thought you were going to mess with her head, I never would have left you alone with her."

Joe mumbled something under his breath.

"What? I didn't catch that." Her voice was still sharp.

His vision of Marly half-floating in a bubble bath had been replaced by Marly and a man, probably that Danny guy from last night. Joe chugged his beer and clunked the glass down on the table. "I think she's messing with mine." He dropped his head against the back of the booth.

Olivia burst out laughing. "That will be the day."

He looked at her through narrowed eyes and decided he'd been heckled enough for the night. It was her turn. Hopefully, a little teasing would get that bruised look off her face and get her off his back at the same time. "*You* oughta get laid, kiddo," he said casually.

"You're not offering, are you?" Her eyes were amused.

"I'd consider it, but why ruin a beautiful friendship? Unless of course—"

She shook her head vehemently.

Joe continued. "You should get back up on the horse, so to speak. You're young, good-looking, and there's no better way to get over Wonder Boy."

"You sound like Marlene," Olivia said. "She swears that the best way to get over the last guy is to move on to the next."

"Smart girl," he said wryly.

Joe sat up straight and scanned the bar. He spotted a middle-aged banker-type hunched over his glass at a table in the corner. "How about him?"

"He's got a daiquiri."

"All right then, what about that guy? Musician?" Joe looked at a scruffy, long-haired guy at the bar staring into his shot glass like he expected a genie to pop out of it. "Finish your drink, and go get him, kid."

"He looks…dirty." Olivia said, but she almost smiled.

"Picky, picky."

She pointed at the door. "Quit playing matchmaker, and go get your stuff. I've got a spare bedroom, and you might as well use it."

Joe raised his eyebrows over his Guinness. "Mrs. Watson? Are you trying to seduce me?"

She laughed out loud, and he felt he'd accomplished his mission.

"That's Ms. Marconi to you, cowboy, and you can keep your horse to yourself. Giving you a room will be cheaper than paying for your motel, and it will definitely piss Keith off. We'll have opposite schedules once you get rolling anyway. *Mi casa es su casa.*"

"Sounds fair." Anything would be better than the motel he had crashed in last night. Fleabag city. "Tomorrow night should set me straight. I've got the menu down already. Why don't you take Sunday off? No offense, but you look like you could use a breather."

Olivia shook her head in amazement. "Sunday is brunch, Joe. Totally different menu. And tomorrow night won't be a cakewalk for you either. We've got a hundred on the books, and that's just reservations. I bet we do one-fifty, at least."

Joe whistled. "I'll take that bet. Easy street, baby. Turn and burn."

"Only you would think you can run my restaurant after two nights on the line." She punched him lightly on the arm.

"Two nights on the line and I *can* run your restaurant. And as far as brunch goes, I'm pretty sure I can cook eggs." Joe stood. "You coming?"

"In a minute. I'll meet you at my place." She gave him directions.

"You sure you don't want me to drive? We can pick up your car tomorrow," he offered.

"Go, Joe." Olivia gave him a shove toward the door. "Gimme some space. I'll meet you at the house. Key's under the mat."

"Think about taking Sunday off, kid. You need a break," he urged her.

"Only if you ask Marly to help you with brunch," Olivia called after him. "Nicely! I heard you two squabbling today."

"Have a little faith," Joe threw over his shoulder, whistling to himself as he headed for his truck. He sat in his Jeep until Olivia left the bar and made it safely to her vehicle. Then he headed for the motel to check out and grab his stuff.

Chapter 8

MARLENE ARRIVED AT CHAMELEON BRIGHT AND EARLY Saturday morning, full of the energy and love of life that only the day after a hangover can bring. She felt more than able to take on any task, and she looked good too, thanks to her new highlights. Her hair now had so many different shades of red and gold and brown that it was hard to put a name to the color. Cranberry marmalade, maybe. Or hot whiskey. She'd definitely talk to Olivia about taking over the line today.

Chameleon wasn't open for lunch on Saturday, so she didn't expect anyone to trickle in until after noon. It was heaven to have the whole kitchen to herself. She spent the morning filling the freezer with rolled pastry shells for future lemon tarts and scones for her shortcakes, and she toasted almonds for her roulades. With every other egg she cracked, her mind returned to Joe. She hadn't given this much thought to a man since, well, her father didn't count, so never.

Joe Rafferty did not want her. No big deal. No problem. Plenty of other guys did. Like Danny for example. He'd been more than willing to stay with her instead of playing poker last night. She didn't need Joe.

Unfortunately, the tiny little traitor that lived somewhere between her heart and her brain wanted to show Joe what he was missing. That inner turncoat was fluffing her hair, checking her makeup, and picking out scandalous lingerie. Oh yeah, and another part of her wanted to show him he wasn't God's gift to the kitchen. Especially her kitchen. That part of her was sharpening her knives. By hand.

Marlene poured egg yolks and sugar into the small bowl of her heavy-duty KitchenAid mixer on the counter. She stirred and scraped once, just to keep the yolks from burning, then secured the whip and let it rip. She turned around to pour egg whites into the bowl of her twenty-quart Hobart stand mixer and began whipping them at medium speed, wrinkling her nose as the egg white smell of wet dog rose from the stainless steel bowl.

"You always come in this early on Saturday?" Joe asked from the doorway.

Marlene looked up for a moment, just long enough to catch an eyeful of his broad chest and the swirl of dark hair peeking out of the collar of his T-shirt as he buttoned his chef coat. A sharp flash of lust arced through her belly, quickly chased by irritation. Not interested, she reminded herself. She began to add sugar, tablespoon by tablespoon, to the meringue. "I can't stay late tonight, so I wanted to get my desserts prepped and my specials done early." Samson had been known to misbehave when left alone too long.

"Can't stay late, huh? Got a date?"

Inner traitor giggled. "As a matter of fact, I do." Sam would share her dinner and her bed—that counted as a date in her book.

"Leaving early shouldn't be a problem," Joe said, making it sound as if he was giving her permission.

She gritted her teeth and added the last tablespoon of sugar to her meringue.

"Got a minute to go over the prep list?" he asked.

Marlene bumped up the speed on the mixer. "Sorry, my nice, fluffy egg whites aren't going to hang around while we chat. Just write it down. I'll get it done."

He stood over her. "I'll wait."

"Your call."

She folded the ground almonds into the yolks, and took her time folding in the whites, gently bringing the denser nut and yolk mixture up from the bottom of the bowl. She would not take her irritation out on her delicate sponge cakes. Just before the streaks of egg white disappeared, she divided the batter among six half-sheet pans and encouraged the bubbly batter toward the edges of each. She slid them into the deck ovens and shut the heavy door with care before she turned to face him.

"Now, what were you saying?" God, it was completely unfair that he was so attractive. She should not want to kiss a man who made her nuttier than the almonds in her cakes.

"Olivia wants to know if you have time to make the garlic mashed potatoes and white beans. She soaked the beans last night. We also need pesto, chimichurri, chipotle sauce, and onions and peppers, got that?" Joe asked.

"I'll get right on it. Anything else, chef?"

He cocked his head to the side. "You make the word chef sound like an insult. You have something against chefs?" he asked, leaning a solid shoulder against her reach-in, blocking her in the bakeshop.

"Absolutely not, *chef*," she repeated. "Just doing my job."

"Uh-huh," he said with a sardonic grin. "Which job?

Pastry chef? Prep cook? Troublemaker?" Joe pushed away from the reach-in and began to walk toward her. She swallowed, resisting the urge to step back.

"All of the above." She lifted her chin and met his eyes, hoping he couldn't read the bluff in hers. She wasn't going to cause any more trouble. She just wanted her real job back, which unfortunately happened to be his job at the moment.

Joe stopped right in front of her. His blue eyes went gray, like an ice storm. "You don't have any other nasty little tricks planned for me during service, do you, sugar? Because if you do, neither one of us will be laughing this time. I'll turn you over my knee and give you the paddling you deserve."

"Well, that would be something new." She gave him a tight-lipped smile. He was so close that his breath feathered over her face and another lightning strike of simple, straight-up lust hit her in the gut.

His eyes dropped to her mouth, and she saw a muscle in his jaw twitch. Maybe he wasn't unaffected by the tension that charged the air between them. Frustration, pure and simple, made her crave some sort of satisfaction, and inner traitor wanted to remind Joe what he was missing. She reached out to smooth the cotton of his chef coat across the expanding width of his chest. "I don't need dirty tricks to take down a schoolboy like you," she said.

"You don't, huh?" His deep voice rumbled quietly in his chest. "What do you need?"

"Not a thing." Her palm slid over his firm muscles, caressed the warm column of his neck, and finally felt the rasp of his shadowed cheek. It did make a sound. She drew his face down to hers. "Just this," she whispered against his lips.

Joe leaned into her kiss.

Heat rose between them. She hadn't imagined how good their last kiss had been, after all. Their lips moved together in a perfect synchronization of shared breath, movement, and desire. She kept her eyes open. He did too. His strong arms sought her waist, pressing their bodies together from groin to breast, searching for a seamless fit. He surged into her, pressing her against the table behind her, lifting her onto its surface. Her back hit the storage shelf, and she didn't care what precious garnish got destroyed as it hit the table.

His tongue found the sensitive inner edge of her upper lip and stroked along its length. She wrapped her arms around his neck and held on as he moved against her, creating more heat with his lips. His hands caressed her back, and she felt him tug the strings of her apron loose. She welcomed his hand on her breast beneath her T-shirt and wished he would get rid of her shirt too. Arousal spiked hot in her center, and insistent, insane heat consumed her. She watched his eyes drift shut, and shut her own to better concentrate on the breathless awareness between them.

You're losing it, her inner traitor warned. *You made your point. Now walk away. Show him what he's missing. Do it now. If you wait another minute, you'll be on the floor, on your back, and it will be too late.*

With effort, she loosened her hold around Joe's neck and slid down his hard body until both feet touched the floor. Her kiss became teasing, deliberately seductive instead of spontaneously combustive. She gave him a playful shove and stepped back. "See? It's not so hard to take you down."

He crossed his arms, cocked an eyebrow. "I distinctly remember you saying that my virtue was safe from you."

"Oh, I don't think I hurt your virtue. Besides, if you can't take the heat, stay out of the kitchen." She grabbed her dirty dishes. "Let me know if you need anything else before service, *chef*."

Joe caught her arm as she sailed past him. "Don't forget about your cakes, sugar."

Marlene wanted to continue her triumphant march to the dish room, but she knew from the nutty smell perfuming the bakeshop that he was right. Her almond roulades were done, maybe even overdone. She dropped her dishes on the table and pulled her cakes from the oven in the nick of time.

"Thank you," she said formally, when all her cakes were safe.

"You're welcome," he said, just as politely. Marlene heard amusement ripple in his voice and barely controlled the urge to heave a hot half-sheet pan of cake directly at his head. Instead, she picked up the dirty bowls again and made her way to the dish room.

Olivia was coming in the back door.

"Are you all right?" Olivia asked, giving her a worried look.

"Perfectly fine," she responded calmly. "But I need you to sterilize a knife. Quickly. I'm either going to kill Joe or slit my wrists."

Olivia's laugh echoed behind her as she swept out the back door to run home and let Samson out to pee.

In spite of her agitation, or perhaps because of it, the hours flew by after she returned from doggy duty. Marly cooked white beans with fresh rosemary and thyme and made sauces and mashed potatoes while she filled the almond roulades with caramel mousse and baked a new batch of chocolate cheesecakes.

Tonight's special dessert was a crème brûlée infused with star anise, basil, and ginger, and spiked with a bright green herbal liqueur called Chartreuse. The customers loved it. In fact, they had sold so many brûlées last night that the waiters had burned more on the fly. This morning, she had walked in to a huge mess in her reach-in because the no-good slackers hadn't bothered to finish caramelizing them all.

Marlene pulled the leftover brûlées, covered with thick piles of white sugar, out of her fridge. She lit the propane torch and tipped it toward the first brûlée. The sugar on top sputtered and burned, spitting hot, black flecks onto her hand. "Ouch!" she yelled. The sugar must have been damp from spending the night in the cooler.

She opened the bin under her table and sprinkled another thin layer of granulated sugar on top of what was already there. She touched it with the torch. That's better, she thought, as the sugar turned amber and rolled toward the edges of the ramekin.

She topped the rest of the custards with extra sugar too, and waved the torch back and forth, covering each custard with a thick, hard sheet of amber sugar.

Joe was right, she thought. She did have something against chefs.

She had been crushed when Olivia brought Keith home and put him in charge of the line, the line Marly had been guarding while Olivia got her pretty piece of paper that declared she was a real chef. At first, Marly had tried to work with him, but there was only so much she could do to cover his mistakes. She'd lasted a year and a half and then hoped his inability to cook good food would be revealed when she quit the hot line. Instead, Olivia had taken over the job of babysitting her husband's plates. Marlene had retreated to the bakeshop to make desserts and pray Olivia would come to her senses. And she had.

But did Olivia give Marly her old job back? Nope, she sure didn't. Instead, she called her buddy Joe in to pinch-hit, and then she put an ad in the fucking paper. Seriously, what did it take to get some respect around here? The torch hissed as Marlene shut it off. She stored it under the table, making sure the hot tip wasn't touching anything remotely flammable.

When she stood, Jacques was peering over the top of the waiters' station. "You let your mama get near your head again, kid?" he asked, grinning and scratching his gray braid.

"Mom's never wrong about hair, Jacques. It will calm down."

"You got a little cake for me?"

Jacques was the best, a solid gold dishwasher with a sweet tooth, which she kept well supplied. She handed him the uneven first slice from the end of the last almond roulade on her table. The rest were tucked in the freezer for the week.

He licked the caramel cream cheese mousse oozing

from the spiral of crunchy cake. "The new guy seems good." He spoke around a mouthful of cake.

"He's temporary," she said flatly.

"Guess you don't like him."

"I didn't say that." She stacked dessert plates in the makeshift window. She had run home once more to take care of Sam, but Joe and Olivia hadn't needed any help from her for over an hour, even though they were really cooking up there. She might as well go home. They didn't need her.

Marlene wiped her table with sanitizer and took off her apron.

"You do like him, then?" Jacques asked, watching her.

"I didn't say that either."

He smoothed cake crumbs out of his drooping mustache and goatee. He gave her a sage nod. "First time for everything, kid."

Chapter 9

JOE FINISHED A PLATE AND SLID IT INTO THE HOT WINDOW.

"Any idea why Marlene wants to fillet your testicles?" Olivia asked him.

He grinned. "She does, huh?"

"You like that idea? You're sicker than I thought. I knew you guys were perfect for each other. You ask her to help you with brunch yet?"

He would die, buried under omelet pans, drowning in waffle batter, choking on hollandaise before he would ask that little minx to help him with brunch tomorrow.

The white beans in his sauté pan were thick and gloppy. He checked the flame under the pan. Not hot enough. The opposite of the problem he was having with Marlene. He cranked the dial sharply to the left. Every time she got close enough to touch him, he remembered how her breasts filled his hands. How her mouth made him crazy. "I've got it under control," he said.

"That doesn't answer my question. Did you ask her to help?" Olivia asked.

"Not yet."

"Joe, Sunday brunch is slamming. You'll need two people, and Anthony isn't up to speed yet. Sorry." Olivia shot an apologetic glance in the salad kid's direction. He flushed.

"Never mind. I'll come in," she capitulated.

"No way. You're running on empty already," he said.

"So ask her already. Or I will. I'm beginning to like the idea of a day off," she said.

Suddenly, flames engulfed his pan, shooting up around its sides. He cut the heat all the way down the stove and dropped a lid over his sauté pan. When he pulled the pan off the stove, flames shot up into the hood. Joe swore.

Olivia stood frozen, tongs in hand. "Salt, girl!" He thrust the box of kosher salt at her and took off for the bakeshop, almost running through Jacques on his way down the short hall.

"I need baking soda," he said when he reached Marlene. She thrust a five pound bucket into his hands and didn't ask any questions. He sprinted back to the line where Olivia was still frozen, kosher salt box in hand. He elbowed her out of the way and dumped soda on the flames. It hit the stove in a powdery whump, and the flames sputtered, still trying to break through the heavy powder.

"I hope this does it," he said. "If the Ansul system drops, we're done." They couldn't serve food from a kitchen covered in flame-retardant chemicals. That's why he hadn't reached for the fire extinguisher in the first place.

Servers and busboys crowded the front of the line, trying to get a good view. Marlene must have followed him up there because Joe heard her shooing them back into the dining room. He poured again, tasting the soda on his tongue, feeling it coat his nostrils.

The flames sputtered, died out, then disappeared.

Olivia swayed next to him. Tears streamed down her face. He grabbed her around the waist, putting one hand on the back of her head, shoving down. "Head between your knees, kiddo. Lean on me." He held her that way for a moment, bent over, cradled in the curve of his body until her shoulders relaxed. Joe pulled her slowly upright, still supporting her weight.

"You gonna make it?" he asked.

Olivia nodded. She sagged against the salad station. At Joe's sharp gesture, Anthony tentatively took her hand and drew her away from the line.

Joe jerked the grease catchers from underneath the burners. The right-hand one was dripping with blackened oil.

"I just changed that a few days ago!" Marlene exclaimed behind him.

Joe raised his eyebrows.

"No, really," she protested. "Wednesday. I was doing it when the dairy order came in."

"Well, it looks like somebody dumped the fryer in there. And then dropped a lit match," he said. "Jacques, would you get me a hotel pan, please?"

"Wait." Marly elbowed Joe out of the way and reinserted the trays into the stove. "Do this first." She grabbed a big ladle and pulled the burners from the stove. As they hit the sink, the hot stink of steaming cast iron filled the air.

Joe brushed the remaining baking soda through the stove into the trays underneath, while Marly rinsed the stove inserts. Then he pulled the trays again and tipped the sizzling oil into the hotel pan Jacques shoved through the window. He teased the sticky, blackened foil away from the edges of the tray and then carried both pans into the dish room.

"Thank you," he said solemnly as Marly replaced the eyes of the stove.

"You're welcome," she returned. Humor lit her coffee brown eyes, which told Joe that the role reversal was not lost on her either. "Order me some baking soda on Monday."

"Sure thing," he said, replacing the now clean trays.

Joe busied himself checking sauté pans full of half-finished dishes, trying to see if anything could be saved. They'd lost ten, maybe twelve minutes while all hell broke loose, and it would be double that before he caught up with the tickets.

What a freakin' mess.

Marlene stood by his side, facing the stove. She bit her lip. The sight of her white teeth digging into her full, pink lip made him stiffen. A waiter called an order. If he didn't get his mind off her mouth, he was going to see some serious weeds. He didn't analyze the urge that prompted him to ask, "You ready to put your money where your mouth is, sugar? I could use a hand until Olivia gets her act together."

"You don't think I should go check on her?" Marlene glanced down the hall toward the office.

"Nah, she's a big girl. She'll be back in a minute, but I've got a dozen tickets to re-fire. Wanna play catch-up with me?"

Oh boy, did she.

Marlene wanted to hop up on the salad station and pull Joe into her body, wrap her legs around him again, and get some more of those soul-torching kisses. She was painfully aware of the tips of her breasts and their round fullness, heavy in her bra. She was tingling at her core, ready to play just about anything, especially catch-up.

Marlene's memory fed the fire. *Joe roughly yanking her shirt over her breasts. His hand tangled in her hair, pulling her head back. Joe thrusting his leg between her parted thighs and pulling her hips to meet his own. Bending her backward…*

Oh, shit. He was waiting for an answer.

Busted.

Marly hoped none of what had just flashed through her mind had appeared on her face, but his smug look told her it probably had. She cleared her throat and turned to the grill, studiously ignoring her dampening panties. This was her opportunity to show this Kentucky boy how to do the job right.

They better get things rolling pretty quick, get those first tables out, or they'd get hammered when the rest of the orders came in. Joe was fast, she had to give him credit for that, but he couldn't put up a hundred dinners by himself tonight. She cast an eye over the tickets hanging in the window and the half-grilled meats dripping on the cutting board, pulled off the flames when the stove caught fire. Joe was almost finished restarting the dishes that had been ruined.

He turned to her. "Well? Are you looking for some action? Can you put your energy into the grill and see if you can keep up with me until Olivia gets back? Or won't your hot date wait?"

What date? Shit.

She was glad she'd gone home so many times to let

Samson out. Marly grabbed a pair of tongs from the rack
and began laying the meat back on the grill. "My date is
very patient, but you better get moving, buddy. I'd hate
for my food to get cold waiting for yours to catch up."
She could take him as long as there was an even mix of
grilled and sautéed items in the orders. She could take
him even if there wasn't.

"Anthony, are you all up on table two?" Joe asked.

"I'm good, chef," Anthony called from the farthest
corner of the salad station. He had returned to the line
alone shortly after he'd left with Olivia. Anthony never
said much, but tonight he was silent, staring at them as
if they were highly unpredictable animals. He must be
worried they'd never get out of the weeds. Marlene gave
him a reassuring smile, but he still looked nervous as he
ran his hands through his short, dark hair.

"Wash those hands, kid," Joe said, pointing at the
sink in the dish room.

"Yes, chef." Anthony ducked his head and all but
sprinted to the hand sink. Marlene flipped steaks. She
could feel Joe standing behind her. Probably checking
her work, she thought acidly.

She didn't want to turn around until he moved, scared
her inner traitor would give her away. She wasn't sure
if Joe actually breathed a mocking laugh into her hair or
if she imagined it.

Thank God it was hot up here. Her flushed cheeks
could be attributed to the heat instead of lust.

For now, she would concentrate on food, narrow
her world to the two perfectly crosshatched rib eyes for
table two. Finish them with a velvety soufflé of garlic
mashed potatoes, a zinfandel demi-glace, and confetti

vegetables. Garnish. Place them in the window at the exact moment Joe wiped the rim of his pasta dishes.

Damn. He was fast.

Marly dropped the oven door and gave her fillets a firm poke, pulled the medium and left the well done in there to char a minute longer. Who the hell would order a steak well done, anyway? A waste of good meat. She liked hers red, raw, and dripping. Steak made her think of wine, and wine made her think of sex, and sex made her think of…

Joe.

Damn it. She slammed the oven door shut.

"Fire table four. And I'm going up on table six. You ready?" He was already plating. That was cheating.

Marlene fired the fish on table four and pulled a smoking hot plate from the heated rack, hissing a bit. "You got the stuffed apple and the sweet potato cakes for my veggie plate?"

"Sure do, sugar."

They came together in the middle of the line. Marlene unmolded a timbale of toasty quinoa pilaf onto the plate and Joe reached around her with the apple. She held still, enjoying the feel of his body against her arm. She breathed in his scent, a mix of soap and sweaty man— the most potent aphrodisiac she knew.

Joe turned to snag the sweet potato cakes and lean them up against the rice. It wasn't the usual presentation, but she had to admit it looked good. "Sauce?" he asked.

She nodded and finished the plate with pinot noir– dried cherry sauce and some spiced walnuts. She put the veggie plate in the window and pulled down three more hot plates. Joe piled a good handful of rosemary roasted bliss potatoes on two of them and she spooned polenta onto the third. "Grab that well-done steak will you?"

He nodded and reached into the oven with his gloved hand.

"Show off," she said.

He grinned and returned to the stove.

Marlene plated the two steaks and a half a chicken, precisely piled bâtonnet vegetables next to the meats, and sauced everything. Plates in the window. She snagged a potato that was escaping from the herd on the plate and popped it in her mouth.

"New York State has a glove law, you know."

"Oh, shut up," Marlene shot back. "Your pasta is late on table six."

"Wrong. It's on her tray." Joe gave Beth a charming smile. "Don't pull anything out of the window until all the plates are up. I don't want my food getting cold waiting for hers to catch up."

"Yes, chef." Beth had the grace to look abashed, but Marlene was sure her blush had more to do with the way Joe's eyes crinkled up when he smiled. It was very George Clooney. *Or very shar-pei*, she thought uncharitably.

"Don't worry, sugar, maybe you'll catch me on the next table," he said.

Marlene considered beaning him with a handful of vegetables from her station, but she didn't want to set a bad example for Anthony. Instead, she grabbed a wet towel, stretched it between her hands, and twirled it into a tight rope.

"Don't even think about it." He gave her a warning look. She gave the towel one more twirl and let it fly.

Joe caught it, midair, and used the towel to haul her

forward. Her clog caught in the mat, so he caught her too, pulling her roughly into his arms. Their bodies fit together, instantly and perfectly. She felt satisfaction burst in her chest when Joe didn't let her go. She tipped her head back, felt him harden against her belly, even as she saw shadows darken his blue eyes.

"Uh, guys, do you really think this is an appropriate time for that?" Olivia said from the hot window. Her eyes were red-rimmed and watery, but her expression was calm. She walked behind the line and examined the board.

Marlene and Joe had put out six tables in twenty minutes. Joe's hands slid down Marlene's bare arms to her wrists, leaving every tiny hair raised in their wake. He took the towel out of her hands.

"Your pastry chef should do something about her impulsive streak," Joe said to Olivia.

"She's tried. It's hopeless," Olivia said.

"Order in! It's a ten top." Eric dropped the ticket.

"Time to rock and roll." Joe glanced at Marlene. "You in or out?"

She itched to cook him into oblivion, but a look at the clock told her it was pumpkin time. Samson had probably tried to dig a hole in her couch by now. "I'm out," she said, keeping the regret from her voice.

"Right. Your date." He turned to the board, then the stove.

Dismissed. It was a slap in the face.

"Who's the lucky guy?" Olivia took her place in front of the grill.

"Sam," Marlene shot her a wink as she turned away.

"I love Sam, he's a sweetheart," Olivia said, playing excellent backup.

"Yes, he is. A real sure thing." They shared a grin. Marlene gave Joe an encouraging nod. "Nice work, *chef*, but I don't have time to continue your lessons tonight. I usually don't mind keeping a man waiting, but Sam is very special to me."

"How about tomorrow?" Joe looked up from the stove. "Olivia needs a day off. I'm doing brunch. Want to help me sling eggs?"

Olivia smacked his arm.

"Please," Joe added. "Pretty, pretty please."

"You're on." Marlene headed for the bakeshop to get her purse, disturbed by the intense pleasure she felt at the idea of cooking with him again.

Joe reluctantly pulled his attention from Marly's retreating backside and laid two pans on the fire for the next table, automatically slowing his pace so Olivia could keep up with him. He watched her lay steaks on the grill, frown, and turn around to check the ticket again.

"Salmon," he prompted gently. "Hey, Anthony, could you get me some more onions and peppers from the walk-in?" He had two backups underneath, but he didn't want an audience.

"Sure thing, chef." Anthony cleared the line.

Joe turned to Olivia. "All right, kiddo. What the hell was that?" Her shoulders hunched as she laid the salmon on the grill. "Olivia Marconi does not lose her shit over a little grease fire."

"Olivia Watson does."

"Gimme a break." He rolled his eyes.

"I'm serious. I told you. I can't do this by myself.

Keith sucked, but at least I wasn't alone. I hate to be alone. I'm beginning to think I married him so I wouldn't have to do this all by myself."

"You aren't alone. You've got Marlene. And you'll hire someone. "

"The résumés coming in are crap, and Marlene's always got a guy. Or six."

"What does that have to do with anything? Marlene can cook, girl. She kept up with me. I know Keith was no great shakes in the kitchen, so I assume someone has been helping you run this place. Marlene, right?" Joe asked.

Olivia sighed. "Marly's a great cook, but she doesn't have the patience to handle the whole kitchen. There's more to it than just cooking, you know that. You have to come up with new dishes, write the menus, handle the staff. You've seen it yourself. Marly is a loose cannon. If you piss her off, she'll either rip you a new one or walk out the door. She asked to leave the line, Joe. I think that's a pretty clear sign she doesn't want to run the restaurant."

Joe laughed. He saw her point. Siccing the waiters on him wasn't exactly a sign of the maturity needed to run a restaurant. Still, he didn't want to point out that Marlene had kept her head when the line had gone up in flames, and Olivia had run away, weeping. Nobody was perfect, and it seemed to him that Olivia and Marly made a great team.

Olivia checked the tickets again before she spoke. "Don't get me wrong, Joe, Marly is a great friend and a great cook. I just…I don't know. I don't feel like I can put the whole restaurant in her hands."

"Why not? You put it in Keith's hands," Joe said.

"That was different."

"Please tell me you're not buying into that whole gotta have a culinary degree to be a chef mentality."

Olivia's cheeks turned pink. "Of course not."

"Because that would be really stupid. Talent is talent, and I have no doubt you could teach anyone anything they need to know. Anthony, here, is a perfect example."

Anthony had returned to the line, automatically checked the orders, fired his salads and appetizers, and was now furiously prepping his station for the next day.

There was one ticket hanging. Joe turned to Anthony. "C'mon, kid. Get me a roll of masking tape, a marker, a wet towel, and a bucket. We're on cleanup duty until Olivia has more than three tickets hanging in the window. You can get the salads too, right?" Joe kept his expression blank. Olivia returned his look through narrowed eyes.

"Of course," she said tightly.

There was only one way Joe could think of to give Olivia her confidence back, and he and Anthony could set the kitchen to rights at the same time. Two birds with one stone. After that, maybe he would start teaching Anthony how to make some of the sauces. This place needed a damn prep cook.

"Uh, chef?" Beth peered under the heat lamp and caught Joe's eye as he sliced a roasted vegetable stuffed chicken breast into neat, colorful rounds. Olivia had been swearing, but doing fine when they'd returned to the line, so Joe had taken pity on her and sent her out to schmooze the dining room. He was almost done with the last reservation, and Anthony was hanging on his every word as he explained basic sauce techniques.

"My table says their crème brûlée is terrible. They said they were expecting something unusual, but it sucks. Their word, not mine." Beth slid the ramekin into the window.

Joe grabbed a spoon and dipped it into the uneaten side of the custard. "Oh, Jesus! That's salty." He leaned over and spit the custard into the garbage can. "Hang on a sec." He finished plating the chicken and placed it in the window next to a pair of lamb chops. "Buzz Eric, will you?" Anthony hit the button that would page the server and let him know his table was ready for pick-up.

"Follow me."

Beth trailed after him. Joe pulled open the door of the reach-in and looked at the remaining crème brûlées. There were four that were caramelized and ready to go. Joe pulled one out and grabbed another tasting spoon. This time he took a smaller bite. "Ugh, I don't know who would like this even if it wasn't salty as hell."

Joe tried one of the uncaramelized brûlées. It was fine. Not his favorite flavor, exactly—in fact, it was kind of a cross between melted ice cream, mouthwash, and Chinese food. He took another bite. Then he polished it off.

He found a torch under the table and liberally sprinkled the top of the custard with the sugar he found in a labeled container on top of the dessert station. He fired up the torch and touched the blue tip to the pile of sugar. It had been a while, but he remembered that the trick was to tip it almost 90 degrees and roll the caramelizing sugar over the custard. He waited for the sugar to liquefy and caramelize.

Instead, it sputtered and blackened, and the custard underneath scrambled with the heat of the torch. Joe was glad Beth had gone back to coffee her table and tell them dessert would be on the house tonight.

He stared at the blackened mess of another dessert, the fourth one to bite the dust tonight. He had never seen sugar behave this way. He rubbed his face and then brushed his cheeks as the sugar from his fingers stuck to his five o'clock shadow. He licked his lips. His mouth watered. He licked his fingers. Salt.

Joe tossed some of the sugar from the labeled container into his mouth. It was definitely salt. That little bitch.

It was one thing to sic the waiters on him. That was pure fun and games. Deliberately sabotaging the food at Chameleon was another matter entirely. No wonder Marlene had been baiting him in the bakeshop this afternoon. He wondered whether she had planned this before or after her little come-hither routine. Was she responsible for some of the other bullshit that was happening around Chameleon too? Olivia was absolutely right. Marlene was a loose cannon.

Joe pulled the large sugar bin out from under the table and slid the lid open. He tasted it to make sure it was sugar. Just to be absolutely certain, he nicked a tiny bite out of a fifth brûlée. Satisfied, he washed his hands, then covered the custard with a quarter-inch thick layer of sugar and torched it to deep amber. He was careful not to get any caramelized sugar on his hand. Next to roux, it was the hottest thing in the kitchen, and it stuck like glue.

Beth returned, and she set the finished dessert on a doilied plate, added a homemade fortune cookie and a sprig of basil, and then headed back out to the dining room.

He cracked open another fortune cookie and read the slip of paper inside. "You will get what you deserve." He snorted. Yeah, he wasn't the only one. Joe gathered up the dishes from the dessert disaster, plus the mislabeled salt container and the remaining questionable brûlées, and took them to the dish room.

Jacques eyebrows shot up beneath his hair. "Did you eat all those? Marly's gonna kill you."

"Not if I kill her first." The dishwasher gave him a look that could have torched another brûlée. "Just kidding." He looked at the older man's thin chest and saggy jeans. In his experience, kitchen help were the hungriest people on earth. "If you keep my secret, I'll hook you up with dinner. You like fish?"

"Yup."

"Coming right up." Joe slung the salt container into Anthony's station. "Here, kid, do something with that. It's salt."

He wouldn't tell Olivia about the brûlées yet. That was between him and Marly. He'd set her straight himself—tonight. Too bad for her if he broke up her little love fest with her special guy. The job came first—always.

Chapter 10

MARLENE SURFED THROUGH TWO HUNDRED CABLE channels and gave up. Usually the eleven o'clock news could send her into oblivion, but she'd watched every news story, wide-eyed, while demolishing half a large spinach pesto pizza from her favorite pizzeria. Why was there never anything decent on television? She was tired, but she couldn't sleep.

It was going to take something a little stronger than television to knock her out tonight. She'd given up her no booze rule an hour ago, after the Ghiardelli hot chocolate had failed her too. Two glasses of wine later, she was still wide-awake and considering busting into her emergency stash of cigarettes and heading up to the roof. Or heading to Johnny's. Samson wouldn't mind. He'd been a good boy while she was at work, so she'd been petting him for the last three hours to reward him. He was exhausted from the attention, asleep on the couch, belly up, nose tucked under a pillow.

She walked into her bedroom and pulled open her underwear drawer. The way she saw it, she had two options. Go to Johnny's and find someone to put out the fire that was raging though her body. Or stay home and put it out herself. Marlene pulled her vibrator out of the drawer. How desperate was she?

Not desperate enough to show up at Johnny's and admit her date was a dog, she decided, as Samson followed her into the bedroom. He jumped up on the bed, turned around three times, and collapsed into a furry heap.

She could handle this herself. A man, while nice, was not necessary. Pride makes a cold bedfellow, but a very efficient vibrator can do wonders for a girl's state of mind. She was going to make herself come so many times she'd forget her own name, not to mention the name of the man who had gotten her into this state. She crawled into her bed and stretched out on her back, shoving her cut-off sweatpants down to her knees, already heating up in anticipation.

A loud knock at her back door made Samson raise his head, but Marly ignored the summons. There was no one, absolutely no one, she wanted to see in her condition. She might consider answering the door in ten minutes if anyone was still there. She flipped the switch on the vibrator.

The knock at the door sounded again, louder. Samson got up and began to howl.

God damn it. Was the universe trying to kill her? She turned off the vibrator. Was one orgasm asking too much?

Marly rolled out of bed and onto her feet, dragging her sweatpants over her hips and slamming the door on her way out of the bedroom. God, if this was Bill or Thomas coming to pick up Samson because they'd had another stupid fight, she was going to go postal.

Marlene peeked through the window and saw Joe's tall frame outlined by the porch light. Right on cue, her blood began to simmer. The way her hormones went on high alert every time Joe came on the scene was pathetic.

She was beginning to feel like one of Pavlov's dogs—one of Pavlov's inbred, slightly slow, first-cousin-loving dogs, who responded to cues without the benefit of positive reinforcement. This was not good. So not good.

She knew her hair was going in every direction, and her sweatpants and sweatshirt were so old she was entering *Flashdance* territory. She had a feeling her cheeks were flushed, her eyes were heavy, and her mouth looked, well, ready. Not a good time to answer the door, especially when the guy responsible for her frustration was on the other side.

On the other hand, maybe he was into girls with stick-up hair, ratty sweatshirts, no makeup, and "Fuck me," tattooed on their foreheads. She indulged in three more seconds of hot flash fantasy where she opened the door, pulled Joe inside, and had him flat on his back on the kitchen floor before he could say a word.

Since that was just not going to happen, maybe she could ignore him and head back to her bedroom. She peered carefully out the door again. Nope, he'd seen her. Joe stood with his feet planted on the deck and his arms crossed as if he was gearing up for a fight.

Hallelujah. Since she couldn't get laid, a good fight wasn't a bad second option. She unlocked the bolt and opened the door. "Yes? Is there something I can do for you?" she asked.

Joe smiled at her, but he didn't look happy.

Marlene braced her hands on her hips and lifted her chin as his eyes raked over her. It took an effort Joe could hardly appreciate to look regal in the clothes she had on. Thank God she was still wearing her bra.

"Yeah, you can do something for me," Joe growled.

"Quit screwing around at Chameleon. You need to grow up and get your priorities straight because Olivia does not need any more trouble."

Marlene was dumbfounded. "What the hell are you talking about?"

"You know what I'm talking about. The salt on the crème brûlées. It's one thing to have a little fun with the waiters. I can handle your childish bullshit, but what you did tonight was unprofessional. If you've got a problem with me, don't take it out on Olivia. The restaurant is her business, her livelihood, and she's got enough on her plate right now. Enough is enough. Leave the coolers alone, don't ruin the fucking produce, and for God's sake, clean the grease trays properly."

All of the blood that had been circulating south of the border shot straight to Marlene's head. "I don't know what the hell you're talking about, Joe. I told you, I cleaned the grease trays on Wednesday. Maybe Olivia spilled some oil. Maybe you did, hotshot. I didn't touch the coolers, and I don't know what the fuck you mean about the produce." Marlene shook her head in disgust, then remembered his original point. "Wait, what do you mean about salt on my crème brûlées?"

Joe glared at her. "Don't play innocent. You covered them with salt."

"Why the hell would I sabotage my own desserts?" she asked. Was he serious? Or crazy?

"To get back at me," he said. "I told you I wouldn't put up with anymore of your bullshit tricks. If you're still mad at me for—"

"Wake up, Joe! I'm not mad at you. There's way more going on around here than you, buddy. I've made a few mistakes lately, but ruining my crème brûlée isn't high on my priority list. The restaurant is my life too. I've spilled just as much sweat in that kitchen as Olivia has. Maybe more. After all, she left for two years to go learn how to cook—something she could have learned just as easily by staying at home. You're nuts if you think I would do anything to hurt Olivia or Chameleon, and think what you want, but I'd never ruin my own desserts. I only use kosher salt in the bakeshop just to avoid that kind of mix-up. That's the big kind, and it's pretty damn hard to mistake it for sugar. If you can't tell the difference, you should reconsider your profession," she said sarcastically. "You're an idiot, Joe. Go home. I'm sure Olivia will back you up, just like she backed Keith up. I'm too tired for your bullshit."

"Yeah, I'm sure you're exhausted," he jeered. "Burning the candle at both ends, huh? If you're so tired, maybe you should get some sleep instead of staying up half the night entertaining your dates."

Marlene heard a sharp bark, followed by a whine, then a howl. Joe looked over her shoulder, trying to see into the kitchen. "Where'd the dog come from? Are you sure your social schedule permits enough time to take care of an animal?"

She stared at Joe in fury. Not even fit to take care of an animal? That was what he thought of her? This was just getting better and better. Not good enough to sleep with, unprofessional, and now a dog abuser. Well, at least he thought she was popular. "Since you're not interested, I don't see how my social life is at all your concern."

Joe held the screen door open with his shoulder, so

she moved to shut the inside door, but it bounced off his steel-toed boot.

"Do you always run when the going gets tough?" he challenged. "You hightailed it off the line the minute Olivia married Keith, didn't you? Did you ever think about helping out when the food went to hell, or did you leave her hanging? Any idea why she hasn't told you, her best friend, about the problems she's having at the restaurant? Maybe she thinks you're just as unreliable as he was."

Marlene envisioned herself slamming Joe's foot repeatedly in the heavy door. Boing! Boing! Booooiiiinnnggg!

That was the second time he'd struck to the core. She pictured her heart nailed to the back wall of her kitchen with a quivering arrow right through its center. At least her sense of humor was still intact. That was comforting.

Her eyes watered a bit, but she met Joe's cold blue stare. "No, cheffie boy, I don't know why she hasn't told me she's having problems. But I do know that I didn't leave her hanging when she married Keith. I stuck around and filled in the cracks. I did everything I could to cover for him without actually taking the sauté pan out of his hand and knocking him upside the head with it. I didn't fail Olivia. If you want to know the truth, she failed me. Keith was slinging food into the window that I wouldn't feed a dog, and every time I mentioned it to her, she said the food was fine. I've worked at Chameleon for half my life, but you're right: when push comes to shove, Olivia never turns to me. First, she turned to Keith, and now she's turning to you.

When you're gone, I'm sure she'll find some other man, some good *chef*, to help her."

"So why do you stick around?" he asked.

The dog was barking like a maniac, but not so loudly that she couldn't hear Joe's quiet question. She could definitely see the pity in his eyes, and it made her blood burn. Marlene exploded, finally, in the direction of the bedroom, "Sam! Shut up!"

The dog stopped howling.

The absolute silence screamed her mistake. When Marlene turned back to Joe, it was too late.

"Sam? As in Sam your sweetie? Sam your sure thing? A little Saturday night bestiality, huh? You're even kinkier than I thought." His voice was kind.

Marlene gave him an echo of a smile and automatically responded, "You have no idea." She felt a little sick.

Joe's rough hand was gentle as he touched her arm. "I'm sorry, Marlene. I shouldn't have blown my stack tonight. You deserved the benefit of the doubt."

She frowned at him, annoyed. A decent, straight up the middle apology was not what she was expecting. Most of the apologies she received from men were of the "if apologizing will get me laid, I'll do it, but it's all your fault" variety.

"That's so unfair," she said, jerking her arm away from him.

"Huh?" He looked confused.

"You can't just apologize. I'm mad at you. I want to make you suffer."

"Sorry," Joe said, his lips beginning to curve.

She crossed her arms. "Fine. I forgive you."

Joe was grinning now, not the wicked grin, thank

God, just a friendly, average, rip-your-clothes-off smile that wasn't much easier to bear. "That's it? You aren't going to make me grovel? Are you sure you're female?"

"You don't seem the type to put much energy into an insincere apology, so I'll take what I can get," she said, surprised that she meant it.

"Yes, I've heard that's your standard approach," he said.

She ignored the gibe. The accusations had cleared the air between them, and she really did want to know more about what had been happening at the restaurant. "I don't give a crap what you think about my sex life, but I didn't put salt in my crème brûlées."

"Not in. On."

"Well, there you go. Waiter error. Somebody grabbed salt instead of sugar and fired away."

Joe didn't look convinced. "I thought you said you only keep kosher salt in the bakeshop."

"I'll remind the waiters."

"Don't do that."

"Why not?"

"Let's just keep this quiet for now. We don't know where that salt came from or who put it there."

"You think someone did it on purpose?"

"I don't know that they didn't, and if someone is running around causing trouble, I want to find them my way."

"Sherlock Chef?" she asked.

"Maybe."

"Keith was in the back yesterday, but there's no way he could have caused that much trouble in ten minutes, even if he came in with a plan," Marlene mused. "He just isn't that fast, or that smart. So is he sneaking in or does he have someone on the inside?"

"I think he's got someone on the inside," he said.

"Who?"

Joe shrugged.

"You're starting to freak me out, Joe. I've known most of the staff for years. No offense, but I think you're a little paranoid. You know how restaurants are. Confusion abounds, and we've been balls to the wall for a while covering for Keith."

"Just to bring you up to speed, he cleaned out the safe when he was in the office yesterday." Joe toed the inside door open with his foot. "Do I get to meet the dog now, sweetheart?"

She took a step back, still trying to process all the things that Olivia hadn't told her. "Do you ever call women by their first names?" she asked to buy time to decide how she felt.

"Nah, too hard to remember," Joe said, walking into the kitchen.

"Try."

"Marlene," Joe said patiently. Her name on his lips gave her a zing. "Do I get to meet the dog now?"

She might have been able to say no if he hadn't chosen that exact moment to give her his wicked smile. The one that made her want to crawl into his lap. Naked. She felt her cheeks get hot. On second thought, she'd better get him out of here before she jumped him.

Too late.

Samson was barking again. Joe stepped past her and walked down the hall toward the bedroom. "What took you so long to get to the door, anyway? Were you sleeping?" he asked.

"Uh, not exactly."

Oh God, where had she left the vibrator? In the middle of the bed? The floor? "I couldn't sleep. Tried hot chocolate. Tried wine. Didn't want to go out so—" She held her breath as Joe opened the bedroom door.

The barking cut off abruptly and Samson tore out of the bedroom, wagging his tail like mad. He raced down the hall, claws scrabbling on the hardwood. Marly and Joe followed him to the living room. As he rounded the corner of the couch, picking up speed for another lap, Marlene saw her vibrator clamped firmly between his jaws.

"Hot date, huh?" Joe observed.

Lucky for her, inner traitor returned, re-armed. She didn't have any reason to be ashamed. It wasn't like she'd been having sex with the dog, after all. Samson just happened to be there. And, apparently, he liked her vibrator as much as she did.

Marlene walked over to the pizza box on the bookshelf and grabbed a leftover slice. She hadn't been willing to sacrifice any gourmet pizza when it had arrived earlier, but now she was. Now, she was definitely willing to sacrifice just about anything if it would get her vibrator out of the middle of her living room.

She approached the dog and waved the pizza. As the scent hit his sensitive hound nose, Samson stopped. She held the pizza high as she slowly, carefully placed her hand on the business end of the vibrator.

Sam loosened his jaws. She made the swap, then stood, casually checking for damage. There was none. She held the vibe in a loose fist at her side and gave Joe an apologetic smile. "Man's best friend is dog, but woman's best friend is vibrator. You'll have to forgive me if I don't ask you to stay."

Joe moved toward her. He took the vibrator out of her hand and sent it sailing into the bedroom where it landed on the bed with a solid thump. She was mesmerized by the heat in his eyes.

"I've got a better idea," Joe said.

He placed his hand on the small of her back and urged her toward the couch.

Chapter 11

JOE WAS TIRED OF SAYING NO.

All the way over here, he'd been telling himself that he was coming to give her hell about the crème brûlées, but when she answered the door, looking pissed as hell and about as fuckable as any woman he'd ever seen, he had instantly recognized his ulterior motives. He'd come here because he couldn't stay away from her. Now he was in over his head. He could barely resist the temptress witch who threw her body at him followed by rapid insults, but he had no defense against the girl in sweatpants who shared pizza with a dog. The fact that she had been home alone on a Saturday night taking matters into her own hands made him crazy.

He didn't believe Marlene was responsible for any trouble at Chameleon. As she'd pointed out, she'd lived through two years of Keith's cooking without killing him. That girl had self-control and stamina. She was a natural-born chef, and she clearly loved Chameleon or she would have jetted years ago. In fact, he was still curious about why she hadn't.

Joe grabbed the remote control from the couch. "How about a slumber party?" he teased. "Olivia's house is as silent as a tomb, and I'm not ready to go to bed yet. You got any more pizza in that box? A glass of wine would be nice too. Is that TV real?"

"Blu-ray, high-def, forty-inch screen," Marlene

said. She was looking at him like he had lost his mind. "You're kidding, right?"

"Kidding?" Joe asked, keeping up his innocent act.

Marlene stood in front of him. Her hips were at eye level. Panties? He looked for lines. Hard to tell.

She crossed her arms. "A slumber party would be really nice, Joe, but I've already had pizza and wine and about as much TV as I can stand. I want to get laid, buddy. For your own safety, you should get out of here."

"You can do better than a vibrator shaped like an alien rabbit on steroids," he said.

"Don't knock the rabbit," she replied. "It can do things most men can't even imagine."

Joe raised an eyebrow.

"If you're angling for a demonstration, forget it. You haven't earned the privilege," she said.

"I'm angling for more than that."

She didn't resist when he pulled her onto his lap, but she didn't reach for him either. Now that Marlene was so close, Joe could smell her. Hot vanilla and arousal. He stroked the soft skin of her legs where her strong thighs framed his own. She scowled down at him and grabbed his shoulders, squeezing hard.

"Joe, I'm not kidding. It's one thing to play around at work, but I've had enough. I can't take anymore. Get naked, or get the hell out of here."

She was strung so tightly, Joe was sure that when her self-control broke, she was going to shatter into a million pieces. He was going to pluck her strings and see what happened.

"The bunny can rest. I've got what you need, sugar," he promised. He settled her on top of his erection.

Marlene gave a closed-mouth groan and pressed into his lap.

"Feels good, doesn't it?" he asked.

Joe watched her eyelids dip as she swayed above him. Watching her grind was like watching her eat. She wasn't self-conscious about going after her pleasure. She knew what she wanted, and she took it, riding him, even though they were both fully clothed. He couldn't wait to do this naked, buried to the hilt inside her body.

He throbbed against her, making her gasp. Her eyes flew open, hot, hazy, and disoriented. Joe gave her a knowing smile. "Not quite enough to get you there, huh, sweetheart?"

Her shorts were loose, and he worked his hand into the leg hole and slipped his thumb under the crotch of her panties. Her folds were swollen and full. She felt like honey under his thumb.

"Don't stop," Marlene begged.

"I wouldn't dream of it. I just need a little more room to work." He rolled to the left and tossed her onto the couch next to him. Impatient with the barrier between them, he pulled her shorts down to her ankles, deeply appreciating her cooperation. She didn't play coy like a lot of women would. She just lifted her ass, opened her knees, and wordlessly begged him to dive in. Which he did.

Joe dragged his tongue straight up the middle to get the lay of the land, groaning as her clean, sweet-salty taste and smell went straight to his head. He found her stiff bud and latched on, guessing she wouldn't want the gentle stuff right now. She was too close. He worked one finger into her, moving it in and out slowly to loosen her up for the next finger. And the next. She gasped. He had her now. Any minute.

Marlene screamed when her orgasm hit. Her voice rose in an intense, wordless wail of relief. He worked his fingers in and out of her body in time with the spasms that squeezed his fingers. Some women were done after one orgasm, but Joe had a feeling she wasn't that kind of girl. He hoped she wasn't that kind of girl.

He looked up at her face, blissed out, and gave her ten seconds to recover before he rotated his palm and crooked his fingers in a "come here" gesture inside of her.

Her body came to life under his hands. She swelled, quickened, and broke swiftly, drenching his palm. He bent his head to her again, enjoying her scent, her taste, and the sounds of pleasure she made as he moved against her. When Marlene was silent and still, well nearly so, he crooked his fingers again, harder. She groaned and offered her hips.

He laughed softly and slid his fingers out of her. "My turn, I'm about to bust a seam, here." Joe stood. He pulled Marlene's sweatshirt over her head. Her bra was black lace and barely substantial enough to contain her.

Marlene barely opened her eyes. "If I could move, I'd be happy to return the favor, but my legs are numb."

"Oh, I think it's way more fun if we come together next time." Joe pulled his T-shirt over his head. He kicked off his shoes and socks. In one motion, he thrust his pants and underwear over his hips, stepped out of them, and stood before her, naked.

"Thank God," she breathed.

Joe heaved her to her feet. The feel of her soft skin

against his hard flesh made him groan. "I can't wait another minute," he said, picking her up.

He carried her into the bedroom and dropped her on
the bed.

"Watch out for the bunny," she said.

"By the time I'm done with you, you won't even remember you have a bunny."

"I'd better remember. I'll need it when you're gone."

Joe hit his knees on the bed, and Marlene said, "Wait!"

"Can't," he groaned.

"Condom. Top drawer." Marlene pointed.

"Right. Sorry." He rolled the latex down his length
and kissed her.

Marlene leaned up to meet Joe's lips. This was even
better than what she had imagined. The tip of his tongue
flirted with hers in a way that was tender and hot at the
same time. It took her breath away. Oh God, that man
could say a million different things with his mouth. His
lips made her feel safe, and that word wasn't even in
her relationship vocabulary. A rush of pleasure hit her
as that bizarre thought and Joe entered her at the same
time, rocking her body and her mind with a little mini-
mental orgasm. She convulsed around him again.

"God, you're amazing," he said. He began a slow,
sweet, gliding thrust, and she opened to him, giving him
everything he was asking for and more. She rotated her
hips against him on the down stroke, rubbing herself
against the base of his shaft. Joe was watching intently,
a little too intently, she thought, but then he changed the
angle of his hips in a subtle, indescribable way. Marlene

felt her eyes go wide. He smiled. "Gotcha," he said and began to thrust in earnest.

Marlene gave up trying to match his tempo and just held for dear life. She took him deep, and each time brought her closer to something, but she wasn't sure what it was. It was a watery, waving sort of pleasure. It flowed through her limbs making her feel heavy and buoyed up at the same time.

He was watching her again, and this time, instead of making her feel uncomfortable, it took her closer to wherever she was going with him. Joe bent and caught her nipple between his lips and tugged. Oh, yes, that was it. His insistent stroking inside of her and the warm tug of his tongue on her breast brought her to the top of the wave, and Marlene began to fall.

"Oh, I'm coming," she whispered into his hair.

"Yes." His voice was a low growl, violent. It put a sharp edge on Marlene's pleasure.

Their eyes locked as orgasm raced through them. It was unlike anything Marlene had ever experienced. She came harder and longer than the other times, his intent regard pushing her to the top of another wave of pleasure, his merciless hips pressing her forward.

"Enough," she panted. "Stop."

"Soon."

Joe slipped out of her, but he didn't roll away. Instead, he slipped one hand between them to caress her ultra-sensitive flesh. His fingers slipped into her, played through her moist petals, and then settled on her clit.

Marlene jumped and nearly howled at the brilliant, blinding shock that lit her fingertips and toes.

"You're not done yet, sugar. One more time. You can do it."

"I can't," she begged.

His finger barely moved at all, yet tiny pulses of electric heat shot through her entire body. Tiny, inexorable, irresistible pulses. She was going to explode. She opened her mouth to tell him, but his mouth silenced her lips and then his fingers did something quick, hard, and damn near impossible. Instead of speaking, she screamed and then shattered beneath his hands.

Chapter 12

MARLENE WOKE UP THE NEXT MORNING WITH A SMALL, warm, furry body in front of her and a large, warm, hard body behind her. At some point during the night, Samson must have decided it was safe to jump on the bed with them. Joe had never left.

His arm was wrapped around her waist, and she was mildly surprised to realize that his fingers were inside of her. Her body was poised on the brink of another orgasm. He wiggled his fingers.

"You've got to be kidding me," she croaked.

"Nope." Joe sounded more cheerful than any man had a right to be at this hour of the morning.

She groaned. "What time is it?"

"It's seven-thirty. Can't you hear the eggs calling us?" Brunch.

She'd forgotten about brunch. "Oh God. Yes."

"Yes, eggs? Or yes, this?" he asked. His fingers were doing things that only a man very familiar with the female body would even think of doing.

"Yes, both." She opened her thighs and hooked one foot behind Joe's knees. "Latex?"

"Not in my eggs. Otherwise, all set."

"Egg-cellent." Marlene guided him in. A quickie, and then someone had better get her some coffee.

It was quick, compared to last night, but they were still late. Fortunately, most of the brunch prep had been done yesterday, by her, but there was still waffle batter to make and hollandaise to whip together and then hold in a water bath. She had to decide what the specials would be, do about four hundred other tasks, and get at least three cups of coffee into her body before ten. She just made it.

Joe had been busy as well. When the doors opened, his station was set. His egg-poaching liquid was at a bare shiver, and he had the flat top full of extra crunchy hash browns.

"Want some?" he asked.

"Not now." The first ticket was all her, and Joe was lounging against his station watching her fly between the waffle iron and the grill. He had a plate full of hash browns, sausage, and at least four poached eggs.

"Gotta keep my strength up," he said.

Marlene closed her eyes until her knees felt solid again. Every so often, a memory from last night would blindside her, and she would go liquid, instantly aroused. There didn't seem to be any way to stop it. It wasn't unpleasant, but Marlene was afraid she was beginning to scare Anthony.

The poor kid was high-strung to begin with, and he looked exhausted today. After closing with Joe last night, Anthony was back this morning to open the pantry. Restaurant work was hard labor if you weren't used to it, and Anthony was just a kid. So far he was working out fine though. He'd even brought his cousin Mario in to do the dishes until they found a replacement for Kevin.

Marlene resettled her baseball cap on her head and flipped a waffle onto a plate.

"May I speak with the chef, please?" She ducked to catch a glimpse of the face attached to the reedy, unfamiliar voice coming from the dish room.

The middle-aged man standing in the doorway had a pinched expression of concentration that may have had something to do with the fact that his glasses were too small for his face. He was holding a clipboard, pen poised, and his eyes were darting around the kitchen. He made a mark. Marlene's heart skipped a beat.

Chameleon had never had a visit from the health inspector on a Sunday before. And never during service. They weren't even due for inspection until August. *All the better to catch a violation, my dearie.* Mario wouldn't have known to stall the inspector at the back door until someone could sweep through the kitchen and sound the alarm.

Marlene stepped forward, but Joe was already in front of her, holding out his hand to the little man.

"I've got this, sugar. Keep cooking."

The health inspector hesitated before shaking Joe's hand, as if he didn't want to get anything on him, but he took it. Joe's friendly manner seemed to thaw him a bit. He didn't look like the kind of guy who expected to be met with a smile, and Joe's man-to-man grin was hard to resist.

Automatically, Marlene ran through a mental catalog of everyday health code violations. For once, everyone in the kitchen was wearing a hat, thank God. At warp speed, she gathered their mostly empty coffee cups and dumped them in the bus tub to get rid of open containers.

Joe and the inspector headed toward the bakeshop. As they left, Marlene dropped the lids on the work-stations to lower the temperatures before inspector man could return with his little thermometer.

Thank goodness Joe worked clean. Marlene had never seen him prop a sheet pan on the garbage can and use it as an impromptu table when he ran out of work-space, like Keith used to do. Of course, Joe cleaned up his mess as he went along, so he never ran out of room. He even had a bleach bucket under his station, and Marlene would bet he had measured it out to the right concentration too. She dumped half of it into another bucket, labeled it and set it under Anthony's station.

Marlene sent up a quick prayer that her ingredient bins were also labeled and tightly shut and that she hadn't left the scoop in the flour again. Was everything in her reach-in labeled and covered?

She grabbed Anthony's Caesar salad bowls and jammed them into the refrigerated bottom of his reach-in. Then she tossed him a pair of disposable gloves. "Put these on," Marlene said.

"But I'm not doing anything," he protested.

"I don't give a shit. Put 'em on anyway. You're on waffles now too."

Marlene checked the tickets, the ovens, the stove, and the grill. She called for two waffles, dropped an egg into the poacher, cracked two on the flat top for over easy, and laid four pans on the fire for frittatas. Joe had better schmooze the health inspector fast and get his ass back up here.

Anthony went up on his Caesar salads, and Marlene pulled a pair of tongs off the oven door handle. Another violation. They were so screwed. She tossed Anthony the tongs. "Shrimp them." He crisscrossed two skewers of shrimp on each salad.

"It's you and me, kid. Do exactly what I say, and we might make it out of here alive." She took the tongs out of his limp hand and replaced them with a wide offset spatula. "Hash browns on three hot plates. Keep them neat. Then I want those waffles. Keep your gloves on. Keep your hat on. Don't touch your face. Got it?"

Anthony nodded, jumping to pull plates down for her.

They kept cooking.

By the time Joe and the health inspector made it back to the line, Marlene and Anthony had cleared the board once and had a whole new line of tickets hanging. Marlene was swearing, quietly, fluently, and in two languages. Anthony looked terrified, even though the brunt of the orders had fallen on her.

Joe gave the inspector another man-to-man look. "If I were you, Bill, I'd get in Marly's way as little as possible. She's never burned me on purpose, but I always get the feeling that she wants to."

The health inspector nodded solemnly. He zipped behind Marlene once, then twice, to take temperatures in her station, taking his time over the deep, iced six-pan of raw eggs. Marlene knew damn well it was below forty degrees, so she didn't even look. She just kept cooking.

They went up on three tables, and Marlene added a third language to her quiet invective. The inspector cleared the line. Joe escorted him through the dish room and out the back door, handing him a cup of coffee for the road.

She wished Joe would hurry the hell up. The tickets were piling up and she was running out of eggs. She couldn't make a run to the walk-in when she was working this many tables, and Anthony had his own problems.

It was another ten minutes before Joe returned, frowning at the white copy of the health inspection form. "After all that, we still got three violations. I guess he had to find something," he said with disgust. "He did say it's the cleanest kitchen he's ever seen."

"How is that possible?" she asked.

"Anthony and I got bored last night and cleaned house."

"Nice timing," she said.

"Thank you very much." Joe moved to take over the sauté station.

"No way, you big suck-up." Marlene pointed to the walk-in. "I need eggs. Then you can play monkey in the middle for a while. I've got five tables fired, and I'm not in the mood to explain the tickets to you."

Joe leaned to whisper in her ear. "You gonna call me 'cheffie boy' again? It gives me a hard-on."

"Get your ass in gear."

"Yes, chef," he said with a mocking grin.

It was hot, and they were busy. Marlene and Joe worked the board together like they'd been doing it forever, and she discovered that he could take orders as well as he could give them. Every so often, they'd reach to pull down the same plate, at the same time. Their hands would touch, and the kitchen would heat up another couple of degrees.

When the tickets slowed down to a trickle, she finally

asked, "Did you ask the health inspector why he was working on a Sunday?"

"Yeah, somebody called in a violation." Joe said.

"What?"

"Yup. He didn't say what it was, but it was serious enough to bring him in here on a Sunday. He searched the walk-in like he was looking for a dead body."

"Did he find anything?" Marlene asked.

Joe shook his head. "I cleared out Keith's petri dishes two days ago."

"Any violations in the bakeshop?"

"Not even one," he assured her.

"Well, that's something." She fired the last ticket and began to stack sauté pans in the hot window.

"You still think I'm paranoid?"

"I'm too tired to think. Somebody kept me up too late last night." Marlene leaned against her cutting board. "And I still have to hit the farmers' market before I can go home and collapse."

"It's already three o'clock, sugar. There isn't going to be anything left at the farmers' market by the time you get there."

"Wanna bet?" Marlene said.

Marly shut down the line in record time, unplugged everything flammable, and double-checked all the plugs on the coolers. Since they couldn't leave a rookie dishwasher in charge of closing down the back, Joe offered Anthony ten bucks to mop the line while they put away all the leftover brunch prep. In twenty minutes flat, the four of them shot out the back door into the late afternoon sunshine.

The Norton City Market was twenty minutes from town and the oldest farmers' market in Western New York. Local vendors had been gathering at the corner of Robins and Paine to sell their wares for a hundred years now. She looked forward to going every week to load up on fresh basil, locally made cheeses, seasonal vegetables, and flowers for the hostess stand. Today, her first purchase was two flats of gorgeous Fourth of July tomatoes.

Since she came every week, she didn't have to arrive early to get the good stuff either. The farmers saved it for her. No one else was leaving with the first crop of haricots verts. The tiny slips of green, delicate and crunchy, along with those early tomatoes, would be perfect for a tuna Niçoise appetizer. "Now remember, Chuck, when the heirloom varieties are ripe, I want them. Got anything new this year?"

"Black Pearls," he said. "They're gonna look like cherry tomatoes, but darker, and sweet as candy. The Red Lightnings are gonna be pretty too."

She handed him a business card. "Call Chameleon and ask for me. I'll drive out to pick them up."

"Sure thing, Marly."

Marlene put an extra sway in her step as she walked away from the young farmer. She wasn't above trading on sex appeal if it would keep them in good tomatoes all summer. Green zebras, yellow pear, brandywine, rainbow—nothing was better than a ripe, homegrown tomato. "I'm feeling an heirloom tomato salad with ginger soy vinaigrette and a chiffonade of fresh basil coming on," she said.

Joe leaned down to whisper in her ear. "Say that again, but talk real slow."

It was convenient to have him along to make trips back to the car with her purchases—three flats of straw-berries, great sheaves of basil, adorable baby carrots with their tops still on, ten pounds of late rhubarb, and three kinds of mint.

"What are you going to do with all that mint?" Joe asked.

"Covet it." Pineapple mint, chocolate mint, lime mint, they all appealed to her sense of whimsy. True, it usually came right back to the kitchen parked on the side of the dessert plate, the very definition of a non-functional garnish, but mint was cheap. She didn't care if anyone nibbled it or even sniffed it. The customers could tuck it behind their ears and do the cha-cha for all she cared. She had to have it.

"And the basil?" Joe queried.

"Pesto. We make it all summer and freeze it. Pesto sells out the house in January."

Marlene paused to smile at Ben, her favorite squash guy, a rawboned and rangy strawberry blond whose face and forearms challenged the sun to find another spot to place a freckle. "How're the pumpkins coming along?"

"I've got three the size of my head. We'll have to see which one takes off, hard to say who's got the best position," he told her, brushing dirt off his orange Carhart overalls.

"Ben had a six-hundred–pound pumpkin last year," she told Joe.

"Gonna break my record this year," the farmer said, glowing. "You should stop by and check out the vine." He handed her a small box of baby zucchini. "On the house. Should have some patty pans by next week."

"Thanks, Ben. I can't wait."

She sneaked a glance at Joe as they walked down the aisle. His shoulders were shaking.

"I bet big pumpkins get all the babes. It's hard to resist a man with a really big—"

"Enough." She shoved the box at him and surveyed the market. "We're almost done."

"Let's take a break." He pulled her over to a grassy spot in the commons and pulled her to the ground. He sprawled out beside her and gave her a very lazy, very inviting grin. Marlene rested on one elbow and gazed down at him.

His hair was sticking up, not swept neatly off his forehead, like usual. She fought the urge to smooth it out of his eyes. His T-shirt was so ancient and thin it barely qualified as clothing, and he wasn't wearing the traditional checks today either. Instead, his jeans rode low on his hips.

She saw a quick flash of Joe's tight stomach as he stretched out on his back. Her blood began to warm at the sight of his hipbones and the delicate line of hair heading south from his navel. She licked her lips, dying to run her tongue along the smooth hollows of muscle and bone, right here, right now. If they had been in a backyard, instead of the parking lot of the Lutheran Church, she could imagine doing just that, closing her eyes and learning his skin with her mouth. And then wrapping her body around him and—

"Sorry, what?" Marlene came back to earth at the sound of Joe's voice.

"I could really go for some Thai food," he repeated. "Does Norton have a good Thai restaurant?"

"A couple in Amherst, by the Boulevard Mall, if you feel like driving," Marlene offered.

"I don't. Can I cook you dinner tonight?" he said.

"Sure." She'd never had a man cook for her. The idea made her feel peculiar. "My place?"

"Great." Joe pushed himself to his feet and held his hands out to pull her up. "Are you done shopping yet?"

"Almost." With a firm tug, Joe pulled her up to her feet, hard enough to send her bumping into him. He caught her around the waist and pulled her toward him. His lips were salty from the homemade potato chips he had purchased from a farmer earlier, which reminded her of the salty crème brûlées.

As his lips coasted over hers, she pondered the mystery. The crème brûlées in her reach-in must have been covered with salt yesterday morning. She had assumed the white granules wouldn't take the torch because they were damp, even though they hadn't looked it. Now she realized that sugar would have been wet, partially lique-fied from the overnight moisture of the custard and the cooler. She hadn't been paying attention because she had been thinking about Joe. Salt doesn't melt, it burns, and she should have realized something was screwy when she torched them. Instead, in her frustrated haze, she had piled dry sugar on top of the salt and fired away.

Marlene kept her revelation to herself and concen-trated on his mouth. Their kiss had started out sweet, but now his tongue swept against hers with familiar, demanding strokes. She knew where this was going, and she was glad. She'd worry about sugar and salt later, after she talked to Olivia. The restaurant was closed for the moment, but Joe wasn't going to be around much longer. In fact, he'd be at his father's house for half the week. She wanted to enjoy him while she could.

"Are you sure you're not done shopping?" Joe said against her lips.

"I'll shop fast."

Marlene sped through the rest of the market to pick up the items that the vendors had put aside for her, and Joe collected his own bag of supplies for their dinner.

"Drop me off at my truck, and point me toward a grocery store. I need to stop at Olivia's to pick up a few things and shower. Your place in about an hour? Sound good?"

Yes, yes it did.

When they pulled up beside Joe's truck, parked in the street in front of Chameleon, the word "asshole," was written in the dirt on the driver's side door.

"That's the problem with having a black truck," Joe said. "People feel like they have to write their name on it." He cleaned it off with his fist.

"Lucky they didn't use a car key."

"No kidding," he said, giving her a kiss that she felt everywhere. "See you soon, sugar."

Chapter 13

JOE CRUISED AROUND THE BLOCK ON THE OFF-CHANCE Keith had hung around to witness the reaction to his graffiti. The quiet block was pure midsummer Sunday. He turned his truck toward Olivia's house.

He was shocked that he felt peaceful. All day he had been waiting for the guilt to kick in—or the boredom. Instead, he felt lust. Watching Marlene work ten brunch tickets at the same time had been the hottest thing he'd ever seen. He'd been half-hard all afternoon watching her fly around the kitchen.

This was a first for him. He had gone to bed with her, woken up with her, worked all day with her, and then asked her to have dinner with him, with the intention of falling straight into her bed when the dishes were done. When had he ever spent that much time in the company of the same woman?

Never.

Maybe his conscience was quiet because it knew Marlene was his last fling, that he was going to find himself a nice virgin with marriage on her mind the minute he crossed the California border, a girl who would have made his mother proud. His enthusiasm for that idea seemed to have gotten lost with the guilt he should have been feeling for breaking his vow to his mother again.

He needed to stop trying to think of new ways to get

Marlene naked and do something useful, like figure out what was going on at Chameleon and who was responsible. He should at least be thinking about what he was going to say to his father on Tuesday, because that was going to be difficult. He should absolutely be planning a kick-ass menu to impress the resort chefs in California.

Yeah, that just wasn't happening. He couldn't pull his brain out of neutral gear. It was not his usual MO, but then nothing had been usual about his life since he got to Norton. He wasn't feeling even a hint of the usual bored itch, the desire to start fresh and find something new to try. He'd been plenty restless before he got here. Did he even want to go to California anymore?

He didn't have a choice.

No more sluts.

For a second, Joe wished Marly didn't have so many admirers. He shook his head at his hypocrisy and decided not to sweat it. He'd be ready to go when it was time. He and the road were good friends. Its call would eventually drown out Marlene's unexpected siren song.

Joe pulled into Olivia's driveway. The garage door was open and her car was parked inside. He entered the kitchen through the garage.

"Olivia? Where y'at, kiddo?" Joe called.

"In here." Her voice was soft. Tired.

Joe walked into the dining room and found her sitting at the table and staring at her laptop. "What's up?"

"Nothing. My lawyer's on the way over here."

"On a Sunday?" he asked.

"Sean's an old friend. Actually, we went to high school together." Her cheeks reddened.

"Better tell him someone called the health department on Chameleon. We got a surprise visit today," Joe said.

"Are you kidding me? Oh, shit, I wasn't even there. Did they find anything?" she asked.

"Not really. A couple of random citations. I think he only wrote us up so he could come back. I told him to bring a friend and check out the dining room next time. Seemed like the thing to do. Hey, look on the bright side: he said it was the cleanest kitchen he'd been in all week."

"Thanks to you," she noted.

"Don't look a gift horse in the mouth, kiddo. That's why I'm here," he said.

"I shouldn't need you."

"All women need me." Joe got the response he was going for with that remark. Her laugh eased him.

"Hey, you want to bring the lawyer over to Marly's? I'm cooking Thai," he said.

"You and Marly, huh?"

Joe shrugged.

"About time. You were starting to worry me, cowboy. Is that where you were last night?" Olivia chuckled at Joe's terse nod. "Thanks for the offer, but I think we'll stay here."

"I filled Marly in on all the drama at Chameleon. Any special reason you didn't tell her?"

"Denial?" She looked depressed again.

Joe noticed a bottle of wine on the counter, and he gave Olivia an assessing look. Maybe he should insist that she come to Marly's with him. Olivia was in no condition to make big decisions. "Olivia, are you sure it's a good idea to sleep with your lawyer?"

She didn't blink. "A good friend of mine told me to get laid."

"Yeah, he may have been rushing things a bit," Joe admitted. "Are you sure you're ready to move on?"

"I never should have been here in the first place." Olivia leaned back against her chair and stared at the ceiling.

Joe put his hand on her shoulder. "In that case, I recommend you have at least one drink before the lawyer gets here." That got another smile out of her. "I'm going to shower and head out. You sure you don't want to join us?"

"Ewwww, no way."

Joe grinned.

She pointed toward the basement stairs. "Take a couple bottles of wine with you. Pick good ones. The wine cellar was Keith's baby. At least sometimes he had good taste," Olivia sighed.

Joe kissed her on the forehead. "Sometimes he had great taste, kiddo."

Marly answered the door wearing a thin summer dress and no bra that Joe could detect. Her feet were bare, and her hair was wet. The farmers' market ingredients were piled on the island. "Where's Sam?" he asked.

"Thomas just picked him up."

Joe kicked off his shoes and stared at Marlene's ass while she opened the bottle of Cabernet he'd snaked from Keith's cellar.

He wanted to cook for her, he really did. But he also wanted to hike her dress up to her waist and bend her over the island. She handed him a glass of wine. "No pressure, but I'm not wearing underwear."

He set his wine glass on the counter. "Lady's choice: kitchen or bedroom?"

In reply, Marlene pulled her dress over her head and threw it on a kitchen chair. She stood before him, perfectly, gloriously naked.

Joe restrained the impulse to flip her around, press her to the counter, and slide into her. Barely. And, really, only because the smug look on Marlene's face dared him to do it.

He reached out to brush one hand over her collarbone with a feather light caress. He continued down over the curve of a breast, then under it. He pinched her nipple. She gasped.

He was going to take her slow, just to torture her. He enjoyed teasing her. She could take it. She was used to fooling around with guys she could wind around her little finger. Guys who slunk off the porch and called in sick to work when they didn't get what they wanted. He was not one of those guys.

He moved south, keeping the maximum amount of distance between them as his fingers glided through her folds. She felt like satin ribbon spooling through his fingertips. He watched the gold flecks spark in her eyes as she moaned.

"Yes, right there," she breathed. "Don't stop. That feels incredible. A little bit harder and…yes! Oh my God." She braced her elbows on the island and watched his hand move between her thighs.

Joe sped up the motion in slow increments, sometimes adding a finger, sometimes taking one away, but never losing contact with her. He didn't let her go over the edge, but he never let her come down from it either.

When her walls finally broke around his fingers, Joe sank to his knees and buried his face between her thighs. Tasting soap, salt, and Marlene, he searched out the sweet center of her pleasure as she rippled around his tongue. He wanted to make her come again. He sucked and stroked until her little screams shredded his control.

Now, he thought, rising swiftly to his feet.

He ripped a condom out of his pocket, shucked his jeans to the floor and pulled his shirt over his head. He picked her up, groaning as she wrapped her legs around his waist and pressed down on him. He muscled his way across the kitchen and sank into a chair at the cherry-wood table.

With Marlene riding him, he forgot to breathe. She rocked against him, tight, then rose above him, slowly squeezing him in a liquid vise.

When she paused, he finally remembered what his lungs were for, but forgot again when she arched her back to rest her weight on his thighs and began to squeeze and release his cock without moving a muscle that he could see. Circular, tight, stunning. Loose, wet, heating him up.

Joe knew he should do something. This was supposed to be his show. Marlene sank into his lap, undulating, giving a gentle shimmy of her hips. God help him, he couldn't move. All he could do was watch, and let her pull him wherever she wanted him to go. It was her show now, and he had the best seat in the house.

Joe gave himself to her, his breath harsh in his ears. His blood roared. He was dazzled by the goddess rising above him, ruling him, making him hers. Every second felt like an orgasm as she spun him out, stretched his control beyond the limits of his endurance, carried him along with her. Her golden eyes held him captive as her hips mastered him.

She leaned down to place a slow, melting kiss on his lips. His heart swelled with the rest of him. It nearly choked him.

Did Marlene feel it too? Tenderness? Awe? He opened his mouth to ask her, but she silenced him with a kiss, and he forgot his question as she broke him into pieces with the driving, unprecedented, rhythm of her perfect hips. He poured himself into her, felt her walls shaking, his pulse pounding in time with hers, as if they were one body.

From a distance, Joe could hear cursing. There was also giggling, and he was pretty sure that was only coming from Marlene. She collapsed against his chest, panting. Her forehead pressed into the crook of his neck, and her arms clutched his shoulders.

He was still inside her, and he was certain that if he was ever going to be able to move again, it wasn't going to happen until she stopped shaking. Every few seconds, her body caressed him, and Joe couldn't think while she trembled around him.

"God, you are so much fun," she groaned into his neck.

Fun? Joe's heart skipped a beat. Fun seemed a little…well, light. Marlene kissed him again. There it was, that connection, that heat. It made Joe's heart jump and then slam unevenly in his chest. Was he the only one who felt it? The casual smile Marlene gave him as she lifted her body and swung a graceful leg over his lap made Joe think that he was. He reached for the condom before his cock could shrink completely.

Sex, he reminded himself. This was just friendly neighborhood, casual sex. A fling. Right. He could do that. He was good at it. He didn't want anything more than sex. He was leaving, and even if he wasn't—

"I'll be right back," he said.

Marlene had her dress in one hand and her wine glass in the other. She didn't seem affected at all, damn it.

Joe padded down the hall to the bathroom in just his socks. He ignored the empty feeling in his chest. It didn't matter. Marlene was just another girl.

Still, a mocking voice in his head wondered if his mother might have been right, that Joe should have stayed away from loose women after all. Because the only thing worse than sleeping with sluts would be falling in love with one. Was that what she had meant? Fooling around could get him in trouble? It might, at the very least, be bad for his heart.

Chapter 14

MARLENE DOWNED HER ENTIRE GLASS OF WINE. HER LIPS were numb. Her legs were jelly. She had never come that hard in her life and that wasn't even the disturbing part.

What was really killing her was the way her heart pounded every time she looked at Joe. The way his arms made her feel warm and protected. The way she couldn't be near him without wanting to touch him, rest against him, let him hold her and make her feel safe. There it was again. Safe. The word she hadn't thought about before Joseph Rafferty.

Safe was not something she wanted from a guy.

Other women, women like her mother, used men for security. The only thing she wanted from a man was pleasure. Simple pleasure and a rocking good time. Keep it sexy. Keep it simple. What was her other choice? She washed her hands and poured herself another glass of wine. By the time he got back to the kitchen, her high-proof pep talk had done its work. She tossed him his jeans with a teasing grin.

"Get to work, chef. I'm starving." She admired the lean muscles in his back as he stepped into his pants. Her eyes slid over the taut muscles of his stomach as he fastened them.

"If you want me to cook, you better stop looking at me like that, sugar."

"Are you telling me you can't cook with a hard-on,

cheffie boy?" She caressed the hard ridge pressing against the front of Joe's jeans.

"Nope, I'm telling you that if you can't behave, I'll have to make you behave. At least until I get some food into us. After that, all bets are off. You can do whatever you want."

"Promise?" She arched an eyebrow.

"Promise." Joe spun her away from him toward the island. "You want to stuff dumplings or chop vegetables?"

"Stuff, I think." Marlene wasn't sure she could keep her hand steady on a knife at this exact moment. She noticed with irritation that Joe's hands seemed rock steady.

"Got a bowl?" he asked.

Joe chopped garlic and fresh ginger and threw it into the bowl she handed him. He rummaged through her cupboards, adding salt, sesame oil, cabbage, soy sauce, and finally, the ground pork. He worked the ingredients together with one hand. When he was done, she took the bowl of filling from him.

"Hang on." He reached into the bowl and snagged a small piece of raw meat and put it on his tongue.

"Yuck!" she recoiled.

"Trichinosis has mostly died out in the hog population. They keep them clean these days." He took the bowl from her and added a few more glugs of soy sauce. He mixed everything one more time and tasted it again.

Satisfied now, he washed his hands and began rooting through the grocery bags. He tossed her a plastic package of dumpling wrappers.

"What's Olivia doing?" Marlene asked.

"Waiting for her lawyer. With a bottle of wine."

"Oh, that's good." She laughed. "Actually, that could be very good."

"Yeah?" Joe asked.

"Sean's had a thing for her forever."

"Is the lawyer a good guy?"

"Yeah, I think he is. Sean is the complete opposite of Keith, that's for sure. I bet he logs even more hours than Olivia."

She had seen Sean around town a few times since high school. He was still blond and helpful-looking, the sort of guy to whom you told all your boyfriend troubles and then ended up kissing because you were just so grateful someone would really listen. Not that he was slick or sneaky. He was straight, almost to the point of being stiff, but like any good ex-football player, he knew when to press an advantage. That was a good thing in the business of law.

"Speaking of Keith, what do you think he'll do next?" Joe asked.

"Take Olivia to the cleaners. New York is a no fault state, so he'll get half the total assets, half the house, the bank account, savings, stocks, you get the picture," she said.

"What about the restaurant?" Joe asked.

"Olivia's parents gave her the restaurant as a graduation present before she married Keith. Who knows?" Marlene shook her head. "That's why she needs a good lawyer. Sean will take care of her."

She glanced at Joe's hands as he began to dice onions, red peppers, and carrots, working the knife in even, controlled strokes. He was so good with his hands. She could picture them, sliding over her body, stroking it, bringing it to life. The rhythm of the knife on the cutting board echoed another rhythm in her head. She blazed through the package of wrappers, filling each dumpling with total concentration, enjoying the heat dancing along her skin. She jumped when Joe spoke.

"My mom loved dumplings."

"Past tense?" She spooned in a teaspoon of pork filling and crimped the dumpling without looking at it. Her eyes were trained on Joe's face as stormy shadows sailed across his sky blue eyes.

"Breast cancer."

"I'm sorry." She gently placed the last dumpling in his hand. He nodded, only partly in approval of her stuffing speed.

"My parents didn't get along," he said. "I thought my dad would be relieved when she died."

"He wasn't?" Marlene asked.

"Nope. Devastated. He's been drunk ever since."

"Aren't you going to see him soon?" she asked.

"Yup. Gotta pull the old man out of his nose dive. He's had enough time to wallow in his misery."

"What about you?" Marlene pressed—accurately, she thought, from the way Joe twitched. "Have you had enough time to wallow in yours?"

"I don't think there is enough time for me, sugar." His small smile squeezed her heart.

He pulled two large sauté pans down from the rack and fired up the stove. "Make some rice, will you?"

She opened a cabinet, realizing she loved cooking with him, here and at the restaurant. In just a few days, Joe had made his mark. Things ran cleaner, tighter, smoother. He really knew what he was doing. She still wanted her old job back after he was gone, but she was glad she'd had the chance to work with him. As she put the rice on to steam she realized they didn't have much more time together. Joe was leaving to spend the Fourth of July with his dad. After that, he'd be back for a week, and then gone for good.

"Hey, you never told me last night why you stick around Chameleon," he said suddenly.

"Olivia's is my best friend."

"Yeah? And? You know you could run any kitchen in Western New York, right? Why stay at Chameleon cooking beans and baking cakes?"

"I like baking cakes."

"You are wasted in that bakeshop, and you know it."

Pleasure soared through her. "It's fine, Joe. Nobody else can do what I do at Chameleon. I don't need to be the chef to run the kitchen. Olivia is my best friend. She brought me home to her family when mine fell apart. That's a debt I can never repay." It felt like a lie when she said it out loud.

"It's not fair." He crossed his arms.

"It's fine." She glared a warning at him. "Are you going to feed me?"

For a minute she thought Joe wasn't going to drop it. Then he said, "I'll fry, you make the sauce?"

She nodded, relieved.

They ate the pot stickers while the rice was cooking. The pan-fried wonton skins were perfect with the salty ginger soy sauce. She couldn't get enough of them.

Joe began the stir-fry. When the rice was done, he tasted the sauce and added a final squirt of lime and a handful of brown sugar. The sweet scent of coconut milk balanced with acid lime and chili heat floated across the kitchen. He placed a heap of sticky rice in the middle of two shallow bowls and ladled the curry and vegetables over the top. Colorful red peppers, green basil and scallions, and orange carrots swam in the fragrant sauce.

She took a bite of the steaming dish. Exotic flavors exploded across her tongue. Sweet, then hot, garlic, a note of licorice from the basil, and then more spice, a light, addictive heat that made her want to take another bite. And another.

"Will you come with me to see my father? I could use a wing man," Joe said suddenly.

His unexpected question caused a burst of excitement to charge through her. A road trip? Hell yes. She'd like to get out of town for a while. Especially with Joe.

She could imagine what it would be like to spend hours in the car with him, the heat building between them, flaring, raging. They'd probably have to pull over a few times, but that would help burn out the attraction that made Marlene want to spend every waking minute by his side. The more time she spent with Joe, the better. That would help her get over him that much quicker when he left.

"Maybe," she said. "We're only open for dinner on the Fourth, and I don't think we have any reservations. Everybody barbecues."

"I should probably warn you about the pig."

"Pig?"

"It's a pig roast. We're cooking."

"How on earth did you get talked into that?" she asked.

"Dad throws this party every year. He invites every person he knows and most of them show up with children and hard liquor. My mother used to cook up a big pot of chili or a shrimp gumbo while the men in the family had a big old time getting drunk and playing poker."

"What about the women?"

"Barefoot and pregnant, of course," he quipped.

"You realize you're slipping into good ole boy dialect, right?"

"Can't help it. I'm a born and bred Kentucky redneck. Anyway, it occurred to dear old Dad last week that it might be fun to have his son, the chef, cook for the party this year. Something easy. Like a pig." His voice was not filled with affection or respect. Marlene couldn't quite put a finger on the emotion. It was something close to scorn. Fathers and scorn she could understand.

"And you said yes? On a week's notice?" Her mind spun ahead to the practical aspects of such a feat. "Where are you going to get a roaster? And a pig?"

"Not important because I told Dad it would take some planning, and we should cook burgers and dogs this year and do the pig next year."

"That sounds like a better idea. Very reasonable. Not at all what I would expect from you," Marlene said.

"Dad said not to worry about it. He didn't think I'd be able to do it, but he wanted to give me a chance. He said he'd call one of his buddies in the morning to see what they could come up with. He said he had an empty oil drum in the barn, and he remembered reading something about pig roasting, oil drums, and electric garage door openers a while back."

"And then what happened?" she asked.

"I said Wilbur and I would arrive Tuesday morning ready to roll."

Marlene laughed. "Where's your backbone, Rafferty? He was probably bluffing."

"No chance. Once he gets an idea, my father makes it happen, one way or another."

"I'm not touching the pig, Joe. I mean it. No pig." She wasn't normally squeamish, but ugh, a whole dead pig?

"Deal. I'll handle the pig. You handle my father."

"Wait a minute! That doesn't sound like a fair trade!"

"You'll see. My father's going to love you. You are exactly his kind of woman."

That didn't sound like a compliment, but she let it go. "Why couldn't you just tell him no pig?"

"You can't tell him no. No one tells him no. I can't screw it up either. I don't want to give him the satisfaction."

"Of what?"

"Watching me fail. He thinks cooking is a sissy job."

Her jaw dropped. Professional cooking was hard labor. It required quick thinking, the ability to multitask, stamina, and skill. Joe's father must be an idiot. "That's ridiculous," she snapped. "Why do you care what he thinks, anyway?"

"He's my father." Joe shrugged. "Dad went ballistic when he found out I wanted to go to culinary school. He thought I should study something useful, like law or medicine. Like you said, cooking isn't exactly rocket science, but I'm good at it."

The shutters snapped down over his eyes. If Marlene hadn't already decided to go with him, she'd go now just to meet the man who could put that bleak look on Joe's face. And make him pay.

"You see the irony, right?" she asked. "You're going to cook a pig for him. That sounds pretty useful to me."

Joe shrugged again. The shutters turned into armor.

"Wow, I'm really looking forward to the trip now. I get to run interference with an opinionated jerk and cook for a huge, drunk crowd of hillbillies. Now that is my idea of a good time. You did mention there would be booze, right?"

"How do you feel about small batch Kentucky bourbon, sugar?" Joe asked.

"Pretty good, considering."

"I don't suppose you can play poker?" he asked.

"Not as well as I can drink bourbon," Marlene lied. She decided to keep a few cards close to her chest. She might need an ace in the hole. Or four. Perhaps a royal straight flush would help too.

"Then you're up for it? Wingwoman?" His eyes were clear now, laughing.

"When are we leaving?"

"Tomorrow night. Pack your bag in the morning, sugar. We'll take off right after service."

"We've got a wedding at Chameleon this weekend, you know," she reminded him.

"We'll be back by Wednesday afternoon. Piece of cake."

"Easy for you to say. I have to make the cake."

"Is that going to be a problem?" Joe was asking as the chef, not the man. There was no way she would admit it even if it was going to be a problem, so she just shook her head.

"No problem, chef. I've got it covered."

Joe gave her his wicked grin. As usual, she began to heat up under the light of his eyes. "I want you working nights as much as possible when we get back. Just in case I need anything. I seem to need things when you're around. Lots of things. Do you need to clear that with Olivia?"

Marlene shook her head. "Not as long as I get my job done. Olivia's good that way. Is there anything you need now, chef?"

"The nightly news?" he suggested.

Marlene groaned.

"Okay. Not the news then. Just fire up that big television, so I can see what it looks like."

Joe immediately commandeered the remote, and they did end up watching the damn news. His warm body, the food in her belly, and the excellent sex sapped Marlene's will to move, to think, to choose. She was living in the moment, but she had to admit, this moment was pretty darn good. She nestled into Joe's warmth and fell asleep.

It was dark when she awoke. They were tangled up on the couch in a pile of warm limbs. She wiggled her butt, snuggling into the crook of his hips. Joe's hand caressed the curve of her belly and hip, then ran down the length of her thigh.

Marlene could feel his arousal nudge her butt. She faked a sleepy moan and arched her back, shamelessly rubbing against him.

Joe cupped her bare mound under her dress. She was so ready his fingers met no resistance. She held still as Joe slowly circled the center of her desire. In the tiny, fractured part of her brain that was still functioning, she wondered if Joe still thought she was asleep.

And if he did, what a pervert.

"Just so you know, I don't buy it." Joe spoke quietly into her ear, amusement rippling his deep voice. "But if you want to play possum, I'll play along. No snoring though. Screaming, on the other hand, is just fine."

He wrapped a hard arm around her waist and pulled her body on top of him so they both faced the ceiling. He bucked his hips sharply and brought her body into a more yielding position on top of his.

Joe's hands were sure. His arms held her immobile, cradled above his body, while his middle finger slid back and forth, every now and then stopping to slip one or two fingers inside her to gather moisture to ease his way.

Joe didn't tease her this time; he took her straight up to the top of the wave and tossed her over the peak while she sobbed his name, willing to go anywhere with him, as long as he kept her safe in the curve of his arms.

Chapter 15

THE NEXT MORNING, MARLY LEFT JOE SOUND ASLEEP in her bed and went to work earlier than usual. If she wanted to go on the road trip to Kentucky with a clear conscience, she needed to get the wedding cake baked and the layers frozen before she left. She also had to make sure they had enough desserts on hand so that they wouldn't miss her while she was gone. One more double wouldn't kill her, even if she'd had zero sleep for two days and every muscle in her body felt like room temperature butter.

Olivia was already working in the office when Marlene arrived. Anticipating that, Marlene had stopped at the coffee shop on the corner to get two large cappuccinos. She set one on the desk, and Olivia sighed her thanks.

"How'd it go with the lawyer last night?" Marlene asked.

"He says he can take care of everything." Olivia's voice did not hold the relief Marlene was expecting.

"Everything, huh? I bet he can." Her low tone imbued the words with a meaning that earned an impatient look from Olivia. "Is he still in love with you?" she asked.

Olivia blinked.

"I'll take that as a yes," she said. "Did you sleep with him?"

"Marlene!"

"Just checking. Joe said you rolled out the wine. I thought you might put my theory into action."

"Not likely. I'm not even sure how you developed your theory in the first place. Don't you have to fall in love, first?"

"Semantics." Marlene shrugged.

"Maybe Joe is going to be the one for you." Olivia neatly turned the tables on her.

"Certainly not. He's a maestro in bed though. I haven't slept for two days." She forced a laugh, then ducked out of the office and began assembling ingredients for a mega-batch of chocolate cake.

Olivia followed her. "You can run, but you can't hide."

"I'm not hiding. I'm baking. Hey, do you think you can handle the Fourth of July crowd by yourself? Joe asked me to go with him to his father's cabin." She kept her back turned so Olivia wouldn't see the stupid grin sliding across her face.

"I suppose I can. We've got zip on the books. It'll be deader than a doornail around here. Go have some fun. But would you mind answering one teeny-tiny question first?"

"Fire away."

"What have you done with Marlene Bennet?" Olivia demanded.

Marly's stupid grin got wider.

"No, seriously. Have you taken your temperature? Meeting the parent? Are you feeling okay?" She reached around to touch Marlene's forehead.

"Oh, shut up. At least I'm not sleeping with my lawyer."

"Neither am I."

"Yet."

"Yeah, that's not going to happen," Olivia stated.

"Give it a shot. You might like it."

"No, really, Sean turned me down," Olivia said.

Marlene turned around. "Get out!"

Olivia took a slow sip of her cappuccino.

"Do you want to talk about it?" she asked.

"No." Olivia shook her head. "I really don't. I'll tell you all about it some other time, but right now I don't want to talk about anything that's going to piss me off or make me cry." She took a deep breath. "So, three tiers for the wedding cake?"

"Yes. Boxed." Marlene shook her head at the stupidity of the tradition. Why have a cake, if no one was going to eat it? Especially an amazing bittersweet chocolate cake filled with whipped raspberry ganache, iced in chocolate buttercream, and then enrobed in more bittersweet chocolate ganache. The cake was going to be delicious.

She sighed.

The cake was going to be sliced and jammed into boxes where it would melt in the guests' cars for a week before they remembered it was there. A total waste of good chocolate.

"Don't blame me," Olivia said. "I tried to talk her out of it. You know you can't argue with brides. If the bride wants crème brûlée for dessert and her cake in a box, she gets it. Actually, I like this one. She didn't cry when I told her I'd fired the chef."

"I hope you didn't tell her why. No one wants to hear about divorce when they're planning a wedding."

Olivia flinched.

"Oh, honey, I'm sorry. I was just kidding! Any news from Keith?" Marlene held her breath.

"Voice mail, text message, email. He calls so often his cell number shows up in all forty slots of my caller ID."

"That's a little creepy."

"Once in a while I pick up."

"And?"

"He's sorry. He wants to make it up to me. Same old story," Olivia said tiredly. "He says I need him. I can't run this place without him. If I let him come back everything will be different."

Marlene's laughter was harsh. "Different how? Is he going to learn to cook?" Olivia shook her head, but she didn't laugh. "Olivia? You aren't buying that crap, are you? Oh my God. Sweetheart! Chameleon is so much better off without him. You don't need him. We will make this work, I swear."

"He says he still loves me. That I was the best thing that ever happened to him." Olivia's voice was small and distant.

"You told him to piss off, right? You were the best thing that ever happened to him, and he screwed you over. Literally. You know Nikki was not the first. How many chances do you want to give him?" Marlene asked.

"Maybe it was just a cry for attention. He says I work too much—"

"Olivia. Focus, here. Keith is full of shit. You don't work too much. A restaurant doesn't run itself, a little fact he would know if he'd ever done any actual work around here. He knew who he was marrying. You can't change yourself for Keith, and you can't expect him to change for you. You can do better than Keith Watson, Olivia. You deserve to be happy."

"But I was happy."

Oh God, she was serious.

Dread rose like bile in Marlene's throat. She tossed

the measuring cup back into the cocoa powder, ignoring the dark cloud that rose up and settled on her table.

Olivia sniffed. "I mean, I wasn't unhappy. At least everything was working around here. The restaurant was staffed. The bills got paid. Ever since I kicked him out, everything is falling apart. *I'm* falling apart. I almost called the repairman because a plug fell out of the wall. A grease fire made me hyperventilate, for God's sake! We only passed our health inspection because Joe cleaned up the damn kitchen. I can't do this by myself."

"You don't have to do it by yourself. You've got me. You've got Joe—"

"Joe's leaving. Then I'm back to square one."

"You've still got me." Marlene took a deep breath. "You don't have to get a chef—just someone who can cook. I'll fill in, and I can train anybody. I don't mind working doubles."

Olivia laughed. "You aren't going to want to spend every waking hour at Chameleon after Joe leaves. No offense, but your social life is pretty intense. I don't want you getting all bitchy on me because you haven't gotten laid." Olivia smiled as if she meant that as a joke, but it was still a dig.

Marlene put her hands on her hips, smarting from Olivia's instant dismissal of her offer but unwilling to give up yet. "Olivia, we need a body. Get a cook in here, get two cooks in here, whatever, but for God's sake, don't put Keith back on the line. I'm begging you."

"That's easy for you to say, you're heading off on a fun little road trip with Joe while I try to figure out how to run this place—"

"I'm not leaving until everything is under control—"
Marlene was losing her patience.

"I haven't made a decision yet—"

"A decision? Whoa! You aren't serious? You can't
take Keith back!"

"Sure I can. He's my husband."

"Olivia, listen, I know I'm not supposed to take a side
because if you do take him back you'll hate me instead
of him, but I can't let you think this is okay. This is not
okay! You've changed. You aren't the same girl who
came home from culinary school and turned a family
restaurant into Chameleon, the hottest joint in town.
You used to be fearless. What did Keith do to you?"

"Keith didn't do anything to me." Olivia stalked into
the office.

"Is that the problem? Lack of sex? Please don't tell
me you're doing this because Sean turned you down,"
Marlene guessed.

"Not everyone is motivated by sex. Divorce is complicated, Marlene. Keith is going to get half of everything, including the restaurant. It might be easier to
stay married."

"Having Keith at Chameleon doesn't make anything
easier."

Olivia shrugged. "It's all been going to hell since he
left anyway."

"Amen to that, sister, but did you ever think Keith
might be causing the problems? Weird things have been
happening around here since he left. That health inspector, for one thing. The grease fire for another. What if
Keith has been sneaking in to make trouble around here,
trying to get you to take him back?"

"A conspiracy theory? How about plain carelessness? Speaking of which, Ms. Know-it-all, you left the fryer on yesterday."

"No, I didn't. I pulled the plug."

Olivia didn't look convinced. "Well, maybe the heat between you and Joe spontaneously plugged it back in. It was on when I got here this morning. Double-check next time, okay?"

Marlene nodded shortly, too angry to trust herself to speak.

"I'm going to go through résumés. So far I haven't come across a single guy who has done anything more than flip burgers." Olivia sighed. "Let me know when Danny gets here. I need to talk to him."

Marlene shut the office door.

A million thoughts whirled around in her head as she cracked eggs and added water, milk, and oil to the mixing bowl. Olivia hadn't even taken her offer seriously. What was up with that? And she knew damn well she had unplugged the fryer yesterday. She remembered doing it. If someone had plugged it back into the wall, then it had to be someone who worked Sunday brunch. Or someone who had a key to the building.

Marlene put the bowl on the Hobart mixer. Was it a mistake to go with Joe this weekend? What if Olivia let Keith come back and he did something really destructive? Olivia didn't seem to be listening to anything Marly was saying, and she wasn't listening to Joe either. Marly glanced at the wall clock and did the math. It was past noon in Italy. She set aside her dry ingredients.

The new bartender, Mikey, spent more time smoking and talking on his high-tech cell phone than he did making drinks, so the bar was empty and quiet. Marlene looked up the long-distance number and grabbed the bar phone. She should have made this call last week, when she found Keith with his checks around his ankles. Olivia was going to be truly pissed, but enough was enough. It was time to call in the cavalry.

—∿∿—

Marlene was filling her wedding cake pans with chocolate cake batter when familiar arms slipped around her. She stiffened. They were the wrong arms.

"Hey, Danny," she said, twisting around and stepping away from him. He was freshly showered, his still-damp, dark blond hair pulled back in a thick ponytail. "Feeling better this week?"

"Yeah, but I heard you've got a new boyfriend," he complained, crossing his tan arms and leaning on her table. His wide, thickly-lashed, milk-chocolate brown eyes usually made her melt, but this morning the wounded look in his dark eyes annoyed her.

"Don't even start with me, Danny Boy," she warned.

"Whatever. You never made me any promises. I get it. I don't have to like it, but I get it. Rumor has it he's leaving soon anyway. That's not why I came in early. I need to talk to you about Keith," he said.

"I'm not discussing that shithead." Maybe she had misread the pleading look in his eyes. Danny wasn't looking to get back in her bed if he wanted to talk about Keith, that was for sure. Everyone on the staff who had a brain knew how she felt about Keith, including all the new guys.

"Look, I know you two don't get along—" he began.

"Understatement." She nudged Danny out of the way with her hip and measured chocolate cake batter into pans.

"Keith's in big trouble, Marly."

"Damn right. The next time I see him, I'm gonna kill him," she said.

"There might not be much of him left. He's hanging with a bad crowd, Marlene. He's making mistakes, and—"

"Good. A couple broken legs would do him a world of good. How tough is this crowd? Tough enough to maim?" she asked.

"Probably. They are not nice people."

"So why are you telling me about it?" she said.

"Because we're friends, and I don't know who else to tell. You *are* my friend, Marly, even if, well, whatever. Keith's my friend too, and he needs help."

Danny's skewed logic made Marlene shake her head. He was just so young sometimes. "You're standing between me and the oven, Danny."

He jumped out of the way.

"Danny, I am your friend. I'd help you in a minute, but Keith? No way. You're asking too much. Keith will manage to squirm out of whatever problem he's having. He always does."

"Not this time. He's playing poker at the Niagara Falls Casino. In the big room."

"Oh, shit," she breathed.

High stakes poker would explain why Keith had taken money from the safe, all right. Keith was a lousy poker player, so bad that whenever he was playing, Marly couldn't keep herself away from the table, even though she hated to listen to his stupid game chatter. It was just so darn easy to take his money. Apparently, she wasn't the only one who thought so. "How come you're telling me about this?"

"Because there's another game this week," Danny said. She groaned.

"I don't know how much he's in for now—"

"I'd say at least five hundred dollars. That's what he took out of the safe," she said dryly.

"We have to get him out of there before he loses again. I know you don't care about him, but he'll take Olivia and the restaurant down with him," Danny said.

"What do you expect me to do? I can't play for him."

"No, but you could be my date. That might get you into the game. Then you could win his money back." Danny played his last card so carelessly she almost folded.

"Your date, huh?"

"It's invitation only, but the guys like to have women around. Especially hot ones. I bet you could talk one of the guys into staking you if you work it a little."

"Nice try, Danny Boy. If these guys are dangerous, there's no way I'm going to get involved. Let Keith hang. He deserves it. Call the cops if you really care," she suggested.

"I'm pretty sure one of the players is a cop. No help there. Come on, Marlene. It will be like Vegas. We had a good time, remember?" His warm eyes lit with memories of a great weekend in a free hotel room with complimentary room service and a huge Jacuzzi. Olivia and Keith had gone with them. Keith had won big, luck being blind, and he remained convinced to this day that he had poker skills. She shook her head.

Danny edged closer to her. He put his hands on her arms, and she let him, just to see how it made her feel.

Nothing. Danny's eyes weren't blue. Or hot and cold at the same time.

Gently, she pushed him away.

He frowned. "I've heard stories about Joe Rafferty. You know he's leaving right? He's a user, Marlene. And I—"

"Maybe after he's gone, Danny Boy, but not now."

Danny sighed. He really was a puppy.

"Olivia wants to see you," she added. "Maybe you should tell *her* about Keith's little problem."

"She'll probably fire me," he said.

"You called in sick two days in a row and she saw you at Johnny's. She might fire you anyway. Better come up with something good."

"The next game is Saturday night. Let me know if you change your mind, Marlene. About anything."

"You'll be the first to know," she promised and gave him a nudge toward the office door.

Danny knocked. When Olivia answered, he stepped into the office and shut the door behind him.

Marlene turned back to her prep list.

"You left me in bed to come in and flirt with a toddler?" Joe asked from the doorway.

She turned around. "Jealous?" The sight of him made her pulse throb.

Joe walked toward her. "Nope."

He stopped in front of her and slid his arms around her waist. Her head dropped back as his lips feathered her neck. Joe lifted her until she was sitting on the prep table, straddling his hips, and held her still for a kiss that left her wishing she were naked.

"Where did you learn to kiss like that?" she finally asked.

Joe flipped her apron out of the way and rubbed his palms over her thighs. His thumb grazed the rip at her knee and gave her goose bumps.

"My mother's best friend." His grin was so full of memories that Marlene felt a stab of envy. "I was an early bloomer."

"That's illegal," she protested.

"Yup, among other things, but she kept me from getting into a lot of trouble with girls my own age."

"Did your mother find out?" she asked.

"Nope."

"She didn't actually...ummmm." Joe's thumb pressed into her center. Even through denim, he knew just where to touch her. She tried again. "Did you—" His thumb made small circles against her. "Forget it, I don't want to know."

Joe leaned forward, and he didn't pull away from her until the office door opened. She lifted her head and saw Danny's brown eyes chill as he took in the scene in the bakeshop.

"Danny—" Marlene began. Joe's arms tightened around her.

Danny held up a hand and kept walking.

Joe held Marlene still for another kiss. "I guess you made me jealous, after all."

"You're not playing fair."

"I never play fair," he said. "What's the point?"

"Danny told me Keith is playing serious poker at the casino," Marlene said.

"So?"

"You ever played poker with Keith?"

Joe shook his head.

"He's never put a dime on the table that didn't get taken away from him. Well, except once. I bet that's why he took the money from the safe," she said.

"You tell Olivia yet?"

"No."

"Let's go, sugar." Joe pulled her off the prep table.

Maybe Olivia would listen to sense now, and Marlene could talk to Danny later. They still had to work together, and it was just plain bad manners to flaunt her relationship with Joe. Not that she and Joe had a relationship.

They did have a road trip, though, and she was looking forward to spending the next two days alone with him. The thought set her on fire as he took her hand and pulled her toward Olivia's office.

Chapter 16

AFTER A GRUELING NIGHT OF SERVICE, MARLENE hauled herself out to Joe's Jeep. Her feet were aching and her arms felt like lead. Her brain was fried from worrying about what might happen with Joe and Danny on the line together, and trying to talk to Olivia about Keith's poker problem had been like banging her head on a brick wall. She fell sound asleep just past the New York State line.

When Marlene woke up, she was snout to snout with a dead pig.

She screamed. Actually it was more of a gasp with pitch because she didn't want to open her mouth very wide.

"I've been waiting for that." Joe chuckled.

Marlene cranked her seat up until she was no longer reclining into the back, where the grayish-pink, sprouty-nosed pig was stretched out and buckled in. She adjusted her seat belt as if it could protect her from further indignity.

"You didn't seem to mind Wilbur when he boarded. You snuggled right up to him," Joe said.

"Why didn't you put him in the back?" she asked.

"No room."

Right, the food. The back end of the Jeep was full of everything they would possibly need to pull off a barbecue. Joe had packed a huge cooler full of bacon, coleslaw, macaroni salad, an enormous bag of shredded cheese, cooked-off pasta for macaroni and cheese, and dozens of hot dogs and buns for the kids. They also had #10 cans of baked beans, a gallon of barbecue sauce, two watermelons, and a dozen bags of potato chips.

Now, they had a pig.

She glanced in the back. It was whiter than she had imagined it would be. Beneath the clear, plastic tarp she could see several blue USDA stamps. She gave it a tentative poke in the ham with the tip of her index finger. It was disturbingly firm. She craned her neck to get a better look at the head. Its eyes were blue-brown and wide open, and its thick, purple tongue protruded from its snout. It had very small teeth.

The pig smelled, well, dead, like a dish towel that had been used to clean up blood, and then soaked in vinegar. Marlene could not imagine eating it. It was going to take some serious work to make this little piggie smell like dinner.

"I'm sorry I slept so long. You should have woken me up."

"That's all right, sugar, you'll need your rest. I'm glad you moved when we heaved Wilbur in next to you though. I was afraid the hog farmer would think you were dead too," he said.

"Is this what passes for humor in the South? Pig jokes?"

"Get used to it." He signaled a left turn. "We're here."

Joe turned into a mud driveway and headed for a dinky, rundown house on a hill overlooking the river. It was more of a shack, really. Marlene was relieved when he passed it and drove toward a wide, wire fence. The dashboard clock told her it was six in the morning. Her teeth were fuzzy, and she was going to need some coffee before facing that pig again.

He leaped out to open the fence, drove through, and jumped out again to close it. "Keeps the cows in," he explained. Off to the right she saw an enormous thicket of wild blackberries on the edge of a wide-open meadow. The meadow was freshly mowed, the grass yellow in protest to the sudden exposure to the sun.

The truck crunched along the gravel driveway, going down and then up a short, steep hill. When they crested the rise, a two-story log house appeared behind the trees, facing a barn with double doors large enough to drive a truck through. Up top, an open hayloft welcomed the morning sun. Two deer took off into the woods.

Marlene felt like they had driven straight into a forest wonderland. "It's like Norman Rockwell goes country up here," she said as they climbed out of the truck.

"That'll change when you meet my father," Joe said.

"Oh, I don't think so. This just gets better and better." Marlene had just caught sight of an old man sleeping in a wooden rocking chair on the front porch of the cabin. His feet were propped up on an upturned tin washtub. "Is that your father?"

Joe nodded.

Mr. Rafferty was decked out in worn-out bib overalls. His side-flaps were unbuttoned, and his thin cotton shirt hung out of one side. His bearded chin rested on his chest. He looked like a cross between Grizzly Adams and Santa Claus.

"Damn. I wanted to get the pig rolling without any help." Joe sounded glum.

"Then why am I here?" she asked.

"Garnish."

"Very funny. No more jokes before coffee."

"My father's coffee is strong enough to stand a spoon up in. It'll put hair on your chest, for sure." Joe's Kentucky good ole boy voice was going to take some getting used to. As defense mechanisms went, it was a beauty.

"I can't believe the truck didn't wake him," she said.

"He can't hear a damn thing when he's snoring like that," Joe said as he leaned down to shake his father's shoulder.

The old man woke up fast. His mouth closed and his blue eyes focused on Marlene. Mr. Rafferty's eyes traveled the length of her body, pausing at her breasts and hips before making their way back to her face.

"Hello, Dad." Joe held out his hand for his father to shake. "I brought you a pig."

"She don't look like a pig. Does she act like one?" Mr. Rafferty asked.

Marlene chuckled. "More pig humor. The apple doesn't fall far from the tree, I see."

"Don't let my boy fool you. The best part of Joe here ran down his Mama's leg." The old man gave her a sweet grin that belied the obscenity of his words. "Call me Frank."

Marly felt Joe stiffen. She wrapped her arm around his waist and wedged herself under his arm. Joe's dear old dad was no match for her. Growing up with a succession of stepfathers had taught Marlene many things, not the least of which was how to deal with lecherous older men.

"Oh, I doubt you've seen the best part of Joe in a good many years, *Mr. Rafferty*." She cocked her head to the side. "Aren't you supposed to stand to greet a lady in this neck of the woods?"

Frank Rafferty shouted a laugh and got to his feet. He was almost as tall as his son. "Sorry, princess. I thought I was dreaming." He held out his hand, and Marly took it, even though she knew he was going to hold on to it too long.

She had planned to take her cues from Joe, but his sullen silence wasn't giving her much to work with. He looked about ready to pile back in the truck and head home. She was going to have to nudge them along.

"Boys, if we want to eat by three, you'd better get that pig rolling. Point me at the coffee pot, and I'll brew us up some inspiration." Oh God, now that damn dialect was rubbing off on her.

"Coffee's made," Mr. Rafferty said. He disappeared into the kitchen and returned with a full pot. She pretended not to notice when he doctored his own cup with whiskey. "I was just resting my eyes for a minute. Joe said he'd be in by seven this morning. That boy may be peculiar," Mr. Rafferty said, "but he ain't ever late."

Joe ignored the coffee and stomped off toward the truck. Mr. Rafferty followed him. Marlene sighed and sipped her coffee. It was strong, hot, and thick, as promised.

Caffeine filled Marlene's veins with cautious optimism. Birds chirped and bugs hummed as sunlight began to spread through the forest. It was going to be a beautiful day. She wouldn't let a couple of stubborn, redneck men ruin her damn picnic, she thought, as she followed them to the truck.

Wilbur was laid out on the tailgate, and she had to look away as Joe forced a thick metal pole into the center of the pig. He threaded large metal brackets onto each end of the bar and cranked them tightly into place. Then the debate began on whether to wrap Wilbur in chicken wire or just put him on as is. Mr. Rafferty maintained that chicken wire was a waste of time and might be hard to get off later, but Joe was firmly in the chicken wire camp.

"What do you think, Marlene?" Joe said. Mr. Rafferty looked shocked. Women must not be consulted much around here.

"Better safe than sorry, don't you think?" she said. "You've only got one shot at this."

Joe heaved the pig up into the air, and his father grudgingly slid the fence around it. They cinched it neatly with bailing wire.

"Well, we are aiming for falling off the bone tender," Mr. Rafferty conceded. "We don't want to lose any. Let's see if Sal's pottery wheel motor can handle all this cyborg pig," he said.

"I thought it was a garage door opener," Joe said.

"Didn't work out. This one turns like a charm."

Joe nodded. "Coals ready yet?"

"Gettin' there," Mr. Rafferty reported.

They each took a side and heaved the pig into the bisected and hinged oil drum.

Joe's dad hooked the motor onto one side of the drum and checked to make sure the pig was locked in tight. He flipped the switch. The motor hummed and the pig jerked, caught, then began to turn. Mr. Rafferty adjusted the speed and grinned, showing tobacco stained teeth. "She's a beaut."

He closed the lid. "You kids hungry?"

Joe smothered a yawn. "Sure, what would you like?"

Marlene dug her elbow into Joe's side. "How about

you take a nap before people start getting here? I'll keep
an eye on Wilbur."

"I'm all right," Joe said. "The pig is going to need a
pretty close eye on him for a while."

"Don't ever say no to a lady, son. I got the drunk
house all fixed up for you, and I'll watch the pig." Mr.
Rafferty gestured at a small building just off the main
house, and winked at Marlene. "That's where I put anybody who gets unruly and needs a place to sleep it off."

Joe shook his head. "We'll take the hayloft. I brought
sleeping bags. Give the drunk house to somebody who
needs it." Joe gave his father a pointed look. "Make sure
you keep the coals toward the back."

"Git, boy. This ain't my first rodeo."

Joe was silent as they climbed the stairs into the hayloft.

Marlene perched on one of the three bales set in front
of the open shutters as Joe spread blankets and sleeping
bags out on a bed of hay. She peered down at the front
of the cabin, the "drunk house," and the driveway. Mr.
Rafferty was back in his chair on the porch. She turned
to Joe, who was lying on the blankets with his arms
above his head, staring blankly at the rafters.

"Your dad really gets to you, huh?" she asked.

"He doesn't bother you?"

"Nope. He's just an old man to me, slightly faded
around the edges. I enjoy seeing big, bad Joe Rafferty
thrown for a loop though." She lay down beside him and
put her head on his shoulder. Joe's arm snaked around
her waist and tucked her into his side.

The sweet, dry smell of hay surrounded them, making

her feel lazy and relaxed. She rolled over and stretched out on top of Joe's big frame, settling her body onto his. "You poor thing. Intimidated by your old, drunk, heartbroken dad."

Joe's snort made her bounce. "Heartbroken men do not throw parties."

"Sure they do. If that's all they know how to do."

Marlene took his upper lip between her own. She kissed him, gently, sweetly, so attuned to his breath that she felt the exact moment he surrendered. She scooted down his chest, pausing to flip his shirt up so she could nibble her way down his stomach and follow the delicate line of hair to his navel. She made quick work of his belt. His clothes melted away under her hands.

She spoke into the strong hollow of Joe's thigh. "Some men choose other ways to hide their emotions." Her lips and tongue danced a delicate waltz around his hip.

His hands encased her skull, angling her head up to meet his gaze. For a minute she thought he might push her away.

"Some women do too," Joe said.

Marlene smiled and held Joe's eyes as she took him in her mouth. A hectic flush spread across his cheekbones, and the blue of his eyes, sharpened, flashed. "Somebody needs to tend that pig."

She lifted her head. "I'll take care of the meat, Joe."

His laugh consisted of one indrawn breath.

Marlene bent to her work. Bales of hay were stacked around them. From below, their cozy nest was invisible, but not inaudible. *Frank*, as she had finally decided to call him, deserved a good earful after the comments he'd made earlier, and she was going to make sure he got it.

Marlene grasped Joe with one hand, sliding her fingers over his silky shaft, pulling back the soft skin, thrilling to the way he grew and hardened beneath her touch. Her tongue flashed against him, catching the ridge on the underside of his cock in a strong, sure stroke. Her mouth slid over him, taking him deep, deeper into her mouth. She relaxed her throat, pushing the boundaries of her reflexes.

Her lips inched farther.

Past her limits.

Farther.

"Jesus Christ," Joe groaned.

If Marlene had had room to giggle, she would have. She eased back, took a breath, then did it again. Joe's moan was hoarse, thready, his breath harsh.

She bent to finish him. Her lips worked in concert with her hand, sliding up and down. Completely focused on him, Marlene brought her other hand beneath Joe and gently cupped him. He fishtailed beneath her, lost to her now, she could feel it, feel him fill in her mouth, feel the subtle change in his body. She glanced up at him. He was watching her every move with an avid expression that made her lose her rhythm. She shut her eyes, sucking hard to catch her balance, her world centered on him.

Joe's control broke. He shouted, filling the rafters with his cries of release. When Marlene was sure she had him, she let go of him and thrust one hand into her jeans. She came instantly.

With a contented sigh, she flopped down onto her back next to him.

"Don't forget to check the pig," Joe said in an uneven whisper before he fell asleep.

———∿∿∿———

Marlene left him like that, snoring slightly, and went to visit the small outhouse that overlooked the ravine. She used a pump and what she assumed was well water to wash her hands before she checked on Wilbur. The coals were cranking hot and the skin was beginning to sear, but it would be a while before they would need to keep the lid open. She opened the vent halfway to keep the coals fed and tiptoed past Frank, who was sleeping on the front porch again, coffee cup empty. She went into the kitchen to do some reconnaissance.

Frank had clearly made an effort to stock the small kitchen. Plenty of flour, sugar, butter, and eggs waited for her. Marlene grabbed a big bowl and headed down the driveway, humming, determined to find the black-berry bushes she had spotted on their way in this morn-ing. The country air must be going to her head. She felt positively domestic.

The men were still sleeping when she returned with her bowl full of blackberries. She tossed a half bag of fresh coals under Wilbur and shut the lid again. The pig was getting brown and almost starting to look like food. She had no idea what time the guests were going to ar-rive or how many people to expect, but judging from the supplies Joe had packed, they were expecting an army. Marlene could handle an army.

An hour later, the blackberry cobbler had filled the kitchen with a heavenly scent, and she was frying bacon for the barbecued beans.

Joe walked into the kitchen, rubbing the back of his neck. He had straw in his hair. "What smells so good? Bacon?" He opened the door of the punched tin refrigerator in the corner of the kitchen and popped the top off a beer.

"Joe, it's eleven o'clock."

"When in Rome, sugar. Want one?"

She shook her head.

Joe shrugged. "My father always said that the day my mother died, he was gonna go around the world with a ten-dollar whore who could suck the chrome off a bumper hitch. I think he's looking for you, sugar. You really knocked me out."

Marlene fought down her anger and raised a cool eyebrow. "Is that your way of saying thank you?"

He met her challenging stare with a shrug. "Maybe." He dropped his eyes first. "Sorry."

"You should be." Marlene turned her back on him to pull the bacon out of the pan and turn off the fire. She set the pan in the sink and stood still, gazing out the small, dusty window over the kitchen sink.

After a minute, Joe stepped behind her to rest his chin on top of her head. She didn't soften.

"My father makes me crazy," he said, arms stealing around her waist.

"I can see that. I get a little nuts around my own father. Don't take it out on me though. I'm one of the good guys. I made blackberry cobbler."

Joe kissed the side of her neck, and Marlene turned to face him. She pulled the piece of hay out of his hair. "I think I changed my mind about that beer."

Joe handed her his can. Marlene took a long swig. It did help.

"Have you checked on Wilbur?" he asked.

Frank entered the kitchen just as the sound of crunching gravel alerted them to the arrival of their first guests. "Your girl knows her pig, son. 'Bout halfway done, I reckon. Go see for yourself," Frank challenged. "You're the professional."

"So is Marly, but I'll take a look." Joe grabbed another beer and took off for the shimmering roaster, leaving her alone with his father.

Frank had a beer in his hand too.

Marlene ducked her head and peered into the dark oven. When she pulled the hotel pan out of the oven, the biscuits were the perfect shade of brown and the deep purple berry juice bubbled through the crust in thick bursts. It smelled like sweet, summer heaven.

Frank grinned. "Now that is a sight for sore eyes, girl. You sure are taking good care of us. Joe must have done something good to deserve a girl like you. Where'd you meet my boy, anyway?" he asked.

"Do you know Joe's friend Olivia? In Norton?" Frank nodded. "I've been working for her family for about fifteen years. We're having some trouble staffing the restaurant, and Joe's helping us out for a while."

"I wondered why he couldn't get here any sooner," Frank said.

"We've got our hands full." Marlene kept the sympathy out of her voice. They both stood and watched Joe out the window. Marlene didn't know what Frank was thinking as he watched his son, but she hoped her own thoughts didn't show on her face.

Joe's white T-shirt stretched over his wide back as he heaved the lid of the roaster open. His faded jeans rode low on his hips. Well-broken in work boots and a brown leather belt completed the workman look. Just watching him sweat over the roaster made Marlene want to have him sweating over her.

"You in love with him, little girl?" Frank asked abruptly.

"Nope." She tried not to sound startled. "I don't do love. Just not my thing."

"Hmm. Well. I didn't think I did either. Sometimes things change." She caught a glimpse past the blustery good ole boy facade to the uncertain man beneath the bold words. Frank knew he had a problem. He just didn't know what to do to fix it. Her dislike of him morphed into, if not exactly empathy, then something closer to understanding. "You don't fool me, Frank."

"I don't have to. I just have to fool him," he replied.

"Why?" she asked, genuinely curious.

"So he'll stay out of my hair." Frank pretended indifference.

"You don't really want that."

"Yeah, well, he does." He emptied his beer can into his mouth.

Joe clomped back into the kitchen. The look his father shot him was full of bitter longing, quickly covered. Frank tossed his empty in the trash can and grabbed another beer. "Looks like your Uncle Sal's on his way up the drive with every brat in the family."

"Should we shoot now or wait until they get closer?" Joe wondered.

"Let's wait. Sal's got the cards and poker chips."

It was obvious Joe was kidding about shooting the children because the first kid to hit the porch got slung up onto his back. And the second. The third he wrapped around his waist. Joe jumped off the front steps and began swinging around the driveway grunting like a gorilla. Soon, he was covered in children, slinging them up and down, tickling the slow ones and trying to snatch the quick ones.

The shouts and squeals bounced between the out-buildings. It was chaos. The game ended with Joe flat on his back in the grass at the side of the house with the smallest of the kids sitting squarely on his face and the rest of them, six in all, draped all over his body.

"Has anyone seen Matthew?" Joe asked in a muffled voice. "I can't find him anywhere."

"He's sitting on you!" the children chorused.

"No, he's not. I can't see him. Has anyone seen Matthew?" Joe repeated.

The two-year-old began to bounce up and down on Joe's head, screeching. Joe gently knocked him onto his side, catching his head before it hit the grass. "Oh, there you are. I was getting worried." Joe blew a raspberry on Matthew's stomach.

Marlene felt like she'd been punched in the gut.

The old man's laugh was low and cheerful. "You don't fool me either."

~~~

Four hours later, the yard, the house, and the barn were full of people. Big people, little people, fat people, skinny people. Some well-dressed, some, like Frank, in tattered overalls and faded shirts.

They were all eating and drinking. The children, even more of them now, raced around like mad fools. A few of them had water pistols; the rest had cap guns.

The kids were jubilant and completely out of control. Marlene was breathless.

Joe handed her another beer. "I told you it would be fun."

"No, you didn't," she said.

"Yeah, well, I forgot."

Marlene's head was fuzzy, but it was all right because the food was all out on the table, and everybody loved it. The pig took up an entire folding table and finally looked like food.

"What on earth is that?" she asked, pointing at the flour tortilla in Joe's hand.

"Pork, sliced avocado, Sriracha, and a big handful of cilantro."

"I didn't see that on the table." She frowned.

"Packed extra," Joe said.

"That can't possibly be as good as what I'm eating." Marlene gestured to her straight-up pulled pork sandwich with coleslaw right on the bun, North Carolina–style. Sauce dripped over her palm.

Joe held out his burrito, and Marlene took a big bite. As she chewed, her eyes began to water, and she had to swallow before she was done chewing because her tongue was on fire. Heat torched her stomach like napalm.

"Is your mouth made of asbestos?" Marlene croaked, nose dripping.

"Just about," Joe said. "You want another bite?" His eyes held a dare she could not resist.

"Hell yes." Joe switched plates with her. He handed her extra napkins too. The noise buzzed pleasantly around them as they sat on the steps of the drunk house and watched the action.

When Marlene was finished, Joe took her plate and put his arm around her. That was even more pleasant, so she leaned against him.

The pack of children paused around them. "Uncle Joe and Marlene, sitting in a tree! K-I-S-S-I-N-G!" That was as far as they got before Joe pulled her in for a kiss. With tongue. The children ran away screaming and screeching. But not before soaking them with their water pistols.

"The wet T-shirt contest is next," Joe said.

"You wish," she returned.

"Uh-huh."

"Are you really their uncle? Where are your brothers and sisters?" Marlene was curious. Were there more like him?

Joe shook his head. "I'm an only child."

"That explains a lot."

"Takes one to know one?" Joe asked.

She nodded.

"I'm more like their second cousin or something like that. My Dad's brothers had zillions of kids. Then they had kids." Joe waved his hand around the yard.

"Got it." Marlene nodded. "Think there are any kids in the hayloft?"

"Definitely," he said.

"Too bad." Marlene could go for a roll in the hay right about now.

"Later?" Joe offered. "Much later, probably. When the kids settle down, the poker will start. Hardcore. You up for that?"

Marlene frowned. Poker made her think of Keith.

"Stop thinking about the restaurant."

"I can't believe she blew us off like that," she said.

"Would you want to hear that your loser husband stole money from you and then blew it at the casino?" Joe asked.

"I think forewarned is forearmed. Did she tell you she's thinking about letting him come back to work?" Marlene said.

Joe didn't look surprised. In fact, the look on his face fell into the I-told-you-so category.

"Don't give me that look," she said. "I tried to tell her the things going on at the restaurant are a little too strange to be coincidences. She didn't want to hear that either."

Joe shrugged. "She might be right. Keith let a lot of things slide around Chameleon. Olivia was spread too thin, and you've got your hands full too. You have to expect the shit to hit the fan sometime. We'll get things back on track next week. Don't worry about it, sugar."

"What happened to Chef Sherlock? You going soft on me?"

"Sherlock's on vacation. Relax, sugar, we've got our own poker game to play. I'll even front you some cash if you're nice to me."

"You will? I can be nice. Real nice." Marlene pulled his lips down to hers and forgot all about Chameleon. This trip was already turning out to be more fun than she had anticipated.

And a pickup game was pure gravy.

―∾∾―

"I wouldn't do that, sugar," Joe advised her a couple hours later, just as it was starting to get dark.

They were sitting on the front porch. The locusts

were singing and lightning bugs danced at the edge of the trees. "Uncle Mikey's got a set of cowboys. I can tell by the way he's scratching his armpit."

"Uh-huh," Marlene said. "Call." She laid down a straight.

Joe looked over at her with respect. "Nice."

"Your Uncle Mikey's been looking down my shirt," Marlene whispered, loudly. "He didn't watch the turn or the river. I knew I had him."

"Auntie Carol's not gonna like that."

"See, then I did him a favor."

The game continued. Marlene knocked Joe out next.

"Nothing personal," Marlene said sweetly. "It's just a game."

He sighed and tossed his cards to the center of the table. "You gonna be okay here if I go tell the kids some ghost stories?" Joe asked Marlene.

"I'll be fine. It's not like we're playing for clothes or anything." Marlene's smile was full of innocence and sharp teeth.

"Is that even a possibility?" Uncle Sal looked hopeful.

"No," Joe said firmly. He looked around the table. "I guess I asked the wrong question. Are you boys gonna be okay if I leave her here?" The men hooted.

Joe got Marlene a fresh beer and headed for the barn, yelling a round-up call as he went. Kids came from all corners, following Joe up into the hayloft. Marlene hoped none of them fell asleep up there. She had plans for later, and they didn't involve more than two bodies, no matter how cute his devoted uncle routine was.

First things first though. She was going to take Uncle Sal's money too.

Chapter 17

JOE THOUGHT MARLENE LOOKED DISAPPOINTED WITH the flop when he came to fetch her.

"Call," his father said. They were the last two sitting at the table.

Marlene tossed her cards into the muck and stood up, pushing her chips across the table.

"Just like that, huh? You fold?" his dad asked.

Joe pulled Marlene to her feet. She reeled against him, probably from sitting for so long and spending the better part of the day guzzling beer.

"Frank, there's only one thing more fun than playing poker, and I know a better deal when I see one," she said, stealing a kiss.

Joe smiled against her ninety-proof lips. At some point she'd switched to bourbon. No wonder she was about to fall on her ass.

His father put a wad of cash into Joe's hand. "This ought to cover the pig."

"I've got it, Dad," Joe said, pushing the money back at his father.

"Hell no." His dad gathered the cards. "Put her to bed, son."

Joe shoved the money in his pocket. Marlene sagged against him, and he wrapped his arm around her waist. He half-carried, half-steered Marlene up into the hayloft. "Playing with that crowd has its drawbacks."

"Your family is great," Marlene slurred softly.

"Can you wait up for me? I need to talk to my father."

"I'll be asleep before you hit the bottom of the stairs, sucker."

"And you didn't even win," he chided her.

"Bullshit. I had four of a kind," Marlene mumbled into her pillow. Joe pulled a blanket over her shoulders.

He found his father sitting in the kitchen with the top half of the Dutch door open to the night air, pouring himself another drink. Joe walked into the cabin and sat down at the table. "You haven't had enough yet, Dad?"

"I knew you were going to start in with that." He tipped another shot into the glass.

"You've been drunk since Mom died."

"So what? I'm getting along."

"Are you?" he challenged.

"Sure." His dad took a slug of his drink. "Gotta tell you, son, I sure am sorry your mother didn't get to meet Marlene."

Joe snorted. "Mom was very clear about how she felt about the women I date. Her last words to me were, 'No more sluts, Joe.'"

His father glared at him through narrowed eyes that showed no sign of the vast quantities of alcohol he had consumed that day. "Boy, you disappoint me."

"Tell me something I don't know," he said flatly.

His father ignored him. "If you can't tell the difference between a woman like Marlene and a simple piece of ass, then you haven't learned a damn thing from me, that's for sure. That girl is smart as a whip. You think I don't know she just beat my ass? She was just being polite. Not only that, she's so easy on the eyes that everybody wants to look at her. Your Aunt Carol had to clout Mikey upside the head before he got his eyes under control. Pissed Carol off good too, but then I pointed out that Marlene can't see any man but you. That shut Carol up quick. She's the toughest of all your aunts. If she liked Marlene, then your mama would have loved her, for sure. That girl is a keeper." His father took a drink, swallowed. "Sounds like she fucks like a mink too."

Joe's hand curled into a fist, and his dad's dirty laugh turned into a wheeze.

"Go ahead, boy, take a shot at your old man. Might make us both feel better."

For one raw second, Joe considered it. He would purely love to feel the crack of his knuckles against his father's jaw.

It was his fault Joe was afraid to settle down and fall in love with a good woman. His wanderlust blood that ran in Joe's veins, making him afraid to make promises he couldn't keep. He hadn't shown Joe how to be faithful.

He flexed his fingers and relaxed his arm. His father smiled, but it wasn't a nice thing to see.

"Yeah, love's a bitch, ain't it?" he said.

"How would you know?" Joe retorted.

"I loved your mother like nothing else on earth. She was too good for me. Beautiful. Strong. And too smart to take shit from any man. A real wildcat—" Joe held up his hand. "Sound familiar? Women like that ain't a dime a dozen, son. Pay attention. I know you don't want to hear it from me, but your mama ain't here anymore to set you straight."

"She ain't here anymore to set you straight either." He took the bourbon out of his father's hand.

"Huh." The old man sank down in his chair.

Suddenly that's what he looked like to Joe. An old man. Diminished, somehow. Not the towering giant of Joe's youth. Not the father who would always be smarter, stronger, and wilder. He looked like an old man who had lost his heart and then tried to drown the leftovers with whiskey.

"Enough booze," Joe said. "It won't bring her back."

The men sat quietly for a few minutes, taking each other's measure. Joe saw his father reach for the drink that was always nearby. His mouth worked convulsively for a minute before he laid his hand flat on the table, pressed it down until it quit shaking.

"I promised Mom I'd pull you out of the bottle," Joe stated. "She knew you wouldn't know when to quit. So here I am. I need to know if you're done trying to drink yourself to death."

Silence settled between them again as his father considered the question.

"I reckon I am," he finally said.

"Good."

His father took a breath.

"We're leaving in the morning," Joe said before he could speak.

"I figured as much." His father exhaled. "Didn't expect you to stay."

There was so much that was better left unsaid between them. Joe didn't want to open up another can of worms tonight. He didn't want to hear about all the things he should be doing with his life, all the ways his dad could do it better. He'd spent his whole life listening to that.

Joe stood up and pushed his chair under the table. "Good night, Dad."

"'Night, son. Remember what I said about Marlene."

Joe shook his head. "I'm leaving for California next week." He opened the bottom door, stepping through. "I'll find another 'piece of ass' out there."

Joe shut both doors behind him and took a deep breath of the damp night air. He had fulfilled his promise to his mother, but he still felt the sharp sting of her disappointment pierce his heart. His father's take on Marlene had opened his eyes, and the clues washed through his head, making him feel exposed and stupid. The fact that his father had seen her so clearly, when he had not made him feel even more like a dumb ass.

Joe had assumed Marlene was easy because she had a lot of guys circling around her, and she came on strong. On the surface, she seemed to be like all of the women he had left behind. The kind of girl he could fuck and forget. He had been fooling himself. He had flat-out ignored all the signs that she was different, far different, from his usual fare.

Her kitchen should have tipped him off immediately. It was the kitchen of a professional cook and a homemaker: practical, comfortable, and top of the line. It was the kitchen of an equal, a room Joe envied. Hell, her kitchen had made him yearn for banana pancakes, for home and comfort. How could he have forgotten that the first time his mother had let him touch the stove, they had made pancakes?

Then, of course, there was Marly on the line at Chameleon, a force to be reckoned with. She single-handedly ran the bakeshop and had her finger in every other pie in the kitchen—ordering, training new cooks, filling in during service, acting as the prep cook, and even washing dishes when necessary. Joe had never worked with someone who challenged *him* to keep up with *her*.

There was also the fact that he hadn't willingly left her side since Saturday night, and he was perfectly content. Truth be told, he had never spent every minute of the day with a woman and been at ease. Hell, he'd never spent every minute of the night with a woman and been at ease. Okay, he had never spent an entire night with a woman, period. That fact alone should have told him she was different.

He wanted to sleep with her, cook with her, and work by her side. He wanted to make love with her every night, every morning. He wanted to make breakfast in that excellent kitchen and then go into Chameleon and fix all the restaurant's problems with her help. Then he wanted to go home, make dinner, and start the process all over again.

Marlene made him want to stay.

Joe took a half step back toward the log cabin and his father. It was ironic that he had fallen in love for the first time in his life, and the only person who knew it couldn't possibly give him any advice worth taking. He took another step. He might not want his father's advice, but he sure as hell wanted that bottle of bourbon that was sitting in the kitchen. When he reached the door, he heard his father move inside the kitchen.

It was better to stay sober. They had a long drive back tomorrow, and he had a feeling Marlene was going to be in rough shape in the morning. He was glad she wasn't

waiting up for him because it spared him the temptation
of blurting out his feelings to her. She would probably
jump out of the hayloft. He knew exactly how she felt
about their relationship, the same way he had felt until
five minutes ago. He stepped off the porch and headed
for the outhouse, instead of the bourbon.

His glorified vision of finding a nice girl and settling
down in California seemed crazy now, but there was no
place for him in Norton. Sure, he could find a job. Hell,
Olivia would probably hire him if she could afford it.
He could easily find a place to live too. That wasn't the
problem. Marlene was the problem. He might want to
stay, but that didn't guarantee she would be willing to
keep him.

That wasn't the only problem either. It was all well
and good to think about inflicting himself on a name-
less, faceless California girl, but he actually cared about
Marlene. Just because he had decided to try to settle
down and honor his promise didn't mean it was going to
go well. Rafferty men were cursed. They hurt the women
they…loved. If he really cared about her, he should get
away from her before he did something stupid. He had
to get the hell out of Norton as fast as possible.

God, he was such an asshole.

Joe pulled his cell phone out of his back pocket, won-
dering if anyone would be in the kitchen in California.
Test-cooking was only a formality. He knew they were
waiting for his call. Maybe he could even move his in-
terview up a week. He punched send and waited for the
call to go through. Marlene might be a "keeper" as his
father had said, but she knew the score. He hadn't made
her any promises. She didn't know he cared for her, and

he wasn't going to tell her. He would enjoy the rest of his time with her in a way they both understood: naked, wordless, and uncomplicated.

Just as the phone began to ring, his cell phone dropped the call. He had been surprised to have coverage in the middle of all these trees anyway. No worries. He would stay in Norton for one more week, like he'd promised. His presence at Chameleon was only a Band-Aid, but he could never leave Olivia hanging, especially with a wedding on the books. He'd keep his word, and as an added bonus, he would figure out who was causing all the trouble at the restaurant before he left.

As his final act of service, he would also give Olivia a much-needed wake-up call. Joe knew exactly who should replace Keith, and it wasn't him or anybody on one of the résumés in the office.

Marlene flattened herself against the side of the log cabin and watched Joe head down the path to the out-house. She'd just come from there. The slight ache in her head became a flurry of hammer strikes.

She hadn't planned to eavesdrop, but Joe's quiet voice had carried across the driveway. She'd heard her name mentioned, so she had drifted closer, close enough to catch the tail end of a conversation that left her in no doubt as to how Joe felt about their affair.

She was a piece of ass.

And to think she'd been acting like a girlfriend.

Hot shame made her feel dizzy. She shouldn't have gotten carried away by the warm family picnic mood today. Joe couldn't help being cute with the kids. He hadn't asked her to make blackberry cobbler, and he hadn't known she was making a play for his father's approval. She had thrown herself into the role of girlfriend with gusto, completely ignoring the fact that it was all an illusion. Joe was temporary. Their relationship was only about sex.

She slipped up the hayloft stairs and settled herself into her sleeping bag with her back to the stairs. Hot, angry tears slid from her eyes and soaked the pillow under her cheek. A few minutes later, Joe climbed the stairs and slid into the bag next to her. He nudged her hip. She didn't stir.

Not a chance, buddy.

It might be all her own stupid fault that she had allowed her emotions to get involved, but she was mad at Joe. Tomorrow she'd get her head back on straight. She would remember that she didn't want to be a girlfriend, ever. Tomorrow, she and Joe could pick up where they left off this afternoon in the hayloft. He thought she was a piece of ass? By God, she'd be the best piece of ass he ever had. She'd be unforgettable. She would ruin him for other women. He would leave Norton, but he would think of her every time he got hard, and when he climaxed, she hoped he'd choke on her name.

But not tonight.

Tonight, she was going to pass out and try to forget that she'd broken all of her own rules. The smartest thing to do would be to move on to the next guy immediately, but she knew she wasn't going to do that. Joe was leaving soon enough, and this was too good to give up. She would deal with the emotional backlash, if there was one, after he was gone. Until he left, she was going to spend every minute she could with him and have as much sex as possible.

Tomorrow.

Marlene forced her eyes to stay shut, her body still, her breath quiet. She ignored Joe's warm hand on her hip and the silent tears sliding down her cheeks. Instead, she welcomed the swirl of alcohol in her blood that carried her into black oblivion.

Chapter 18

"MY LADY AT TABLE SEVEN WANTS TO KNOW WHAT THE specials are tonight." Eric leaned against the wall looking as if he wanted to grab a nap while standing there. There were hardly any reservations on the books tonight, and Eric generally slept on the job when he knew he wasn't going to make any money.

"Thai curry. Weren't you listening at the staff meeting?" Marlene scowled at the lazy waiter. He thought he was tired. She and Joe had pulled over to have sex three times on the way home. It was a miracle they made it back in time for service. Maybe it was a good thing he was leaving soon. She couldn't keep up this pace for much longer.

The drive back to Norton had restored her equilibrium, just as she had hoped. She was still angry at herself for behaving like a girlfriend at the cabin, but all that sex on the ride home had helped her get her mind back in the game. She had her eye on the ball again, so to speak.

Sex.

As much sex as humanly possible until Joe left. No thinking about the future, no expectations, no tomorrows. Just hot sex. And lots of it. After a nap, that is. She was dog tired, saddle-sore, and still just the tiniest bit hungover.

In contrast, Joe seemed to be getting more energetic by the minute. He was still running in Thai mode, and the scent of sweet ginger and onions, sharp garlic, and full-throated summer basil filled the kitchen.

Eric dropped another ticket in the window. "Table seven wants some curry then. She's already worked her way through half the menu. A real pain in my ass. She wants to know every ingredient in every freakin' dish," he grumbled.

Marlene and Joe looked at each other.

"Food critic," she said. "Definitely."

Joe turned to Eric. "Little notebook, maybe a tiny tape recorder on the table, a million questions? Did she ask you to pair a wine with her appetizers? Any of that ring a bell? Make you think, hmmm, that's odd, all my years of experience waiting tables tells me that these people are either spies or perhaps, say, food critics from the newspaper? Are you a fucking idiot? You've been lollygagging around all night, dragging your heels and thinking about tonight's TV topics! You waiters kill me."

"Olivia's gonna flip. She knows them all by sight," Marlene added.

Joe sent her a dark glare.

"Just thought I'd throw that in there." She took a perverse satisfaction in his frustration.

Eric put his hands on his hips. "Hey, you didn't seem to notice that you sent four appetizers to a two-top, so don't yell at me! Just make some freakin' curry and get off my back!" He stormed off, presumably to improve the level of service at table seven.

Marlene bit her lip. "Shit. He's right. We did send four appetizers to that table." She would have sent another four too. She wasn't thinking about cooking at all.

She was thinking about Joe, naked. And clean sheets. And soft pillows.

"I guess we better make some freakin' curry, and get it to table seven," Joe said with equanimity. "We'll send them some dumplings too."

"Excuse me, are you the same guy who was flipping out and ripping Eric's head off five seconds ago?"

"He caught me off guard. Eric's a waiter. He's used to getting yelled at. If he didn't deserve it now, he'll deserve it some other time," he said.

"You're just full of surprises today."

"Part of my charm, sugar. Now do me a favor and find some wonton skins." He tossed the filling together while Marlene hunted through the reach-in.

"What do you want me to do with these?" she asked when she had a dozen dumplings stuffed with Joe's hastily made filling.

"Drop them in the fryer." He grabbed half of the dumplings. "I'll turn the rest into pot stickers. A little chicken chili sauce, a little ginger soy, a pretty plate, a nice pile of cilantro, and, darlin', we've got a dumpling duo. Two styles, two sauces, they'll love it."

Marlene plopped her dumplings into the fryer basket and lowered it into the hot grease. The oil bubbled and sizzled. When they were golden brown, she pulled the dumplings out of the fryer, and shook them onto a sheet pan covered with paper towels.

Joe pulled the lid off the pot stickers and used a heatproof spatula to gently roll them out of the pan. He carefully arranged the pot stickers, her dumplings, and the two sauces on a black and white plate with geometric designs. The dumplings looked hot and inviting, and the green cilantro and bright orange chili sauce popped against the black and white of the plate.

"Buzz Eric, and I'll finish the curry," he said.

When Eric returned, he gave Joe a filthy look when he took the dumplings and dropped a stack of tickets in the window. Joe winked at him.

"Looks like we're gonna get busy after all," Joe said. "Fire the chicken and salmon on table five and give me three Caesars, a caprese, and two grilled asparagus apps."

"Yes, chef." Marlene kept her head down so Joe couldn't see her smirk.

Much-needed adrenaline began to pump through her veins, burning away her exhaustion. Nothing like a food critic to get the juices flowing. Well, a food critic and Joe Rafferty.

Working on the line with him was an education and an inspiration. He had everything under control. Since her thoughts were only about two steps from the bedroom whenever he was in the room, she thought about how his kitchen manners compared with his bedroom manners. Bossy? No doubt. Ambitious. Definitely. Talented? Oh dear God, yes.

She laid the chicken on the grill, dredged the salmon in a sweet Indian curry oil, and laid it on the hot side. She wiped her forehead with her arm as she got her chilled salad bowl out from under the salad station. A container labeled sugar fell out from underneath the station, and she set it up on the shelf where it belonged. Marlene tossed three Caesars and put them up on the cold side.

Man, it was getting hot in here.

"Are you all right?" Joe asked. The fire in his eyes told her he knew exactly what was going on with her.

"Perfectly fine," she said, watching Joe lick red curry sauce from a tasting spoon.

"Got any sugar over there?" Joe said.

"Sure," Marlene handed him the container from the shelf. He dumped some into his sauce and tasted it again. He made a face.

"Not funny, Marlene." He added more coconut milk and chicken stock, readjusted the heat and stirred in a bit more red curry paste. "You want to get me some sugar this time? Brown, just to be safe, smart ass."

"That was sugar." She held up the labeled lid.

Joe took a pinch out of the container and dropped it on her tongue.

It was salt. "What the hell?" she asked.

"Good question. That's the container I found in the bakeshop Saturday night." Joe put the finishing touches on the curry dish for table seven. "Let's get these plates out of here."

"Think you made enough?" She eyed the sauté pan full of chicken curry. "Are you feeding an army?"

"I'm practicing. Might do a Thai menu for the resort in Napa."

"Thai and wine?" she asked, wrinkling her nose.

"Think fusion."

She turned her attention to the grill. In the nick of time, she flipped the chicken and salmon, then stepped out from behind the line.

"Watch the grill, will you? I want to go take a peek at table seven." Marlene rounded the corner to the dining room and ducked into the bumped out supply closet they used as a bar. Mikey was clumsily opening a bottle of Riesling.

"For table seven?" she asked.

"Uh, yeah, how'd you know?" he asked.

"Lucky guess." Riesling would actually be great with the fried dumplings and the sweet, spicy curry. Maybe Joe could use it on his damn menu. Did they make Riesling in Napa? "I'll take it out." She grabbed the tray and headed into the dining room.

The woman at table seven was fiftyish, on the hefty side, with painted on eyebrows and dark lip liner. Her hair was medium length, mostly blond, and had the remnants of a spiral perm kinking out the ends. She totally had that on-the-ball, rabid reporter look in her eyes. There were two plates on the table, but no sign of a companion.

"With the compliments of the kitchen," Marlene said, placing the glasses on the table.

"Are you the chef?" the woman asked.

"I make the desserts. I'm Marlene Bennet." Surprise lit the reporter's eyes. "Are you enjoying your dumplings?"

"They're marvelous. New chef?" she asked.

"On the record?" Marlene gave her a conspiring smile.

"My secret is out, huh? I'm the new food critic for the *Norton Herald*. Somebody tipped my editor that Chameleon had taken a turn for the worse. I thought I should check it out." She slid her voice-activated tape recorder into her purse.

"In my opinion, the food has gotten a lot better lately," Marlene said.

"I'd have to agree. Please join me." The reporter indicated the empty chair. She looked apologetic. "My friend went to get something out of the car."

"Since we're off the record, I can tell you that the owner, Olivia Watson, fired her co-chef and husband and replaced him with an old culinary school friend." Marlene glanced up and saw Joe making a slow beeline for their table. "He's coming this way."

Joe's long legs carried him fluidly through the dining room. He was carrying two bowls of curry easily in one hand. He caught customers' eyes and smiled as he passed them, eliciting smiles in return. "Chef Joe Rafferty has cooked all over the country. I'll handle the kitchen while you two chat. When you're ready for dessert, just let me know. Joe, this is our new friend…"

"Margaret O'Leary from the *Norton Herald*." The reporter extended her hand. Joe placed the bowls on the table and took her hand with both of his. The reporter blushed.

"Always happy to have more Irish in the house. I bet they call you, Maggie, don't they?" Joe asked.

"Actually, no. But you can," she said.

Marlene grinned as she headed back for the kitchen. Mission accomplished. Margaret O'Leary wouldn't know what hit her. Before Joe was done with her, she'd think Chef Joe Rafferty was actually Emeril Lagasse, and that Eric, the slowpoke, was the finest waiter in Norton. She headed for the bakeshop, determined to join the cast and make Margaret O'Leary and her date believe that she, herself, was the reincarnation of Julia Child.

"Marly?" Olivia's voice broke the silence of the bakeshop, where Marlene was making a special dessert for table seven. "Do you know your dad's in the dining room?"

"Huh?" She felt another surge of adrenaline, this time not the good kind.

"He's at table seven laughing it up with some old blond," Olivia said, tucking her own blond hair behind her ears.

"The food critic?" Her goodwill toward the reporter sailed out the window.

"Food critic!" The panic on Olivia's face probably matched the horrified expression Marly knew she was wearing.

"Don't freak. We've got it covered. What are you doing here, anyway? I thought you were gone for the day." Olivia had shot out the back door to meet her lawyer as soon as Joe and Marlene had pulled into the parking lot this afternoon.

The stricken look on her friend's face made Marlene forget all about her father and the food critic. Olivia looked at the floor. "You're going to kill me."

"What did you do?" Marlene asked.

"Keith kept calling and calling, and since you and Joe were both gone, and I booked a late party, I let him come in to work last night."

"Oh God." Dread wrapped its fist around her heart.

"Yeah, tell me about it. He walked in the back door, took one look in the bar, and ran back out to his car. With the way he peeled out of here, you would have thought somebody was standing in the parking lot with a machine gun. You were right. It's just…I thought maybe if I gave him one more chance, it would all go back to being fine again."

"Oh, Olivia, it hasn't been fine for a long time. You know that. There isn't going to be a quick fix for

Chameleon. We're going to have to work really hard to get back up on our feet—"

"Keith took more money too."

"What? How? I thought the accounts were frozen?"

"Everything but the restaurant overdraft. He cashed a check this morning, and the bank covered it. That's why I ran out of here. I had to meet Sean at the bank before five. I'm tapped out. No credit. Can't even order from Sysco. I didn't want to tell you."

"How much did he take?"

"Ten grand."

Marlene gasped. Her heart began to race as her mind searched for a solution to this new problem.

"There's more." Olivia pulled a chair out of the office and sank down into it. "I got an offer for Chameleon."

"No fucking way." Marlene's rejection of the idea was unequivocal.

"It might be the best thing to do, Marlene. Just liquefy everything and start over. I don't know if I want to do this anymore. I'm not good at it. Sean is looking into the buyer, and I'm going to talk to my parents. I want to consider all my options."

"Options? You don't need options. You just need to get your shit together. You picked a bad husband, Olivia. Big deal. It's happened to a lot of other women too. It isn't the end of the world. It isn't the end of your life, or your career. It's just the end of your marriage. Life goes on." Marlene dropped to her knees and took her hands.

"You don't get it. I can't change gears this fast. I'm not like you. You barely flinched when the line went up in flames. You just cleaned up the mess and kept cooking. I should be able to do that—"

"Olivia, nobody said you have to be perfect."

"Perfect! Ha! I'd settle for adequate."

"You're way more than adequate. You're fabulous." She squeezed Olivia's cold hands. "There isn't anybody I'd rather stand next to on the line. We've had each other's backs for half our lives. You can't quit on me now."

They both jumped when the swinging door banged open, and Joe strode into the back room followed by a tall, gray-haired man wearing a tan linen suit. Marlene stood up and gritted her teeth, trapping a low hum of frustration in her throat. Olivia stood beside her.

Not now. Not this too.

"Marlene? You have a visitor. Actually, he's dining with Ms. O'Leary. I assume I don't have to introduce you," he joked as he stepped back. "Nice to meet you, Dale."

Her father nodded. "Nice to meet you too."

He held an unwieldy, paper wrapped package under one arm, and he offered Marlene a hug with the other arm. She scowled at Olivia over his shoulder, giving her a "we're not finished yet" glare. Olivia tugged Joe out of the room. She waited for them to clear the door before speaking.

"Hello, Dad. This is pretty far off your route."

"I'm taking some vacation time this month." Her father set the package on her table. "Callebaut. Bittersweet, your favorite, right?"

Marlene nodded grudgingly. "Business must be good if you can afford to bribe me with eleven pounds of Belgian chocolate."

"It's a late birthday present. Do you have a minute to talk?"

"Sure. I was just fixing you and your *date* dessert."

"Margaret felt horrible about not telling you I was here. She wasn't quite sure how to introduce herself."

"Honesty would have worked," she said.

He watched her add swirls of raspberry sauce to the plate. In each section of the long, divided platter, she had arranged a small portion of her three favorite menu items. She wasn't only doing it to impress the food critic now either. After all these years, the teenager inside of her still wanted Daddy's approval. It was hopeless. She should let Anthony plate their desserts and walk out the back door.

A week ago she might have done just that. To hell with the food critic. She didn't need to surround the berry shortcake with raspberry sauce and crème anglaise hearts or pipe quick chocolate fans to garnish the cheesecake. Her desserts could speak for themselves. This sampler usually sold for twenty bucks. However, her father and Margaret would enjoy it on the house tonight because Chameleon needed good press.

She had downplayed the challenges with Olivia, but they were understaffed and changing chefs could cause them huge problems. Customers would come to check out the food, and if it wasn't up to snuff, they'd write Chameleon off as a has-been. As long as Joe stuck around, they would be fine. When he left, though, all bets were off. Chameleon needed help.

Therefore, as much as she wanted to cut her father cold and walk out the door, she wouldn't. It wasn't just about her. It was about the restaurant, and Olivia, and even Joe too. She would do the right thing, even if it made her feel like screaming.

"Why are you here, Dad?" The word felt strange on her lips. Marlene always felt like the grown-up with both of her parents.

Her father shifted, glanced at her, and then glanced away, as if he'd already done something wrong. "I know you and I don't have a very close relationship."

It was true, but it made her angry to hear him say it. Her father's words put them on even footing, as if she were equally to blame for the awkwardness between them. Her father had deserted her. He'd had all of the power, and she'd had zero. To expect that dynamic to change because of the passage of time was unfair to say the least. Some wounds never healed. Marly felt like it was a major triumph just to be civil to the guy.

"You gave Mom custody. I haven't seen you more than twice a year for most of my life. It's hard to be buddies with a father who never calls, never writes, and never sends birthday presents on time. What do you expect from me?" She saw the door from the kitchen swing open and Joe saunter to the coffee station.

Get out! Get out! Get out of here! She didn't want Joe hearing any of this. She had a bad feeling her inner teenager might throw a tantrum, and she didn't want any adult witnesses.

"I guess I expected that one of these years your mother might step up and take some responsibility for what happened between us. That never really was her thing though," her father said.

"Don't even go there. Mom took care of me. You don't call that stepping up?"

"She did do that," he allowed. "But I think you're

old enough now to understand that your mother expects someone to take care of her. I loved her, but I couldn't do everything. She wasn't happy with me. I couldn't make her feel whole. She needed something more, something I couldn't give her."

"I can't imagine that you deserting us helped her out a whole lot."

"I gave up, Marlene. I'm sorry, but I gave up. I convinced myself that someone else could do a better job of making her happy. I thought it was the least I could do. When she wanted sole custody of you, I thought that might help. I know it's too late. I know that trying to make your mother happy made me lose you too. I made a terrible mistake. I won't ask you to forgive me, but I'd like the opportunity to become a part of your life again. On whatever terms you'll have me." Her father paused. "I keep thinking this will be easier if I can just think of the right way to say it."

He took a deep breath.

Suddenly, Marlene knew what was coming. She held up her hand. Even with Joe listening on the other side of the waiter's station, it was impossible to ride herd on her inner teenager. "Why don't you just mail me an invitation to the wedding? I'm sure it will be lovely. I'll turn it down, send a nice gift, and we'll be done. End of story. Your little girl doesn't need you anymore; she doesn't need anyone. She's all grown-up now."

Her father crossed his arms. "I had a feeling you'd say that. I'd still like to get to know you better, be a part of your life again. I *am* getting married, Marlene. Margaret is an amazing woman, and she's helped me discover what's important in life. Like family. She's a widow, has four kids. We'd really like you to come to the wedding."

"Really? So you can show me what a family looks like? Forget it. I don't want to see you playing father. Go ahead, get on with your new life. You don't need me in it. You have my blessing. Just make sure Margaret gives Chameleon a good review."

Her father touched her arm. "Marlene, don't you ever wonder where you got your sweet tooth? I bet your mother still skips dessert, doesn't she?" he asked. "Do you know chocolate is my favorite food? I bet you're like me in other ways too. For example, I can tell you're stubborn." He smiled and Marlene saw her dimples on his face.

She looked at her father. His curly hair. His height, and, yes, the stubborn gold light in his warm brown eyes. It was all there. All of the things that made Marlene so different from her mother. "I have wondered," she said. "That's the thing, Dad. For fifteen years I've wondered about a lot of things. But you weren't there for me to ask, and Mom doesn't talk about you. And now...it's too late. What difference does it make?" The words were as kind as she could make them. She stepped away from him. "You should go."

Marlene heard the coffeepot touch down on the burner and saw the flash of Joe's white jacket through the baker's rack as he headed back to the line. Now she could tell her father what was really on her mind. "The only thing I haven't ever wondered about is why I've never wanted a long-term relationship. Why bother getting attached to a man? They all leave. I have you to thank for that little gem of knowledge—well, you and

Mom, I guess. She's getting married too. Number five, every marriage more miserable than the last. She just doesn't learn. I'm sure you guys both saved me a lot of heartbreak by setting such a good example. So, thanks for that, I guess, and really, good luck with your marriage. From what I've seen, you're going to need it."

"I'm sorry, Marlene. I hope you change your mind." He pulled a thick, square envelope out of his pocket and placed it in her hand. He turned to go.

Marlene's eyes followed him to the door, and she saw that Joe held it open for him.

"Damn it!" she whispered. She whirled back to her table and saw that the dessert was still sitting there too.

She grabbed it and marched over to Joe. "Buzz Eric. This is for table seven." She shoved the plate into Joe's hand. "Mind your own business, next time."

"I just wanted a cup of coffee," Joe said, handing the dessert plate off to a busboy and gesturing at Eric.

"Yeah, right." She glanced at his still full cup.

"Don't you think you were a little hard on him? I mean, give the guy a break, he's reaching out to you."

Fury made her teeth ache. "He doesn't deserve a break unless it's in one of his bones. And you are so not the guy to give me advice about my father. You won't even talk to yours."

"Bullshit. I drove sixteen hours to roast a pig for him."

"Yeah, but you didn't actually talk to him. You stormed in, showed off, made your big declaration, and then left him in the dust. Or the woods, as the case may be."

"He doesn't want to talk to me, Marlene."

"Sure he does. He's just terrified he'll say the wrong

thing, and he'll never see you again. You don't exactly cut Frank a lot of slack. Why is that, anyway?"

Joe's eyes were gray, his mouth a cold, uncompromising line. "None of your business."

Marlene burst out with a bitter laugh. "Touché."

She turned her back to Joe and began carefully wrapping the block of Belgian chocolate in plastic wrap to seal it against the odors of the kitchen. She needed something to do with her hands until she calmed down.

"So, you gonna go to the wedding or what?" he asked.

"Hell no."

"He seems like a decent guy. He might stick around for you now."

"Joe, you aren't listening to me," Marlene said with exaggerated patience. Inner teenager had reached her dizzy limit. "I don't want a guy to stick around. I have no use for men in a supporting role in my life. That's why I like you. You're entertaining. You can cook. You're a great lay. And, best of all, you're leaving. I'll have fond thoughts of you when you're gone. Feel free to look me up whenever you come to see Olivia. Or your father," she added nastily, because they both knew that Joe visiting Frank once he'd crossed the California line was a long shot. "I don't need a daddy in my life to make me feel complete. I don't need a boyfriend either. I've got all I need right here." She tapped her chest.

Joe set his untouched coffee down and covered her hand with his own. His fingers spread out over her exposed collarbone, then his hand moved to caress her throat. "Yeah, you've definitely got that self-sufficient thing down pat. I have to hand it to you, sugar, you've got the best bad girl act I've ever seen, bar none. You almost had me convinced. Marlene, the heart-breaker, the good-time girl. Not a care in the world." His voice was mocking. His hand on her neck was just on the safe side of threatening. Desire, unwilling, flared within her. "You even had me thinking that playing the field was more important than your job, sugar, but I've got your number now." She tried to jerk away from him, but he snaked an iron arm around her waist and trapped her to his chest.

He bent his head to whisper in her ear. "I can see that fourteen-year-old girl who just didn't get it. You had your own ideas of love, and your parents ripped them apart. You never put them back together again, did you? There wasn't anybody to show you how except your mother, and she failed you over and over again."

Joe's words were hypnotic, his hands gentle on her body, and she leaned against him, remembering the loss. It hadn't been so bad though. Olivia had always been there for her. And then Marlene had discovered boys. She didn't need love. Love didn't last. She just needed sex. Skin. Joe's body to make her forget. Desire pinged through her.

"You focused on Chameleon, even though it really belongs to Olivia." She froze as she processed Joe's change of subject. "Unfortunately, Olivia buys your bad-girl act, hook, line, and sinker. She thinks you can't commit to a job any more than you can commit to a guy. She has no idea that you can run her restaurant, absolutely no clue that the best line cook in town, the hottest chef I've ever seen in action, is hiding in her very own bakeshop. It's one thing to avoid a relationship. Hell, I'm on board with that, sugar. The idea of falling in love scares the hell out of me. But look me in the eyes and tell me you don't want to run this kitchen."

Marlene couldn't speak, couldn't think, couldn't breathe.

"If you don't try, you don't fail, huh?" Joe dropped his arms and stepped away from her.

Fury rose above her sadness, above her pride. For a moment she considered smacking him upside the head with eleven pounds of highest quality extra-bittersweet.

But she didn't. The truth was enough to knock him out, and Marlene used it. "I can't believe I just heard those words from the man who never sticks to a job—or a woman, for that matter—long enough to see if it's a good fit," she said. "Don't talk to me about failure. Why do you move around so much, Joe? Still looking for a job big enough to impress Daddy? You think California is going to be the answer for you? You keep trying, chef. Just do me a couple favors, okay? Keep your amateur psychoanalysis to yourself, and stay the hell out of my head."

She put both hands on Joe's chest and gave him a shove into the prep table. "Why do you care, anyway? You're leaving. It's not your problem. In fact, why don't you get out of here right now? Go find yourself another piece of ass. I don't feel like company tonight."

Joe crossed his arms and leaned on the table. "Sounds like you did a little eavesdropping of your own, sugar."

"Not my fault. I had to pee." She shrugged. "No worries. A piece of ass was all I was looking for from you too." She met his hooded stare, knowing that she could bluff with the best of them.

"I don't think you're just a piece of ass, Marlene."

"Too bad. That's a perfect way to describe our relationship."

Joe put his hands on her body like they lived there. "Then why stop now? I'm free tonight."

"I'm done talking about this," Marlene said, ignoring his lips on the side of her neck, soft and cruel, his thigh between her own, his hand on the back of her head. He cupped her face in his palm and held her, one hard hand in her hair, the other gentle on her jaw. Her mouth fell open, and he brushed his thumb tenderly over her lower lip.

The breath rushed out of her lungs, and she shuddered. Her hands trembled on his chest, and the softest parts of her body melded to the hardest parts of his. She could feel him throb against her, smell the bleach on his jacket and the curry on his skin.

His eyes glittered, shadows gone, replaced by something darker, harder. He took a breath, and Marlene held hers. She tried to duck her head, afraid of what he was going to say, but his hand in her hair held her still.

"In another life, I could fall in love with you," he murmured against her lips.

Marlene's instant response was equal parts *Hallelujah* and *Oh, shit*. Her body responded instinctively, going nuclear, but her brain was detached from his intensity.

Talk is so cheap, she thought, then gave herself a sharp mental slap to remind herself it didn't matter. In another life, she could be in love with Joe too. If she were another person, with another job. Another family. But she wasn't. She was living this life, this story, and falling in love with Joe was so not going to happen.

Marlene broke their kiss. "You should go, Joe."

"I'm not like your dad, Marlene. You're going to have to point me at the door more than once to get me to go."

"Really? Well, I can wait a week."

Joe's gaze wavered, then he looked away.

"No? Less than that? Shocking. Get Olivia to finish service with you. I'm out of here."

Marlene twisted out of Joe's arms and turned to her prep table. She picked up the block of Belgian chocolate and lifted her father's gift high above her head. The chocolate hit the tile like a thunderbolt and broke into dozens of pieces within its protective plastic wrap. Breaking something could almost make her feel better, she decided. And she had an excellent idea of what would definitely do the trick.

She tossed the chocolate, now in small, usable pieces, up onto her prep table and swept past Joe. His blue eyes followed her as she headed for the back door.

She'd slam that too, just for good measure.

"Get a drink with me?" she asked Danny as she passed the hot window. She didn't look at Olivia.

"You bet. Am I done, here, boss?" Danny's eyes lit up.

"Yeah, you're done. Thanks for sticking around," Olivia said slowly.

"Sure thing," Danny said, untying his apron.

"Let's go, Danny boy," Marlene said, hoping her voice carried all the way back to the bakeshop.

It was time for the next guy. Or the last guy. Whatever worked.

Chapter 19

Joe left the bakeshop and walked up to the line to take his place beside Olivia at the grill. Good thing she had stepped in without being asked when she saw Marly hit the door. Somebody had to think about the food around here.

"What's going on with you and Marlene?" she asked.

Flip, flip, slide. They were ready to plate the first ticket.

"Well?" Olivia shot him a sideways glance as she fanned plates out on her cutting board.

"The usual. Why do you ask? Are you looking for a cheap thrill and some dirty details, or do you actually need an explanation?"

"I've seen your usual, and it doesn't involve spending the night, road trips, and mooning around like a lovesick schoolboy."

"I'm not mooning around," he said.

"How many times have you been back to that bakeshop since you started working here?"

"It's cooler back there." Joe's words were short and precise, a mirror of his movements as he arranged lamb chops and truffled mashed potatoes on the plate.

He tucked matchstick vegetables into the potatoes at three points around the plate, sauced with lamb demi-glace and stuck it under the heat lamp. "At least she doesn't give me any attitude." He tried to lighten the mood.

"You don't call that attitude?" The last three plates

were Olivia's, two easy paellas, and one complicated pasta dish involving white beans, prosciutto, and Herbes de Provence. Joe wiped the rims of her plates and slid them up into the window.

"Buzz Beth," he said to Anthony.

"If you hurt her—" Olivia crossed her arms.

"You'll what? Don't be a hypocrite, Olivia. You served her up to me on a silver platter. 'Help me, Joe. I need you, Joe. Run my restaurant, Joe. Take my best friend, Joe.'"

"I did not!"

"Uh-huh."

"Well, I didn't know she'd fall for you." Olivia checked the next ticket and lined four clean pans up on the burner. "If someone is going to break her heart, I don't want it to be you. I don't want to have to choose between you."

"I'm not going to break her heart."

"Joe, you're leaving next Sunday."

"I'm not gone yet."

"Keep it clean, cowboy. I'll pick up the pieces when you go, but for God's sake, don't make her any promises."

"I don't think you're giving Marlene enough credit."

"No? Well, I don't think you're thinking at all. Fire the salmon, hotshot. You're falling behind."

Joe looked over at Anthony. "Go get me some—"

"Got it, chef." Anthony shot down the hall to the walk-in.

Olivia frowned, looking at Joe from underneath lowered brows. "Since when is he your fetch boy?"

"I know how to get the most out of my staff." He met Olivia's glare head-on. "Olivia, I hate to say this because I don't have many friends, and you're more than a friend. You're like a sister to me. You made a good move getting rid of Keith, but you are screwing up big time now, kiddo. Pull your head out of the sand, girl! Look around. Your staff is crumbling, and if you don't get a move on, you're going to run out of options. Get some people in here. Do it fast. You gotta start working smart, not hard. You don't have the luxury of feeling sorry for yourself anymore."

"Doesn't matter. I'm out of options," Olivia said.

"What do you mean?"

She sighed. "Keith cashed a ten thousand-dollar check on the restaurant overdraft. We've got a hundred on the books Friday night, and the wedding on Saturday. None of the prep is done, and I can't even afford to buy potatoes. There's a buyer interested in Chameleon, and I'm considering the offer. Oh, and Marly just walked out the back door with Danny. So who knows when she'll be in to make the wedding cake. Not to mention the fact that Danny will probably call in sick again if Marlene really works him over. I'm totally screwed."

Joe ignored the anger that shot through him like a rocket at the thought of Marlene with Danny tonight. This was about Olivia. Joe would deal with Marlene later. While he and Olivia were on the subject of his leaving and Marlene, Joe had a few things to say. "See? That's just what I'm talking about. You don't give Marly enough credit, and I just don't get it. She works her ass off around here. She gets her job done in the bakeshop, she preps your station for service, she shops at the farmers market, she does everything you ask her to do—"

Olivia opened her mouth to speak, but he held up his hand. "And I don't want to hear that bullshit line you gave me when I got here, about how Marlene is irresponsible. I don't buy it. She gets the job done."

"Do you know how long I've been hearing that?" Olivia interrupted him. "My whole life. Marlene and I have been together our entire working lives. She's amazing, she really is. When Marlene cooks on the line, she's fast, clean, and her food is perfect every time. Her desserts are perfect too. Wait until you see her wedding cake—it will be flawless, I guarantee it. Everything is so easy for her. Cooking, baking. You're absolutely right. Marlene could run this restaurant. I went to culinary school, and this shit still isn't easy for me. Nothing is easy for me. But Marlene? She can do anything. I think if my parents could have given the restaurant to her, they would have."

"But they gave it to you," Joe stated.

"Yeah, they gave it to me. And I'm screwing it up. You said so yourself."

He took a minute to digest all of that. When he put his salmon into the window with her pastas, he said, "You done, yet?"

"Done with what?"

She checked the stove, the ovens, the tickets. "We're up on everything. Buzz Beth."

Joe held up his thumb and index finger and played the world's tiniest violin. "Done with your pity party."

Olivia glared at him. "Shut up, asshole."

"No way, we're just getting to the good stuff. This is really enlightening. I didn't know life was supposed to be easy. How could I have lived all these years and not realized life was supposed to be easy? I feel really stupid now."

"Shut up, Joe. I didn't say life was easy. I said it was easy for Marlene."

"Yeah, and since you're her best friend, you would know, but I think you might have missed a few things. If you think life's easy for Marlene, you haven't been paying attention, kiddo."

"What are you talking about?"

"You think it was easy for Marly when you went to culinary school and she didn't?"

Olivia flushed and dropped her eyes.

"How about when you brought Keith home? She tried to tell you he couldn't cook, didn't she? But you didn't want to hear it. And she had no place to go but the bakeshop." He saw her throat convulse, but he wasn't done with her yet. "I'm sure Marly took it real well when you finally got rid of Keith, and put me on the line. Easy street, huh?"

Olivia kept her eyes on the floor mat.

"I didn't think so. Yeah, it's going to be a real party for Marly when you put some rookie culinary jock on the line and ask her to train him."

Olivia shifted away from him and started slamming dirty pans into the window. "Well, then that just makes Marlene all the more wonderful, doesn't it? Truly, an amazing ability to overcome adversity. Give the girl a medal."

"You do that," he said with disgust.

"Joe, what do you want from me?" Olivia asked impatiently.

"Step up to the plate, kiddo. You need to put people where they belong around here, and get your own ass in gear."

Olivia gave Joe a level look out of green eyes that were suddenly rueful, instead of flat-out pissed off. She grimaced. "Marlene said the same thing about an hour ago."

"Go figure," he said.

Anthony came back to the line and surreptitiously started cleaning around them.

"Hey, Eric, lock the front door. We're done," Joe called to the waiter. He turned back to Olivia. "Order whatever you need for the weekend. I've got plenty of money, and I know where you live."

"Joe, we're talking about a grand just for the wedding. You don't have that kind of money."

He gave her a look. "You're doing it again."

"What?"

"Selling people short."

"You can't be serious."

"Are you going to start thinking life's easy for me too if I tell you that I am? I've got the money, Olivia. In fact, you can turn down that offer to buy Chameleon. If anyone is going to buy your damn restaurant, it's going to be me. I've banked some cash over the last few years. I can float you what you need until we find Keith."

Joe let that hang in the air for a minute before he shot Olivia a sideways glance. "You really think she's falling for me?"

"God, I hope not. Perish the thought. You're a total jerk."

"Nice. I have feelings, you know," he said.

"Stop, you're making me dizzy. Just warn me if you get serious about sticking around. I might have a heart attack."

"I'll keep you posted." He tugged on Olivia's braid. "Get busy, kiddo. Start moving people around."

Her eyes were uncertain. "Joe, I don't know what you mean by that. Move who? Where?"

Joe threw an arm around her. "Now you're selling yourself short, Olivia, but if you really can't figure it out, why don't you ask Marlene?"

"You just missed Marly." The bartender took no small delight in telling Joe as soon as he reached the bar.

He sat down anyway. Her car was still parked on the street. Even though Marlene had flown out the back door of Chameleon like a bat out of hell, Joe had been sure he'd find her here with her little boyfriend. His chat with Olivia must have delayed him longer than he thought.

"She and Danny just left," Johnny said.

"So why are you telling me?" He was getting accustomed to the flash of annoyance he felt every time the bartender opened his mouth.

"She likes you."

Joe raised an eyebrow. "That must be why she left with another guy."

The bartender laughed softly and polished a few glasses. "I've known Marly for a long time. Since grade school."

"You ever hook up with her?"

Johnny shrugged. "Of course." His eyes met Joe's squarely, as if he expected his honesty to quell any anger Joe might feel. It didn't. "I like head games. Marlene doesn't play them. Nice girl, though." Johnny's tone was dismissive, and this time, his cool indifference felt like an insult.

"Are you in love with her?" Joe asked.

"No."

"Then why are you so interested in my situation?"

"I told you. She likes you, and I've known her for a long time. I've seen her with a lot of guys. I don't know what you're doing to her, but keep doing it. Don't quit chasing her before she figures out if she wants to be caught."

Joe stared at Johnny in disbelief.

Again the shrug.

Johnny set a Guinness in front of Joe with a half-smile. "Sorry, I'm not usually so sentimental. I've got woman troubles of my own."

Joe couldn't believe his ears. The pierced, tattooed, tough-guy bartender was looking for sympathy? He drank his beer and watched Johnny work the bar.

Guys generally ignored each other's sex appeal, but Joe was curious now. He glanced around the bar and watched the women flirt with Johnny while he mixed their drinks, saw the way they kept their bodies open to him, their backs straight, breasts high, even after they returned to their tables.

Johnny saw him watching. The bastard didn't miss much. It dawned on him that it wasn't indifference in Johnny's eyes. It was control. Palpable control, and the bar chicks were grooving on it.

Johnny was back in front of him again.

"Head games, huh?" Joe asked. "Like the kind involving leather? Whips, maybe? Collars?"

"I own a club downtown if you're interested."

"Not my thing."

The bartender nodded. The ring in his eyebrow flashed in the candlelight. "That's good. Marly doesn't like to be spanked."

"You're pissing me off."

Johnny nodded equably. "Just FYI. So, you gonna stick around?"

That was an interesting question. The job in California felt farther away by the minute. A week ago, it had seemed so simple, so necessary to move across the country and start a new life. Tonight, leaving Norton felt impossible. Joe set down his empty glass and faced the bartender. "I've got a job waiting in California." Joe said. "Sticking around isn't something I've ever done."

"I meant tonight," Johnny said, white teeth gleaming in the candlelight. "Are you heading out or can I get you another beer?"

The bartender had tricked him.

Nice.

"No, thanks. Do you know where they went?" he asked.

"Niagara Falls Casino. Big games up there. Be careful."

His heart sank. That toddler had talked her into going after Keith.

"Good luck," Johnny said, his calm, black eyes focused on a lean brunette with furious eyes coming through the door like the Furies were whipping her backside. She looked like the kind of girl who might enjoy that sort of thing, though.

"You too, buddy," he offered.

A faint smile ghosted across Johnny's lips. He passed the brunette as he walked to the door and caught a sharp whiff of patchouli. If anybody could rock that smug bartender off his high horse, that tough chick could. For a moment, Joe almost pitied him.

Almost.

Chapter 20

MARLY RESPONDED TO THE CARDS IN FRONT OF HER, THE events of the past week fueling her cold, calculating play. She usually won when she was angry, and tonight, her mood was positively lethal. She folded a barely decent hand and glanced from table to table. Danny had been dead set on finding Keith tonight, but Keith was nowhere to be found.

Most of the guys at the tables in the main poker room looked slick, sharp, and bored. They wore suits or dark collarless shirts and no smiles. The remaining men and women filling in each table also had a few things in common. They had drinks close to their elbows, and they seemed to be having the time of their lives.

A waitress offered her a free drink, and she surmised which group she was supposed to fit into. Marlene took it and smiled widely, making a show of how thrilled she was to get free alcohol. She looked down at her cards. Oh, crap, too late to fold.

She won the hand anyway.

Marlene turned her full attention to her new hand. It was soothing to concentrate on the cards while her thoughts swirled themselves into order in her mind. She waited to see which thought would emerge on top of the chaos.

Joe, naturally.

No huge surprise there. She hadn't managed to focus on anything else since he hit town.

Her eyes slid to Danny, playing a side game one table over. It was way past time to put her personal theory into practice, but Danny seemed like such a kid to her now. It was hard to imagine being naked with him after being with…Joe.

She folded a weak ace and checked out the rest of the men playing around the room. Not one single guy caused a spark of interest, not even the Italian stallion watching the play from the corner of the room.

Marlene gave Rocky a second look, just to be sure. The guy was big and dense. Two weeks ago, seducing him would have been a no-brainer for her. She would have taken him for a tumble just for the novelty of stripping a silk suit from a man instead of a pair of jeans or checked cotton chef pants.

Damn Joe for taking that away from her. Damn his wicked eyes and his hot, hard hands. Double damn his annoying observations. He was right. Why hadn't she tried harder to make Olivia understand she wanted to run the line?

She knew the operation inside and out, from the dish room to the front of the house and everything in between. She knew every menu item, every vendor and purveyor, every employee's family. She had created the dessert menu, tweaked half of the items on the regular menu, and even made suggestions on the martini list. A cold surge of fury made her clutch the pair of eights in her hand. Snowmen. She called. She didn't just want to run Chameleon. She deserved to run the restaurant.

She had done everything at Chameleon but hire staff and balance the books, and those were the two things that were killing them. She hadn't been blowing sunshine when she told Keith last week that she would be welcome in any kitchen in town. Not as a prep cook either. She could handle any station, in any kitchen. She could run the whole damn kitchen. If she were any other person, she would be running a kitchen. She'd be running Chameleon.

So the big question was, why wasn't she?

She didn't want to face the simplest answer. If Olivia thought Marlene had what it took to handle Chameleon, she would have offered her the job by now. The fact that she had not spoke for itself.

Marlene focused on the game again, afraid of the direction her thoughts were taking her. She caught an eight on the flop. She checked. It was time to slow it down and set a trap.

She was never going to be good enough to run the kitchen at Chameleon. After fifteen years, it was time to stop pretending it was going to happen. Olivia was her best friend, a far cry from a wicked stepsister, but she was feeling more like Cinderella every minute. Maybe she should thank Joe for bringing that to her attention. Maybe that made him her fairy fucking godmother.

She had put her sweat, her tears and, occasionally even her blood into making Chameleon a great restaurant. Chameleon was her home. She didn't want to leave it, but the next logical step for Olivia was to hire and train a new chef, a process that she would expect Marlene to facilitate. A couple of weeks ago, she wouldn't have given it a second thought. Now, she wasn't sure she could do it. She didn't want to stand by and let another chef take the reins of the kitchen while she hid in the bakeshop again.

That left her with a huge decision to make. Continue to do a job she was never going to get credit for doing or leave Chameleon and start over?

Marlene heard her opponent go all in, and she responded automatically, calling and showing her three eights. The other player threw away his pair of aces in disgust.

She looked at the huge pile of chips in front of her. *Quit while you're ahead*, she thought.

Marlene pushed her chair away from the table and gathered her chips. They had the wedding to get through. Then Joe was leaving. If she was actually going to do this, she'd have to give Olivia at least a month's notice. She owed her that much.

Marlene felt as if a big empty bubble surrounded her. Was this what it felt like to have room to spread her wings? She took a tentative step toward the cash cage and stumbled, nearly dropping her chips. Freedom might take some getting used to.

After she cashed in her chips, she walked over to Danny's table and put her hand on his shoulder. "Are you ready to get out of here?" she asked.

He folded without looking at his cards and pushed away from the table.

Chapter 21

JOE PULLED INTO THE NIAGARA FALLS CASINO PARKING lot and killed the engine. He didn't exactly have a plan at this moment, but he knew that he wasn't done with Marlene tonight.

A black Mercedes GLK pulled up next to him, stereo pounding hard enough that he felt the downbeat in his sternum. He glanced over as the door opened and the noise cut off. Mario from the dish room slid out of the SUV with his cell phone pressed to his ear. Through the open door, Joe saw Mikey, the new bartender, hop out of the other side. That was a pretty sweet ride for a couple of kitchen rats. How the hell could they have been talking on their cells with all that racket going on?

Joe watched the two men, ready to give them a smile and a wave of recognition, but they didn't look his way. Nice threads, he noticed, as they hurried away from the truck. Another door slammed.

A familiar figure skulked away from the back of the SUV. The boy kept his head down as he headed for the casino, but Joe had seen him in just that posture every-day for a week now. It was easy to identify Anthony from the back of his head and the suspicious hunch of his slight shoulders, even though he had changed out of his work clothes too.

The door to the casino opened wide, and Anthony ducked into the bushes at the side of the building.

Marlene came out of the front door, laughing and smiling at Danny. Well, wasn't that cozy? Joe gritted his
teeth as Danny wrapped his arm around her waist and
kissed her on the cheek. He gripped the steering wheel,
Anthony forgotten, as he watched the pair cross the
parking lot. Danny held the door for Marlene, and she
slid right into his car.

Joe started his truck.

He kept a careful distance behind them in the casino
parking lot and a few cars between them on the highway during the twenty-minute drive back to Norton. He
wasn't worried about losing them. He knew where they
were going.

His brain slipped out of neutral when they passed
Chameleon where Marlene's car sat on the street. Why
was he following her? She was moving on. He should
stop, turn around, and go back to Olivia's. Marlene was
never going to want to settle down with him. It was time
to go.

Joe watched Danny's car pull into Marlene's driveway. He coasted to the curb one house down the street,
proving that knowing and doing are two different things.
So this was what it felt like to be a total loser. His idea
of heaven had become a sixteen-hour day, six-day work-
week with a woman who was hell-bent on leaving him
in the dust.

Do not turn off the car, Joe told himself.

He twisted the key. The doors automatically unlocked, and he put his hand on the door handle.

Do not get out of the car.

He pulled the latch.

The sound of an engine broke the silence. Instinctively,

he slid down in his seat until his head was below the level of the window, glad as hell that he hadn't actually opened the door. Danny's car shot past his Jeep, the engine loud in the quiet night.

He stayed down for a minute. Shame and an unfamiliar feeling choked his throat. He had read Olivia the riot act about selling people short, but he was doing the same thing to Marlene by assuming she would let Danny stay the night.

He straightened up in his seat. That fear of failure thing worked both ways. He could pretend his sole reason for leaving was that he didn't want to hurt Marlene, but it wasn't the whole truth. If he never told her he loved her, then she couldn't tell him to go to hell again. He couldn't fail. He couldn't get hurt.

He had built a career out of one-night stands with restaurants and women, mastering the art of the great beginning but never having the courage to bother with the middle or the ending. He had started over with every town, every weekend, every woman. Starting fresh meant no one had time to build up expectations. No one made any promises. No one got hurt or disappointed.

But it also meant no one cared.

He chuckled quietly, shaking his head. Too late for that. He definitely cared about Marlene. Hell, he was in love with her. The last thing he wanted to do was throw all his stuff in the Jeep and drive across the country. More than anything, he wanted to knock on her kitchen door right now and tell her he wanted to stay, but he knew she wasn't ready to hear it. *In another world, I could fall in love with you*. He now knew he'd been feeling her out, trying to judge what her response would be to the idea of a longer relationship. Abject horror. Fear. There had been nothing but rejection in her eyes. He stayed in the truck.

She wasn't ready to hear it, wasn't ready to admit it, but he'd lay money on the fact that she cared about him too. She had gone out with Danny tonight to make him jealous, but she hadn't sealed the deal, had she? It didn't mean she loved him, but it was something. It gave him somewhere to start. Convincing her wasn't going to be easy, but didn't he love a challenge?

He and Marly were a lot alike, at least on the surface. What had caused a change in him? His mom, initially. Without her interference, he would still be up North skipping from woman to woman like a rock across a river. The promises he had made to his mother hadn't stopped his trajectory entirely, though. She had introduced him to the idea of settling down, but Marlene had changed the direction of his life. Her hot curves had initially attracted him, but he had fallen in love with her mad, fast kitchen skills and her ability to get the job done under any circumstances. He loved her quick sense of humor and her intelligence; he admired her loyalty to Olivia. Hell, there wasn't anything he didn't love about her, including her stubbornness. What would it take to convince her to let him stick around?

Sex? Not a bad idea. He could touch her until she couldn't bear to think about what it would feel like when his hands weren't on her skin, his breath on her lips, his body inside her walls. Sex was something they both understood, and it might soften her up a little.

He'd use food too. The way to a chef's heart was through her stomach, and the busy weekend ahead of them guaranteed they would be spending a lot of time in the kitchen. He would cook for her, work with her, show her just how good they could be together.

Above all, he would not disappoint her. Her conversation with her father had been enlightening. As that thought hit home, a chunk of his grief disintegrated. Hope—tenuous, trembling, and new—took its place. He started the Jeep and pulled out into the street. *Oh, Mom,* he thought, *I hope you knew what you were talking about.*

Chapter 22

MARLENE HAD GIVEN UP ON SLEEP AROUND DAWN AND was elbow deep in chocolate buttercream by the time Olivia walked into the bakeshop Thursday morning.

"Hey," Olivia said, breaking the early morning silence.

"Hey yourself." She finished scraping the bowl and wiped her hands on her side towel while Olivia stood at the office door watching her. Sadness welled up in her center.

Olivia spoke first. "I'm not going to sell Chameleon."

"I know." Marlene held Olivia's eyes.

Olivia's lips twitched. Looking into her friend's face, Marlene wondered how to tell her that she was going to quit. "I'm sorry I ditched you last night," she began.

"I know," Olivia echoed.

Marlene grinned and threw her chocolate-covered side towel at her friend's head. When Olivia ducked, the towel hit the wall next to her and left a greasy mark on the white tile. They both cracked up. It was easy for Marly to pretend for a little while longer that nothing had changed. "So what's the plan? You need some grocery money or what?" she asked.

"No, that's covered."

"It is? How? I thought you said you were tapped out."

"Joe didn't tell you?"

"I haven't seen him." Marlene scrubbed the mark off the wall with a clean corner of the towel and tossed it in the bin.

"Of course you haven't. You left with Danny last night. So does your theory work? All memories of the last guy erased?" Olivia sounded genuinely curious.

"No."

"Want to talk about it?"

"No," Marlene said curtly.

"Will you at least tell me if I can expect Danny to show up for work? He tends to call in sick every time you break his heart."

Marlene sighed. "Danny will be here. Nothing happened. He dropped me off at my door."

"What about Joe?"

"I have no idea."

"Fair enough. Can you make a list of everything we need for the wedding and call around for prices? I'm hoping we can cut some corners."

Marlene reached into her back pocket and pulled out a wad of cash.

"What's that?"

"We went to the casino last night. Lady Luck loves a pissed off woman."

"Keep it."

"No way. That's your money. I just liberated it from the casino. We'll get the rest when we catch up with dickhead."

Olivia sighed. "At the moment, I've got bigger fish to fry with zero credit."

"Shit. I forgot about that. I'll call Jake at Pymco. He'll give us whatever we need, with or without a credit rating. They love us over there, and Jake owes me a favor."

"I thought Keith handled that account."

Marly snorted. "Yeah, like I'd let Keith order anything expensive. Get real."

"All right, that covers meat. What about produce?" Olivia asked.

"I got a ton of stuff at the farmer's market last week, and if we need anything else, all my favorite vendors are programmed into my cell phone. I can get anything we need. I bet a couple of the guys will even deliver."

"Guys?"

"Most of them." Marlene shrugged. "Interested?"

"No. Are you?"

Marlene shook her head. Olivia's small smile got under her skin.

"Good." Olivia said, moving on. "Now we just have to get the work done. Got any bright ideas about how we can do that?"

Marlene cocked her head to the side. That was an odd question. Start cooking, how else?

Olivia turned her back and unlocked the office door. "I, uh, kind of dropped the ball last week. I'm just— never mind, I'll figure it out." Marlene leaned past her to toss the cash onto the desk.

"Thanks," Olivia said. Her voice sounded thick. She kept her back to Marlene as she shut the door.

Marlene pulled the twenty-quart bowl of chocolate buttercream off the big mixer and set it on the prep table. Guilt made her stomach drop to her toes.

Some friend she was.

Olivia's world had fallen apart and since then, Marlene had come in hungover, sabotaged lunch, gone on a road trip, thrown a temper tantrum, and walked out in the middle of service. The self-righteous indignation that had fueled her fury through her sleepless night abruptly burned itself out. Quit? Ha! She was damn lucky Olivia hadn't fired her.

Marlene set the buttercream on her worktable and crossed to the office. She gave the door two sharp raps and opened it.

Olivia's hair was falling into her eyes, as usual. Her shoulders were slumped as she sat at the desk. Not usual. Marlene wondered when the lines between Olivia's brows had appeared, and whether she'd had anything to do with putting them there. Olivia bit her lip as she stared blankly at the computer screen.

"I abandoned you, didn't I?" Marlene asked in a quiet voice.

Olivia turned from the screen, but she didn't say anything. Her green eyes were watchful.

"Is that what you think?" Olivia said.

Marlene nodded, becoming more sure of her guilt by the minute. "Joe came into town, and I forgot everything important, like you and my job. You wouldn't have even been thinking about selling Chameleon if I hadn't been so utterly selfish, so completely taken over by hormones. God, I've been acting like a stupid teenager."

"Joe has that effect on women."

"Well, not anymore. I'm immune now." Olivia snorted. "No, really, I'm back," she insisted. "I'm going to get the wedding cake filled and iced today, so I can help you get everything else done tomorrow. There's room on the rack for the cake, right?"

"Plenty of room until we manage to get some deliveries," Olivia said.

"Don't give it another thought. I've got that covered."

"You do, huh? Because I feel the walls closing in.

We've got so much to get done, and I don't know what
to do first. My wheels are spinning. I feel trapped. Just
out of curiosity, what would you do if you were me?"

Marlene made a few mental calculations. They had
lunch, dinner, the wedding, and then Sunday brunch to
get through. Overtime? Unavoidable. After the wedding,
there was next week without Joe, which would bring
other challenges, but she wasn't going to worry about
that today.

"We can do this if we start hauling butt right now,"
Marlene said. "I'll divide up the prep list while you get
ready for service. Send Danny to me when he gets in.
He needs to learn the night grill menu. You're going to
promote him. We'll need someone with experience on
the line after—uh, you find a new chef. Joe's on wedding prep. We'll hit up the waitstaff for some prep hours
too. Okay?"

"Sounds great," Olivia's voice held relief and something else. Her tears had disappeared, along with the
lines between her eyes, and she seemed pleased with
herself—odd considering she'd choked on the game
plan. "Who's going to give Joe his prep list?" she asked.
Her small smile was getting bigger by the minute.

"You are."

"Hell no," Olivia said, still sporting her Cheshire
cat grin.

"I'm not speaking to him," Marlene said.

"Get over yourself, Marlene. Be a big girl. Didn't you
just say you were immune now?"

"Right." She gritted her teeth. "I was just hoping
you could run interference for me. Does he know I left
with Danny?"

Olivia nodded.

"Good. That will make it easier." Marlene cleared her suddenly tight throat. "Don't look at me like that. I've got to get out of this somehow."

"Why?"

"What do you mean, why? You're in the middle of a divorce, and you want to know why I don't want to get involved?"

"Joe isn't Keith."

"Joe's leaving, Olivia."

"Is that the only reason you're trying to avoid getting attached? Because I think it's too late. You've already accomplished the impossible, smart ass. Big, bad Joe Rafferty ain't going anywhere anytime soon, so far as I can tell. I think he's in love with you."

"Tell me you're kidding."

"Nope."

"Then I'm definitely not talking to him," Marlene said.

"You have to." Satisfaction made Olivia's green eyes gleam. "I'll be busy cooking lunch, right? Isn't that my assignment?"

"Bitch."

Olivia giggled.

Well, two could play that game.

What she had to say was going to wipe that smirk right off Olivia's face. Marlene flashed her own kitty cat grin. "Laugh it up while you have the chance, Olivia. I called your grandmother last week. She's on her way to Norton at this very moment."

"What?" Olivia's giggle choked off in a gasp.

"Sorry," Marlene said, not sorry at all. "You scared the crap out of me when you started talking about putting

Keith back on the line. And all that shit about selling Chameleon? It just can't happen, Olivia. We've worked too hard. Your parents would hit the roof."

"You called my Nonna Lucia? She's going to kill me!"

"She might if you don't get your act together. She's worried about you. I was angry when I called her, but really, I just want to help you, Olivia. You can't do this alone. Will you let us help you?"

Olivia ignored the question. She leaned back in the chair and sighed. Her voice, when she spoke, was faint and small. "Did I ever tell you my father had a fit when I told him you were working in the bakeshop?"

"No."

"Yeah, I don't think they really liked Keith. I never told them anything about what was going on around here. Did you?"

"I might have filled your grandma in the other night."

"Oh God. I'm so dead."

"Nah, you're safe for a while. Your parents are on a cruise, and I don't think murder is Nonna Lucia's style. She's gonna yell though. I'll hold your hand, just like old times."

"What exactly did you tell her?" Olivia asked.

"The truth. That you kicked Keith out for screwing other women and you were having a meltdown. That was enough to get her to buy a ticket."

"You told her about Keith?" Olivia looked horrified.

"You think Nonna doesn't know about sex?" Marlene raised her eyebrows. "She may be a widow, but her memory is just fine. Um, I may also have mentioned that you have your head up your ass. Sorry about that."

"I'm going to throw up."

"No, you're not. We've got too much to do."

Olivia turned her eyes from the ceiling. "Hey, call me when you trim the wedding cake layers? I could use some chocolate therapy."

"Sure thing," Marlene said.

———

Marlene sawed the domed top off the six-inch layer of the chocolate wedding cake and thought about what it would be like if Joe stayed in Norton.

She didn't do boyfriends. *Even with Joe?* her inner traitor needled. Nope. The sooner he left, the better.

Just because she didn't want to hook up with Danny didn't mean she'd never want any other man again. Okay, so what if there hadn't been a single man in the poker room last night that had struck her fancy? She'd go to Johnny's bar tonight. She would find someone.

What if the next guy doesn't work either?

Marlene grabbed a cake scrap and slapped chocolate buttercream onto it. She folded it in half and crammed her mouth full of cold cake until she could hardly breathe. As the flavors warmed up in her mouth, immediate, dark-chocolate comfort set in. Olivia could have the next cake sandwich. She needed chocolate therapy now.

Panic bloomed, and she took another bite of cake. It didn't have to mean anything. Olivia was wrong. Joe was leaving, she told herself. Olivia had just been torturing her. Joe had a job in California. He was planning his menu. She was fine.

Marlene shoved the last bite of the cake scrap into her mouth and chewed. She had to pull it together. There

was no way she could work like this. She re-wrapped
the wedding cake layers and stuck them in the freezer.
Change of plans. Cake next; list first. She grabbed a
legal pad and got busy.

Twenty minutes later, she picked up the phone and
called Pymco. Jake offered to deliver everything himself
that afternoon if Marlene would make his daughter's
birthday cake next week.

Danny and Anthony would have to work doubles if
they were willing. She made a note on another list. They
needed another garde-manger cook. She'd mention that
fact to Olivia if they survived the weekend.

After she got the cake set up and the bakeshop in
good shape for the weekend, Marlene would take over
on the line so Olivia could start handling wedding details. Thank God she had prepped her desserts so far
ahead earlier in the week.

She bit her lip. Unfortunately, the only place for Joe
to knock out the wedding prep was in the back room
with her. Maybe he and Olivia could switch tasks. She
rejected the idea. Olivia could cook lunch blindfolded,
but she probably wasn't up to knocking out a week's
worth of work in eight hours. It had to be Joe. She could
just ignore him, right?

Marlene pulled the wedding cake layers out of the
freezer again. She gathered cardboard rounds, filled a
large piping bag with chocolate buttercream, got her
dowels and clippers ready, and cranked the lid off the
European raspberry puree. Towel, serrated knife, offset
palette, bench scraper, what else?

Marlene began to cut the layers, engrossed in the
process of building the wedding cake. Saw the layer,

turn, saw, turn. Lift and separate. Measure each stacked tier of cake to make sure they were all the same height.

Now fill them. Make a buttercream dam and spread the filling evenly within the ring of sweet, chocolate icing. First a thin layer of European raspberry puree. Not too thick; a little went a long way with the good stuff. Then scoop and spread a thicker layer of chocolate buttercream. Another layer of cake. Do it again. Keep it even. Keep it neat. Crumb coat. Chill. Do the next tier.

Before she knew it, it was past noon. She looked at her watch. She had heard Joe's voice on the line an hour ago. Even though she had been immersed in building the wedding cake, she had been peripherally aware of him at every minute. Her ears were attuned to the timbre of his voice, and her eyes sought him out every time she saw the flash of a white jacket going into the walk-in.

By the time one o'clock rolled around, Marlene was starving and strung out from hyper-awareness. Before the whole Joe thing, she would have gone up to the line to make herself something to eat before the lunch rush, but it was too late. She'd just be in the way. On the other hand, if she kept sucking down cake scraps, she'd never make it through service tonight without crashing, hard. Marlene's stomach growled, and she rubbed it.

She jumped at a sound behind her.

"Hungry?" Joe asked.

She snatched her hand away from her belly.

"Don't glare at me, sugar. I'm not the one starving you out of spite." He handed her a plate. "Here, I made you a sandwich."

"What is it?" she asked reluctantly. Just the sight of

the bread made her mouth water. She peeked under the grilled baguette. Salmon. Mmmmm.

"Eat it."

She took a firm grip of the baguette and raised it to her mouth. The filling threatened to slide out of the bread. Marlene squeezed tighter and sank her teeth into the crusty bread.

The flavors exploded in her mouth—buttery bread with plenty of lemon basil aioli, acidic tomatoes, smoky bacon, and grilled salmon. It was a salmon BLT. Genius.

Not that she'd tell him. An eavesdropping smarty-pants with too many opinions wasn't getting back in her good graces that easily.

"Well?"

"It's all right." Marlene wanted Joe to leave so she could enjoy the sandwich properly. Something this good deserved her full attention. She didn't want him to watch her licking her fingers and wriggling with delight. He didn't deserve it.

"Go away. I'm busy." She sat down on her stool and inched the plate closer. Mmmm, pasta salad and a pickle too.

Forget it, she was going to start eating.

Marlene wrapped her hands around the sandwich, cradling it to keep the filling from dropping out of the sides. She took an enormous bite. Joe couldn't possibly expect her to talk with her mouth full.

Oh, heaven. Everything is better with bacon.

"That's a girl." Joe leaned against her counter and crossed his arms. His crotch was on level with her head, and Marlene glanced pointedly at the bulge in his checks. She looked up at his face.

He was watching her eat, making no effort to hide his interest. His blue eyes were hot, and his cheekbones were slashed with red. An answering thrill shot through Marlene, starting in her middle and sending warmth through her belly and breasts. She put the sandwich down and, with an effort, swallowed.

Her appetite was gone.

Oh, that was so not fair.

Joe pulled her to her feet and leaned forward, giving her plenty of time to reject him. He licked a bit of aioli from the corner of her mouth. "Missed you last night." The heat in his eyes sparked memories of all kinds of things. "Where were you?" he asked.

"With Danny."

"Oh yeah?" He caressed his way up her arms and down her ribs, slipping his hands under the sides of her apron to thumb her hard nipples with a circular motion. His eyes never left hers. "How'd that go for you?"

"Great."

"Liar." He smiled into her eyes.

"How do you know?" she asked. She wasn't going to admit to anything. Marlene tried to channel inner teenager's defiance. Inner teenager refused to leave her room.

"Danny boy gets on my nerves. We had a talk."

Marlene blinked.

"Don't worry. It's all good. I won't be turning my back on him when he's got a knife in his hand, but I'd say we're cool. Did you have a good time at the casino, sugar?" Joe's hand slid over her breast, and his familiar touch sent heat all the way to her toes.

"Not really," she mumbled.

Joe pulled her into his hips, and she lost her train of thought. His semi had become a full on, raging erection, and God help her, she wanted him. "I'm still pissed at you," she said against his mouth.

"Uh-huh." Joe nibbled on her upper lip, gently flicking the sensitive inner membrane with the tip of his tongue. His slow kisses contradicted the urgency she could feel in his hard body.

"You should really mind your own business," she sighed.

"You're right." He leaned down to brush his lips against her ear. "I've got two pints of Godiva chocolate raspberry truffle ice cream and a beautiful apology just waiting for your invitation."

His whisper made her shiver. Was she really that easy?

His tongue slid into her ear and she shivered. "My place, after service," she said.

Joe gave her a gentle push down onto her stool and dropped a kiss on the nape of her neck before he headed back to the line. "Enjoy your lunch," he said.

"Go to hell," she called after him, but he was already swinging through the doors. She scooted on her stool, fruitlessly trying to ease the ache in her center. At least she had a consolation sandwich.

Shit.

Marlene shoved the sandwich across her table and jumped up to chase after Joe. She hadn't given him his prep list.

Chapter 23

JOE WHISTLED AS HE PREPPED THE TENDERLOINS FOR THE wedding. Marlene was on the other side of her baker's rack, pretending to ignore him. The look on her face when she had told him to meet her at her place? Priceless.

Good thing he was feeling so cheerful. She had given him a monster prep list. Nothing he couldn't knock out, but who the hell did she think he was? Gordon freaking Ramsay?

Something jogged loose in his brain when Beth walked in to grab a salad—the salt in the salad station. The boys at the casino, dressed to kill. Keith. The crème brûlée sabotage. Why hadn't he thought to ask this before?

"Hey, Beth, did anyone help you plate desserts last weekend?" he asked.

She thought for a moment. "Yeah, I was in the weeds and Anthony offered to give me a hand. Why do you ask?"

"Just curious. We're going to need some help burning the brûlées for the wedding Saturday night, and I wanted to know who to ask. Thanks, darlin'." The kid must have gotten inspired after service, because they hadn't had any complaints until the next night. He smiled at Beth.

She flipped her hair back and gave him a look he'd seen a thousand times. He looked down at the steaks so she wouldn't think he was hitting on her, and she headed for the dining room with her salads. He shook his head and grinned again, thinking that he had indeed changed if he had just avoided hitting on a cute server.

———

Marlene caught a drip of chocolate just before it hit the bedsheets. The tart, syrupy, raspberry ribbon was a lovely counterpoint to the rich, dark chocolate, and the chewy bits of truffle kept everything interesting. "You forgot the apology," she reminded him.

"That was the apology." Joe dipped his spoon into the half-empty pint.

"That little thing?" She waved her spoon at the sheet covering Joe's waist.

"Thanks, you flatter me." Joe's free hand stroked her breast.

"Mmm-hmmm. You know, the first time I had this ice cream, Olivia and I were shopping at the mall. I can't remember who dropped it, but we were carrying our spoons, rushing to a bench, then we were running after the ice cream as it rolled down the walkway, picking up speed. We were laughing so hard, we almost couldn't catch it."

"Your pillow talk is fascinating. Really," Joe deadpanned.

"I guess you had to be there," she said. "Fine, you pick a topic."

Joe pulled her into a headlock. "Let's talk about your father."

"Let's not," she said pleasantly, throwing a leg over him. She didn't want anything to ruin her sexed-up ice cream buzz.

"Maybe if we share a few secrets, we won't have to spend so much time eavesdropping on each other." His eyes flashed her a sideways challenge.

"You really want to do this?" she asked.

Joe nodded.

Marlene shrugged. "He walked when I was fourteen. Gave my mother custody and just left. He came back a few times, did the 'My how you've grown bit,' and left again. After him, my mother married three other guys, all assholes, and is currently considering bachelor number five. Her optimism is unparalleled. That's why I really don't feel like I have to be part of my father's pathetic, post-midlife attempt at relationship recovery. Satisfied?"

"Four more husbands, huh? Is bachelor number five the winner?"

"Probably not," Marlene said dourly.

She squirmed out of Joe's arms and climbed on top of him. "Your turn." She balanced the pint of ice cream on his broad chest. "What's your beef with Frank?"

She watched his eyes gray out and go still, but he held her gaze and didn't look away.

"He cheated on my mother. More than once, I think. It broke her heart. My mother used to cry and hug me all the time while he was gone. She'd tell me it was going to be all right. That he would always come back. Like I cared."

She leaned over to erase the shadows from Joe's eyes with her lips, her body, whatever it took, but he wasn't finished. "My father made a promise he couldn't keep, but it didn't matter. Mom took him back, and I never understood why. I've heard, 'You're just like your father,' so many times I've lost count, but it isn't true. I don't make promises I can't keep. I'd never tell a woman I was going to stay unless it was true. Marlene, there's something I need to—"

"Shhhhhh." She covered Joe's mouth with her own.

They really were perfect for each other, she thought. Pathetic, flawed, and perfect. She didn't want to settle down because her mother's marriages had proved beyond doubt that having a mate was not the key to happiness. Joe was afraid to break a promise, so he was never going to make one. Period. She couldn't quite wrap her head around why those realizations made her feel sad.

She rolled to the side, casually breaking their connection, taking the ice cream with her. "You make your mother sound like a doormat. Why did she put up with Frank? Don't you think that if it really bothered her, she would have left?"

"Mom said…it didn't matter. She loved him."

"Hmmm. Codependency is a bitch." She kept her voice light.

Joe made a grab for the ice cream, but Marlene held on to it. "I get the rest of the ice cream because you never said you were sorry."

"In that case—" He tossed her to the head of the bed and pressed her knees apart. Marlene ignored him and fished the last big chunk of truffle out of the pint.

Joe lifted his head. "What time do you have to be at work tomorrow?" he asked.

"Early. I still have to ganache the wedding cake. Did you get all the prep done?"

"Most of it. I had to finish service with you, remember?"

Olivia's lawyer had shown up and taken her out for a late dinner after the second turn. No matter what Olivia said, Sean was hot for her. She could tell. Marlene's next-guy theory might be tanking for her, but Olivia should batter up. Sean was a good man, a little straight, but perfect for Olivia.

"Right. I forgot about that. Busy day," she said.

"Even busier tomorrow."

"What do you mean?" she asked. "I thought you got everything done."

"Almost everything," Joe agreed. "But I think I know who's been sabotaging Chameleon, and it's time to lay a little trap."

Marlene shot up straight in the bed. "Tell me," she demanded.

"Not until I'm sure," he said, forcing her back underneath him and throwing the covers off the bed. Marlene resisted, but Joe gave her his wicked smile and she went boneless, breathless, and brainless at the same time.

"Just eat your ice cream, sugar. Tomorrow is another day." He laughed, obviously remembering, like she was, the last time he'd said that to her.

Marlene was torn. There were only a few bites of ice cream left, but curiosity won out over gluttony and her lust reflex, and she shifted to toss him off. Just then, his cold tongue slid against a particularly sensitive bit of flesh, and she froze, exquisitely.

She tapped him on the top of his head with her spoon. "Yes?"

She gave him a demure smile—at least as demure as she could manage while sprawled on her back with her legs over his shoulders—then spooned a big glob of ice cream into his mouth.

"You should see what I can do with ice cubes." Joe opened his mouth for the last bite and bent his head to his task.

Marly sighed and raised her hips. She hadn't thought about ice cubes since she was a horny teenager watching *9½ Weeks*. If this was Joe's form of apology, then he was going to be sorry for a long time, maybe all night. Maybe right up until he headed to California.

Eventually, she would force him to tell her who he thought was causing all the trouble at Chameleon. However, the restaurant was closed now, so she might as well let horny teenager out of her room for the rest of the night. She had some catching up to do.

Chapter 24

ON SATURDAY MORNING, MARLENE WATCHED JOE WIPE sweat from his forehead and replace his baseball cap. "Feeling in the weeds, cheffie boy?" she asked, giving him an encouraging swat on the ass.

"Never. I was just thinking you might need some help caramelizing the brûlées this afternoon."

Anthony looked up from the salad dressing he was making with the immersion blender. "I could help," he said tentatively.

"Sure, that would be great," she agreed.

"Did you set up the wedding cake yet?" Joe asked.

"What time is it?" Marlene glanced up at the clock. "Shit, no. The wedding party will be here in two hours, and I need to get the flowers on the cake. Have you got things under control in here?"

"Piece of cake," Joe said.

Marlene walked off the line and into the back room to pull the stacked wedding cake out of the walk-in. Friday had passed in a blur of wedding prep, line prep, lunch service, dinner service, and cleanup. Marlene would have thought that after all that work and a hot, shared shower, she and Joe would have both passed out in bed, comatose. Definitely not the case. When her alarm had gone off early this morning, Joe had pulled her back into bed again.

Her good karma had continued through the day. The

wedding cake was a freaking masterpiece of glossy dark chocolate fabulousness. The ganache gods were smiling today. Outright beaming, in fact.

"Hey, Shane, grab the doors," Marlene called as she came out of the bakeshop. She carefully maneuvered the heavy cake through the swinging doors and into the dining room to set it in the center of the skirted cake table, then returned to the walk-in for the roses and berries. Marlene paused to grab a pair of scissors from her station and roll the one hundred and thirty crème brûlées, lined up on a rolling rack like creamy little soldiers, into the cooler where the cake had been. Most of them were already brûléed. They'd have to finish the rest later.

She carried her tools into the dining room and went to work. Twenty minutes later, she gathered stems, leaves, and empty plastic pints of blackberries and raspberries from the table and chucked them into the bucket from the florist. She stepped back from the table.

With buttercream, no matter how seamlessly she iced the cake, no matter how many times she stroked the palette knife over the icing, she could still see air bubbles and lines. No avoiding it.

But ganache was the great equalizer. All it took was a nice base coat of buttercream and viola! A beautiful blanket of warm chocolate covered all imperfections. The wedding cake had been sublime before she added the flowers. Now that it was sporting a cascade of pink roses, blackberries and raspberries, it was sheer heaven. Marlene was overjoyed. The cake was simple, elegant, and absolutely what it was supposed to be. Her work was done.

Well, not quite. She still had to pinch hit in the kitchen, burn the brûlées, and then cut the cake. Oh, yeah—and box it. It was unfair that she should have to assemble it and then completely disassemble it a few hours later, but that was the beauty of weddings. She'd have to sneak a glass of champagne before the cake-cutting ceremony. Cutting the four-tier, messy, chocolate cake and packing it into little tiny white dream boxes might push her over the edge on four hours sleep.

Joe poked his head into the dining room.

"Martha Stewart, eat your heart out," he said.

"I had the same thought," she said with satisfaction.

"Gonna save me a piece of that for quality control?"

"I'll put yours in the freezer." Marlene slipped a tart raspberry into his mouth. Joe's even, white teeth gleamed.

"Everything good in the kitchen?" she asked.

"Hell no. Somebody jacked up the heat on my beef demi-glace. It's pretty toasty, right on the edge of burned. Taste it for me?"

"That's funny. Somebody cranked the deck ovens too. My brûlées almost roasted. I meant to yell at you guys to watch your damn shoulders when you walk by my ovens."

"That wasn't my shoulder, sugar."

She rolled her eyes.

"Our saboteur is not very original, but that will work to our advantage," Joe said.

"Are you finally going to clue me in, Chef Sherlock?"

"Nope. You just do your thing. I don't want you to give it away."

"My little poker demo at the cabin didn't convince you I can bluff? You're starting to annoy me."

"You'll live. Just in case our little devil has an original thought, do you have a dowel in that cake?"

"Duh."

Marlene had doweled the cake before she put it in the walk-in. She'd had to stand on a stool to hammer the stick through the layers of cardboard and cake to create the central support for her confection. Each tier had several wooden dowels for internal support, of course, but for real security, nothing could beat a long, sharp stick.

"Good," Joe said. "Keep an eye on it anyway."

"Sure thing, Sherlock. You want some chocolate for your sauce?" she asked.

"Chocolate isn't going to help my sauce, sugar. Now, if you're trying to cheer me up, you could bring me a piece of your chocolate cheesecake. That might help."

She led Joe back to the bakeshop. "Didn't they teach you anything in culinary school?" Marlene pierced the wrap on the Callebaut bittersweet that her father had brought her the other day. At least he was good for something.

"Here," she said, handing Joe a chunk of chocolate. "Change out your stockpot and stir that in. See if it gets rid of the bite."

Olivia paused on her way to the walk-in and noticed the chocolate in Joe's hand. "Burn your sauce, cowboy?" she asked.

"Does everyone know this trick but me?" Joe scowled as he left the bakeshop.

"Apparently," Olivia called after him. Joe flipped her the bird.

Marlene giggled. "Hey, how come you always call him cowboy?" she asked.

"You've watched him work sauté, right?" Olivia raised an eyebrow.

Marlene nodded.

"I've seen him run the board with ten tables fired and a pan on every burner. He's a sauté cowboy, all right, never loses a dish."

Marlene groaned. "God, that turns me on."

Olivia shook her head and tucked her bangs under her hat. "Admit it: you're a goner."

"Keep it up, Olivia. I'm sure I've got your parents' cell phone number around here somewhere."

"Don't you dare. Nonna Lucia is bad enough." Olivia bit her lip. She was going to wear a groove in that thing before her grandmother's plane landed tonight. "You really think we can pull this off?"

"We have to. But I want to know what Joe has going on. I'm not cooking in the dark anymore."

She'd been too busy prepping yesterday to force the truth out of him, but now that the cake was done and everything else was ready to roll, Marlene wanted answers. No more Chef Sherlock.

"Come on." She dragged Olivia toward the line.

Chapter 25

JOE CHECKED HIS PREP LIST FOR THE TWENTIETH TIME. The guests were due in fifteen minutes. Danny and Anthony were in the dining room arranging the poached pears, blue cheese, and spicy walnuts on top of the salads. The servers were out there too, pouring wine and water. The potatoes were popping along nicely in the convection oven, and the vegetables were ready to go in the steamer. The beef demi was as good as it was going to be, thanks to Marlene's chocolate. The only thing left to do was burn the brûlées. He was looking forward to that.

Hurry up and wait. That was banquets. He usually didn't have a problem with it, but the damn tenderloins were taking forever. He had even put them in a half hour early just to make sure they would get done in time, but at the rate they were cooking, the meat was going to take another hour and still be bloody. Joe didn't think this was a beef carpaccio crowd.

He got down on his hands and knees to check the pilot light under the oven door. Burning merrily. Then he killed the burners on top of the stove that were keeping his sauces and blanching water hot. He put one boot on top of the stove and levered himself up high enough to see behind the ovens.

Son of a bitch.

The plug was dangling dangerously close to a puddle of water behind the stove. No wonder his meat wasn't cooking. With fire on top of the stove, who the hell would think that the oven was unplugged? He hadn't even considered that the stove and the oven might have different plugs on this model. Now the kid got creative?

Joe considered his options. The stove was too heavy for him to pull out by himself. And he was too big to fit behind it.

He turned his head and found Marlene and Olivia at the entrance to the line. "Are you planning on serving yourself up for dinner?" Marlene asked.

"Plug's out." Joe jumped down and surveyed the kitchen, looking for something, anything, with a hook on the end.

Mop handle. Broom. Tongs?

Marlene clambered on top of the oven. "Here, give me that."

She pointed at a ladle.

"Get down from there! Are you an idiot? You're going to burn yourself."

"Shut up, cheffie boy. Give me the ladle. And hold on to my feet," she added.

Joe slapped the tool into her palm with just a little more force than necessary, not enough to overbalance her, just enough to let her know she was in trouble when she got off that oven. He wrapped his hands around her ankles and squeezed. She reached down. He held on tighter.

"Almost got it," she announced.

"And then what? I can't pick you up and dangle you down the back of the oven to plug that thing into the wall."

She held up the plug. "There's an extension cord in the office. We'll run it into the pantry for now. It won't be up to code, but it will get us by for tonight."

"Got it," Olivia said. She hurried back to the office.

When she returned, Joe ran the cord and cranked the ovens up to their maximum.

"Hope for the best," he said. Maybe if they poured the wine before they set the plates, no one would notice the meat bleeding all over the vegetables.

"We can always sauce over the top," Marlene suggested.

"Bite your tongue," he said.

"Quit it, you two," Olivia said, before Marly had a chance to ask Joe any questions. "It's show time."

Banquet plating is completely different from cooking food for a table of diners in a restaurant. Every single piece of equipment, every item of food, and every member of the staff had to be ready to go when the command was given. Usually there was a loss of quality somewhere in the process, whether in temperature, degree of doneness, or creativity of design, but not when he ran the show. It was all in the timing.

Of course, since he had inherited this menu from Keith, it wasn't much of a challenge. Standard tenderloin with roasted red bliss potatoes and baby vegetables. No one ever complained if the food was better than they expected, so Joe had taken the liberty of marinating the tenderloins in roasted garlic, olive oil, sun-dried tomatoes, and thyme. He was also doing the tenderloin roasted whole instead of grilling small fillets. When grilled steaks sat for any length of time, they looked like turds by the time they hit the plate. Always better to carve and plate.

Joe called the round up. When everyone was in place,

he glanced at Anthony, Mario, and Mikey. Standing
side by side, their family resemblance was striking,
almost comical.

The boys had the same dark hair, brushed straight
back from their foreheads and tucked under identical
blue Jets hats. They had the same nose and the same
wary tilt to their shoulders. The only difference among
them was in their eyes. Mario's eyes looked tough.
Mikey's were sly. Anthony's looked worried.

"Okay, this is what it's going to look like," Joe said,
making sure the boys were paying attention. "Marlene,
you sauce. Sauce goes down first, under the meat, it's
a perfect medium, I want them to see that. I'll carve.
Anthony, vegetables right here. Mario, potatoes. Here.
Danny, one scoop of horseradish tomatoes in the middle,
sprinkle thyme, and put it in the window. Every plate
just like that one."

Olivia stuck her head into the kitchen. "The bride's
in her chair. Hit it."

"All right, folks. Give me one hundred and twenty
plates, and make them fly."

<hr />

Joe heaved a sigh as the last plate left the kitchen.
Almost home. Anthony jumped as his cell phone buzzed
in his pocket.

"Get moving, Anthony, no time for chatting. You
and Marly have twenty minutes to burn the rest of the
brûlées. Grab a torch," Joe said.

They were cutting it tight. Marlene was already on
her way to the back. Anthony lagged behind her.

Mario's cell phone rang. He glanced at the display

and ducked toward the dish room. "I gotta go move my truck."

"It's in the lot?" Joe asked.

"Uh, yeah."

Joe shrugged. "Too late now—the guests are here. Why bother?"

A couple seconds later Joe heard another cell phone ring through the open service window of the bar. Joe rounded the line and looked into the bar. Mikey was gone. He turned around and walked through the dish room to peer through the screen door.

No Mario either.

An engine hummed to life in the parking lot. Joe opened the screen door and stuck his head into the parking lot. The black Mercedes GLK, lights off, eased toward the exit. There were two passengers. The truck paused at the street.

Joe whipped down the hall and through the swinging doors into the dining room. "Hey, Shane, where's Mikey?" Joe asked.

"He had to go move his truck," Shane replied.

"If you see Anthony come this way, grab him." Joe dove through the swinging doors.

Chapter 26

"AREN'T YOU GOING TO ANSWER THAT?" MARLENE ASKED.

Anthony's damn cell had been buzzing like crazy for five minutes.

"Uh, no." He reached into his pocket to silence the phone. She noticed he was carrying a plastic container in his other hand, the same one she had found in the pantry earlier that week. She stilled. "Whatcha got there, Anthony?"

"Sugar."

"You sure about that?" Marlene held her torch delicately. She wasn't actually pointing it at the kid. She'd never set him on fire, of course, no matter what he said or did.

Maybe.

Joe burst through the swinging doors and charged into the bakeshop. He stopped when he saw their tense tableau.

"Anthony brought his own sugar," Marlene informed him.

The garde-manger cook's eyes shot to the door, like he was looking for backup.

Joe blocked the door. "You looking for your relatives? Mario had to go move his truck. So did Mikey. For some reason, I don't think that means what I think it means. Care to shed some light?" he asked.

Marlene snatched the container of salt out of Anthony's hand.

"You're too late," Anthony said, shrinking away from her.

"For what?" she asked.

Anthony looked like he was going to burst into tears. "Big Daddy sent me in here when Nikki told him Keith owned a restaurant. Big Daddy's always wanted a restaurant."

"Big Daddy who?"

"Capozzi. My Grandpa. He runs the Niagara Falls Casino."

Marlene's heart plummeted. She'd always thought Big Daddy Capozzi was an urban legend, a clever way to scare off the card sharks. At the Niagara, they put the sharks at the table themselves.

"They don't let me work at the casino because I suck at poker. Mario says I wear my heart on my face." Looking at his sad puss, Marlene had to agree. "I didn't want to make trouble after I got to know you guys, but Big Daddy made me bring my cousin Mario with me. And then his brother Mikey came too. When Keith dissed Nikki, the boys stopped letting him win. Figured if he lost enough money, he'd do something stupid. Like empty out Olivia's bank account so then she'd have to sell."

Marlene had now heard Anthony's voice more now than she'd heard it the entire time he'd been working at Chameleon. He kept talking. "Keith must have done something bad 'cause he brought another ten Gs to the table. Olivia shouldn't have turned down Big Daddy's offer to buy the restaurant."

"That was him too?" Marlene asked.

Anthony nodded. "He thought if we kept causing

trouble, Olivia would finally give up, but it's too late now. Big Daddy don't want to wait. He's gonna sit down at Keith's table tonight. Keith's gonna lose everything he's got."

"He can't get any more money," Marlene said. "Olivia's tapped out."

Anthony shot her another miserable look. "Doesn't matter. Mikey and Mario took off because Big Daddy likes to have the muscle around when guys like Keith lose big. In case things get messy."

"Why didn't you go with them?" Joe asked.

Anthony gave Joe a duh look. "I'm not exactly muscle, ya know? And I couldn't leave you guys like that. We haven't plated dessert yet."

Anthony hung his head. The kid looked truly pathetic. Marlene felt sorry for him, but she was still going to kill him. "Did you turn my oven up?" she asked sharply.

"Not today." Anthony hung his head.

Marlene's eyes narrowed. "Joe's sauce?"

"That was Mario."

"What about the big oven?"

"Mikey."

"Don't play innocent," Joe threatened.

"I'm not. I put the grease in the stove and moved things around in the walk-in. I plugged the fryer back in after brunch last Sunday, but I haven't done anything bad all week."

"Anthony, you could have burned the place down!" Marlene said.

"I told you, that was before!" Anthony protested. "I don't want to make things hard for you guys anymore. You're nice to me."

"Anthony, did you put the salt on my crème brûlées?" Marlene asked dangerously.

"Yeah, but it's gone now, I swear." He pointed at the container on the counter. "That's sugar." He looked up from his Nikes. "I *am* sorry. I just didn't want to get in trouble. You don't mess with Big Daddy unless you have to."

"Oh, I'm gonna mess with him all right," Marlene vowed. "Big Daddy is definitely gonna get a piece of me tonight. How much is Keith in for?"

"About fifty. And he put the restaurant on the table." Anthony didn't look up from his shoes.

Joe blanched. "Jesus Christ."

"Where are they playing?" Marlene fired another question.

"In the pole room."

"Pole room? There's no pole room at the Niagara," Marlene said.

Now Anthony gave Marlene the duh look. "They don't usually let girls in unless they're, you know, working. Like, the poles?"

Joe chuckled.

Suddenly, Nikki's platform shoes made sense.

Marlene poured white granules into her palm and tasted them. They were sweet. She spoke slowly and clearly. "Anthony, after we burn all these brûlées, you are going to get me to that game. Light your torch. If I catch your fingers anywhere near salt, I will personally set your apron on fire, so help me God."

Anthony fired up the propane.

Joe took the torch out of her hand. "Tell Olivia to find the deed to the restaurant. We need to see the names on that paper. Then you two need to get out of here. I've got the brûlées."

"Joe, we just lost a dishwasher, a bartender, and a garde-manger cook." Anthony flinched. "There isn't enough of you to handle everything around here," she said.

"I've got it. Go talk to Olivia."

She went.

The dining room was swarmed with wedding guests, dancing, drinking, and laughing. Even the bride's mother was doing the chicken dance. Shane, Eric, Terry, and Beth swooped around the dining room, refilling wine glasses, fiddling while Rome burned.

Marlene found Olivia in the bar, slinging booze and cursing under her breath. If Marlene hadn't felt a little sick, she would have been impressed by Olivia's creativity.

"Olivia, where do you keep the deed to the restaurant? And is Keith's name on it?"

"Marlene, I'm a little busy here. If you want to play twenty questions, grab some glasses and start pouring. Where the hell is Mikey?"

Marlene took a deep breath and checked the bar printout. She pulled two beer glasses down and bent the tap over the first glass. "Yeah, about that—Mikey and Mario split. The deed, Olivia. Where is it?"

When Olivia looked up from the martini glasses on the bar in front of her, her green eyes were bleak. "Gone. It was in the safe."

Marlene's beer overflowed the glass. She set it down and picked up the next glass. "And Keith's name—is it on the deed?"

Olivia sighed. "Last year. He bugged me and bugged

me. I figured…well, it doesn't matter. What has he done now?"

Marlene checked to make sure she had Olivia's full attention. "I'm gonna give it to you fast and hard. Are you ready?"

At Olivia's nod, she said, "Your restaurant has been taken over by the mob."

Olivia's jaw dropped and a hysterical giggle flew out of her throat.

"Anthony, Mario, and Mikey are Big Daddy Capozzi's grandsons. Big Daddy runs the Niagara Falls Casino, and he's after Chameleon. Keith is gambling with the deed. Anthony is on our side now, and I'm gonna go get Keith. Joe will stay with you and Danny to cover the wedding. Any questions?"

Olivia's eyes glazed over, but she shook her head and started pouring again.

"We're gonna fix this," Marlene promised.

"I'm so screwed," Olivia said.

"No, you're not. I only lose on purpose, remember?" Olivia's smile was reminiscent of the worm at the bottom of a bottle of good tequila: pale, stiff, and dead.

Marlene turned away from the bar wishing she had half of the confidence she had displayed to Olivia. The sheer number of tasks that had to be accomplished in order to pull off the rest of the evening was staggering.

Marlene pulled Danny off the line. "Come on, you're on brûlées." Danny raised his eyebrows and followed her to the bakeshop. The thought of Danny finishing the rest of the brûlées with Joe made Marlene want to vomit, but there was no alternative. The look on Danny's face told her he didn't like it either. Too damn bad.

When they reached Joe, she said, "You need to call Jacques, find a bartender, burn the brûlées, and make sure Olivia doesn't cry in front of the bride." Damage control mode was her natural state lately.

"Right on," Joe said.

She pulled a flat of raspberries out of her reach-in and set it on the table. "Don't forget the garnish on my brûlées."

"Got it."

"You also need to cut the cake, and put it in the white boxes stacked up there." She pointed at the top of her reach-in. Well, that was one good thing. At least she wouldn't have to box the cake. "Use a hot, wet knife, and clean the blade every time."

Joe groaned.

Marlene fixed Anthony with a hard stare. "Where's the pole room?"

"You don't want me to come with you?" He looked relieved.

"I work better alone. Just give me good directions, kid."

He did. When Anthony stopped talking, Marlene nodded once and grabbed her purse from under her station. She didn't even make it to the door before Olivia barreled into the bakeshop, white faced. "Marlene, your cake is slipping!"

Marlene dropped her purse into a bus tub and took off into the dining room. She dodged wedding guests and wove around the dance floor toward the cake table. The cake was definitely a solid half inch off center and still sliding backward. Simply not possible. Where was the dowel? Because it sure as hell wasn't in the cake anymore.

Marlene pulled aside the table's skirting and found

her dowel on the floor under the table. She ducked to wipe the long, wooden stick on the inside of the table-cloth. Ever so casually, she hid the dowel behind the table as she nudged the roses on the top of the cake aside with one finger. She was going to have to move fast, really fast. She glanced left and right.

Marlene rose and struck. The sharp tip of the dowel hit cardboard, shifted, slid. Down through the next tier, and the next, she swiftly knitted the cake back together and then dropped her arms and smiled at no one in particular.

Had anyone seen her? She surveyed the guests. A figure caught her eye at the doors to the kitchen, but it was only Joe, his wicked grin almost made her forget to rearrange flowers and leaves until all evidence of the near catastrophe was gone.

"It's just perfect! Thank you!" the bride called as she whirled by the cake table.

"It is now," Marlene said under her breath as she headed back to the kitchen. A man with a pinched expression and tiny glasses caught her arm.

"I saw that," the health inspector said. She gaped in horror. "But I'm off duty." He smiled thinly. "Is Joe around?"

Marlene nodded, struck dumb by another near miss.

"Tell him I'll be in for brunch Sunday, would you?"

"Sure thing." Marlene finally found her voice. "On the house." She fled.

Joe met her on the other side of the door and handed Marlene her purse. "Nice work."

"Did you. I just saw—" She was babbling.

"Yeah, me too. Don't worry about it. Get moving,

sugar." Joe swatted her on the ass, urging her toward the back door.

This time Marlene got as far as the dish room before she slid to a stop. "Oh, crap! Nonna Lucia!"

"What time's her flight?" Joe called.

"Ten thirty-two. Trans-Air Continental."

His grin flashed again. "We'll pick up Grandma on the way to the casino. Don't worry about a thing. You handle the mobster, sugar. I've got the wedding under control."

Chapter 27

MARLENE STEPPED THROUGH THE FRONT DOOR OF THE Niagara Falls Casino and zipped into the nearest bathroom. She dropped her purse on the counter and dug through it for lipstick and a brush. Thankfully, she found both. She had also been lucky to find a pair of old high heels jammed beneath the spare tire in her trunk.

Her hair was in its usual loopy twist, and she pulled it down to her shoulders. She examined her reflection in the brutal fluorescent lighting. The recent highlights had mellowed, and her hair shone with bright colors. She used the brush to rat her hair, making it big, bigger, biggest.

She unzipped her thin hoodie and wrapped it around her waist. She also made sure her skin-tight tank top showed a couple inches of flesh below its hem. Then she tugged until the lacy top-edge of her black bra peeked above the neckline of her tank. With her red lipstick, she'd be all set.

Pole room, here I come, she thought.

Anthony had given her directions to the entrance the dancers and cocktail waitresses used, and Marlene hoped anyone she passed in the hallway would think she was arriving to work her shift. Lady luck still loved her because the back hall was empty, and when she slipped through the door marked Employees Only, the first thing she saw was a rack of black uniform aprons and side towels. She reached into the bin.

The door opened behind her and a blond walked in.

"You new?" she asked, grabbing an apron and wrapping it around her tiny waist.

"First night," Marlene replied, doing the same.

The blond smiled, showing white teeth that were just crooked enough to make Marlene forgive her for her natural blond highlights and perfect breasts. "I'm Daphne."

Like Marlene, Daphne was wearing a low-cut tank top and heels, but her long legs were bare beneath a short, black skirt. She looked at Marly's jeans.

"Big Daddy likes skin. You bring a skirt?"

Marlene shook her head.

"I think I've got one in my locker. Come on."

Daphne led her through the short hall into a dark dressing room. She flipped a switch and round stage lights lit the edges of a huge mirror. The counter in front of the long mirror was littered with makeup, hair products, and used tissues. It looked like beauty pageant hell. Daphne crossed to the wall of gym lockers and rummaged around until she came up with a small, shiny piece of black spandex. She tossed it to Marlene. "Try this."

Daphne was much shorter than she was, but Marlene said, "Thanks," and kicked off her heels. She shucked her jeans and pulled the skirt over her hips. The damn thing looked like a tube top wrapped around her butt. No more cheesecake. Ever. She was really going to kill Keith when she caught up with him now. Marlene stepped into her heels and tied the short apron around her waist. It helped. A little.

"You good to go?" Daphne asked. "You probably don't have a time card yet, but we'll write your hours down at the end of the night. Are you dancing or just cocktailing?"

"Cocktailing."

"I'll introduce you to the bartender, and you'll be all set. Easiest job you'll ever have. The booze is free, and all the tips are yours."

In short order, Marlene met the bartender, received an order pad and a tray, and found herself standing in the middle of a strip club with poker tables. Each private table had its own pole, rising above the dealer, who stood at one end. In the center of the room, there was an oval stage where several girls were dancing, some alone, some with each other. Catwalks extended into the playing area, to make sure that there was plenty to watch from every seat in the house. The music kept the girls on the beat and was just loud enough to be distracting. The room was dark, thank God. It was only well lit directly over the tables, and there were plenty of other waitresses working the room, making it easy for Marlene to blend into the crowd.

She spotted Keith sitting at a large table, right in front of the center stage. She drifted closer, winding her way between tables, trying not to make eye contact with any thirsty customers.

The nine other guys at Keith's table looked sharp and scary, but the burning in Marlene's stomach eased up considerably when she saw that Keith still had a good pile of chips in front of him. The deed to Chameleon flashed white in the center of the felt table, making her feel sick again.

Marlene spotted Mario, shoulder to shoulder with Rocky, the Italian stallion from Thursday night. Mario's eyes were locked on the play at Keith's table. She skirted the table and scanned the room for Mikey. She found him one table over from Keith, directly under a pole.

A rough hand brushed Marlene's leg. "Hey, I could use a vodka tonic."

From the look in the guy's bleary eyes and the pitiful number of chips left in front of him, the guy definitely could not, but she made a note on her order pad and shot an inquiring glance around the table. She wrote the rest of the table's orders down on her pad and carried them to the bar.

The bar system was simple, and she mastered it quickly. As she returned with the drinks, she noticed Keith was up a little, and that gave her the confidence to pause and examine the table.

Holy crap.

There was at least a hundred thousand dollars in the pot. That would mean the blinds were set at one hundred and two hundred dollars. What the hell was Keith doing? He had to know he was nowhere near the skill level required for that kind of play. She winced as he folded a hand with at least a dozen outs.

Marlene saw Mario shift in the shadows, so she turned her back and leaned down to give the table in front of her a good look down her tank top. She took their order and swung off to the bar again.

After she dropped off the drinks, she approached Keith's table from the other side and began to study the players. She kept her back to Mario as much as possible. Mikey, she wasn't worried about. He wasn't seeing anything but the girl on the pole. All of her.

For the next hour, her ability to multitask served her well. She simultaneously kept tabs on the cards the dealer was laying down on Keith's table and the cards of whichever player she was passing behind at the moment, if they happened to flash them. She also kept track of what everyone was drinking at the surrounding tables and ferried drinks and empty glasses back and forth from the bar.

Keith's chip pile was dwindling. He only had about ten grand left, and she knew it was now or never. She had learned as much about each of the other player's playing styles as she was going to be able to learn before Keith went bust. Her plan was simple to the point of being ridiculous, but it was all she had. It was time to make her move.

She dropped her tray at the bar.

Marlene stopped next to Keith. His eyes caught her short skirt and slid up to her boobs. He began to smile. When his eyes reached above her neck, however, his grin slid off his face like a fried egg out of a Teflon pan.

Marlene leaned down to whisper in his ear. "I had hoped to find you with a couple of broken bones. I'm disappointed."

"I was winning," Keith shot back. "I'm good at this. I'm up and down, but I go home with money every night." He glanced at his chips. "I don't know what happened. I'll get it back."

"You got set up, dumb ass," she said. "You don't belong in this kind of game. Not to mention the fact that you stole from your wife to get the money to play. What the hell are you doing with the deed to Chameleon?"

"I grabbed it the day I got my stuff out of the office." He flushed. "I was pissed that Olivia was kicking me out like the trash and replacing me with Rafferty. I wasn't planning to do anything with it."

"Then why did you put it on the table, Keith?

Chameleon is worth way more than fifty grand, even if you're only signing over your half."

"Shut up, Marlene. You don't know what's going on. I'm having a bad night, that's all. I'll get it back."

"Keith, you suck at poker. If you were winning before, then they were letting you win. I know they were letting you win. This isn't just a game anymore. You have to stop. Get up."

Marlene could feel Mario and his hunky henchman heading toward them. She glanced behind her. Mikey was on the move now too. An old man detached from the shadows and began to slowly make his way through the tables using a hand-carved cane.

Keith clutched his cards to his chest and looked up at Marlene. For once, she saw an emotion in Keith's eyes that didn't piss her off.

Fear.

"I can't stop," he whispered urgently. "Capozzi found out about the restaurant. He's coming after Olivia. He's got half his damn family working at Chameleon already. I saw them when I came in the other night. That's the only reason I took the money from the overdraft. But it wasn't enough. This game is my only chance to get it all back. I never meant for it to go this far. Olivia was a lousy wife, but she didn't deserve this."

Mario, Mikey, and Rocky boxed Marlene in against the table. They didn't say anything. They were waiting for the old man. Marlene felt a shiver go up her spine. She stiffened her shoulders and glared down at Keith. The double doors to the pole room swung open wide, drawing every eye in the room except hers. She didn't have to look up to know it was Joe. She could feel him.

Marlene kept her eyes on Keith. "What the hell do you mean Olivia was a lousy wife?"

"She works all the time. Olivia doesn't need a husband. She needs a business partner."

"That was supposed to be you, asshole."

Keith jumped to his feet, knocking his chair back, but Marlene didn't flinch. The Italians, however, took a step toward Keith, and her estimation of her enemies went up a bare notch.

Keith put his hands on his hips. "No, Marlene, that was supposed to be you. You and Olivia think you're so smart, but neither one of you ever figured that one out. Jesus, it's been driving me nuts for years. Her parents wanted you two to run the restaurant together, but Olivia brought me home and ruined everything. Believe me, if I'd known what I was getting into, I would have run like hell. Who can compete with you? Jesus, you could leave a guy some pride, you know?"

Joe and the old man reached the table at the same time, and the Italians parted ranks to make room for them.

Joe took Marlene's side. "Step back, Watson," he growled.

Keith grudgingly took one step back.

"Things are certainly getting exciting at this table," Big Daddy Capozzi said mildly. His low voice held an Italian accent and the wake of a thousand cigars. He kept his dark eyes on Marly and Joe. "Who have we got here? Where's Antonio?" His boys shrugged.

Marlene and Joe faced off with what was now a veritable army of Italian men. She saw Nikki at the edge of the crowd, making her way toward Keith.

"We're here for Chameleon," Joe said.

"Mr. Watson owes me a hundred thousand dollars," Big Daddy offered.

"I heard fifty," Joe countered.

"Interest." Big Daddy's slight shrug was eloquent. Take it or leave it.

Joe eyed the old man. Neither man wavered.

"Done," Joe finally agreed.

Marlene gasped.

"One condition." The old man held up a hand. "You keep Antonio. He's not happy here. Maybe you make him the next Giorgio Locatelli or Mario Batali. I could use a guy in TV." Big Daddy pointed at Keith. "We'll keep him. My granddaughter likes him." Another elegant shrug.

Joe nodded again. His eyes touched on Marlene before he turned to Keith. "That means you too, Watson, that's it. You're finished. Get it? Done playing poker. Done with Olivia. Done with the restaurant. It's mine now," Joe growled.

Panic shredded Marlene.

What was going on here? Who the hell did Joe think he was, swanning in here and going all man-to-man with Big Daddy Capozzi? She had come here to save the restaurant, and by God, she'd do it.

"No way!" She stepped in front of Keith and wheeled around to face Joe. "This isn't your problem, Joe. Chameleon is *my* life. I'll take the risks. You keep your money for California." She stepped in front of Keith's spot at the table and shifted her focus to the old man with the cane. "Bring it on, Big Daddy."

"Sorry, no chip transfers." The dealer was bald and meaty. He also spoke with the rich, Italian accent.

"You boys afraid of a little girl?" she drawled, look-ing around the table. The men shrugged. They didn't look afraid of anything. Particularly her.

Joe grabbed her arm. "I'm not leaving, Marlene. I don't want to go to California anymore," he said.

"Don't be ridiculous." Now Joe's misplaced hero-rescue complex was working overtime. She pulled her arm away from him, refusing to process the concept of Joe staying in Norton. "What about your dream job?"

"Dreams change. I like what I'm doing now."

"Having a couple bucks doesn't mean you can mus-cle in on my life," she told him. "We had a good time together, but I'm not looking for anything serious. If I gave you any other impression, I'm sorry."

"You think you can go back to all your boyfriends at the bar and be happy again?" Joe asked.

She scowled at him.

"They're not what you want anymore," Joe said. "I'm what you want. Go ahead and play poker, but it's not going to change anything."

"You've lost your mind," she said.

"Nope. I've found my heart. Don't send me away again, Marlene, and don't run away from me either. Try something new this time. Give me a reason to stay."

"No." Marlene took a deep breath. "I'm not doing this. I need to concentrate." She sat down at the table and threw a defiant look at anyone who might dare comment with so much as a dark, tilted eyebrow. "Go away, Joe."

"Do we still have a deal?" Big Daddy asked Joe.

She felt Joe's eyes on her. "No," he said. "Sorry, but I guess I'm out."

She felt him walk away from the table. Marlene

disguised her anguish with her poker face, but not quite fast enough.

"You want us to go get him for you?" Big Daddy's smile was sly, but his eyes were kind as he moved toward Marlene.

"No. Thank you," she added.

The man to her right scrambled to his feet and Big Daddy sat down carefully, heavily. He propped his cane on the edge of the table. "I watched you work my room, little girl." Big Daddy settled his back into his chair and gave the dealer the signal to continue play. His dark eyes gleamed. "Now, let's see how you play my game. Bring it on indeed," he said, with a rough chuckle.

Chapter 28

JOE RETREATED TO THE BAR.

Marlene's eyes had held nothing but rejection. Again. He had gone all in too soon, with the wrong hand, and she had knocked him out of the game. He had hoped that working together all week might make him feel as necessary to Marlene as she felt to him, that his talk of falling in love and making promises might inspire her to give it a shot, that his skill with food would persuade her. Not the case. She liked the sex, but this love thing was something he had been working on all by himself.

He hadn't planned to offer Big Daddy the money, but it had seemed like such a simple solution. Joe wanted to work at Chameleon. He wanted to stay in Norton and build a life with Marlene. Sucked for him that she just wanted her old life back. She had made it abundantly clear that she didn't want to start a new one with him.

Joe knocked back a shot of tequila and grieved the loss of what had been so briefly within his grasp. It hurt, he wasn't surprised to notice. Not the tequila—that was good. The rejection. The rejection hurt. Goddamn, he had really wanted that new life.

Parts of him were waking up, after what felt like having been asleep forever. He jerked his head at the bartender to order another shot and settled back against the bar to let it all wash over him. He had a good view of

Marlene's table, and, for the next two and a half hours, he watched her play, stock-still and staring, oblivious to the buck-naked strippers all over the room. Joe only had eyes for Marlene.

When he saw Olivia edge through the door followed by Sean Kindred and a delicate old woman who must be Olivia's grandmother, he stood. The backup had arrived. He wasn't needed here anymore. There was no doubt in his mind that Marlene could win this game. She'd been gaining chips steadily. The best thing he could do for her was get out of the way. He'd leave, even if he didn't particularly want to go. Hopefully, he'd hear the call of the road before he hit the highway.

Joe had quit drinking after the second shot, but he felt maudlin. He was going to have to embark on his new life alone. He was grateful to his mother for waking him up to love. His heart hurt like hell at the moment, but it would be fine eventually. He knew he would recover. That was the thing about life, it kept moving. He had missed so much already. He'd better get moving. But where?

Another chunk of his grief cut loose and in its wake, he discovered something astonishing.

He wanted to talk to his father.

The game was on.

Marlene checked her cards. Junk. She remembered to tuck her hair behind her ears before she bet. She lost. She would have to work fast. She didn't have enough chips to sacrifice two hundred dollars right and left.

Marlene flopped a straight. Sweet Jesus. She shook

her hair back, trying not to be *too* obvious, and bet half her stack. She didn't want to make anyone suspicious.

Damn. Only one customer.

She raked in the ten thousand dollar pot. A great start, but she still had a long way to go.

More junk. She bet and tucked her hair behind her ears again.

The guys took her money.

With her tell well-set, she began to fold, fold, fold.

In another life, I could fall in love with you.

Guess she didn't have to wonder what Joe had meant anymore. It was a wonder she hadn't known at the time. Maybe on some level she had. Too late now.

Whatever Joe's words had meant to him, Marlene knew what they meant to her. She knew from the tips of her toes in their wannabe stripper shoes to the roots of her too big hair. She had fallen in love with him.

Fat lot of good that it would do her. She was doomed. They were doomed. Joe couldn't even discuss the topic of love without imagining them on another planet, and she had her own issues with commitment.

The sooner Joe left Norton, the better.

Marlene tossed her big hair over her shoulders, bet a solid hand, and collected the pot.

She could tell the old man was getting impatient with her. They'd already been sitting here for three hours, and she'd only tripled her money. Thirty thousand dollars. Marlene could do this all night if she had to, but the old man was beginning to yawn, and the guys at the table were starting to look protective.

Marlene wondered how long she had to win this game fair and square before the funny business began. Rocky looked like he might have a pocket full of aces in his Armani suit, and she didn't think he'd be slipping them to her.

Marlene checked her cards. Aces. This had to be the hand.

She bet five grand.

The tight-assed player to her left raised to ten. Too good to be true. By the time it got back to Marlene, four other players had called, including Big Daddy.

Marlene called. Another five thousand.

She returned Big Daddy's measuring gaze with a vapid stare that almost made her eyeballs cross, and twirled her hair around her finger. She shot a smoky smile at Rocky, who was hovering about three inches behind Big Daddy and had been steady in that zone for an hour now. Rocky gave her a glare.

The flop hit ace, queen of clubs, jack of hearts. That gave her three aces. Marlene was first to act, and she tucked her hair behind her ears as she bet ten thousand dollars.

Everyone folded but Big Daddy Capozzi.

The turn was a junk club, and she checked.

Big Daddy bet another ten thousand. Four to a flush and a straight draw. Marlene knew all along Big Daddy was holding kings, and now she *knew* he had the king of clubs. Damn. Almost any club, any king or any ten would wreck her.

No choice. She was committed. "Call."

"Let me see those aces, little girl." Big Daddy said.

Marlene laid her cards on the table.

It was all up to the river. The table was tight. The room still. Even Keith had escaped from Nikki and was watching the game now.

Marlene sent a prayer and a silent promise up to the heavens. *Red card. Red card. I will do anything for a red card. I will teach Keith to cook. I will clean the employee bathroom. I'll even go to my father's wedding. God, please, no clubs and no tens. Just give me a red card.*

Marlene closed her eyes.

She heard the dealer lay down the river card.

Keith's groan rose above the music.

Her eyes slammed open. It was black. Clubs. The jack of clubs.

Marlene's heart shuddered, beat, then began to pound.

She whooped, "Keith, you jackass, you almost gave me a heart attack!" Big Daddy had hit his flush, but Marlene had a full house. She'd won.

Marlene tossed her hair over her shoulders and shook like the girls on the stage.

She giggled. Whoa. Big Daddy was even better at cursing in Italian than Olivia's father.

A sweetly familiar voice cut through the room. "Benito Dante Pasquale Capozzi, you should be ashamed of yourself."

"Nonna Lucia!" Marlene jumped to her feet and ran to embrace Olivia's grandmother.

Nonna Lucia stood with Olivia, Sean Kindred, and a truly terrified-looking Anthony. Nonna held Marlene in her arms as she continued to stare down Big Daddy over Marlene's shoulder. "These are my children."

Marlene breathed happily. Even after traveling all day, Nonna smelled of lemons and the olive oil she used on her skin. She felt her world spin wildly and then center on its axis.

"Where's Joe?" Marlene asked.

"He said he had to go move his truck," Olivia replied.

"How long ago was that?" She hadn't noticed Joe leave or her friends' arrival. She had been too busy praying for an ace and her own salvation. Joe hadn't seen the end of the game?

"About half an hour. Nonna wouldn't let me interrupt the game. She wanted to see you beat Big Daddy. Apparently, he's had it coming for a while."

"Explain," Marlene demanded.

Olivia caught sight of Keith sitting at a table with Nikki. Her eyes narrowed to slits. Sean frowned and nudged Olivia with his shoulder. Reluctantly, she turned back to Marlene. "Nonna Lucia and Benito Dante, aka Big Daddy, were sweethearts, back in the old country. When Nonna moved here with her family, she met my grandpa and got married. By the time Big Daddy found her, it was too late. He never forgave her. It's kind of romantic, if you squint a little."

"Speaking of romance, is the wedding reception over yet? Did my cake make it through?" she asked.

"Cake was fine. It's still going on though. Jacques came in to dish, and Johnny's working the bar."

"Johnny? From across the street?"

"Yeah. He had two other bartenders at his place, and it was a slow night anyway. I think he and Joe are friends," Olivia said. "Anthony was a big help, and Danny stayed to close so we could pick up Nonna Lucia. Danny said thanks, by the way."

They turned to look at Olivia's grandmother.

"Lucia." Her name on Big Daddy's lips was an explanation, an apology, and a prayer. His eyes silently begged her forgiveness. Then Big Daddy dropped his head.

Nonna drifted toward him. "Ah, Benito," she whispered.

"No squinting about it," Sean said under his breath.

Marlene shot Olivia a look. "What's he doing here?"

"Actually, Sean's the one who put it all together," Olivia said. "He discovered Capozzi made the offer on Chameleon. In addition to carrying a torch for Nonna, Big Daddy always wanted the restaurant."

"He was willing to give it up pretty easily." She told them about Joe's offer and Big Daddy's agreement and condition.

"Joe was going to lay down a hundred grand to cover Keith's losses? Just like that?" Olivia said.

"Not quite," Marlene shifted in her high heels. "I think he really wanted Chameleon too. He said he didn't want to go to California anymore."

"No shit, Marlene. I've been trying to tell you that all week," Olivia said.

Marlene shook her head. "I told him I didn't want him to stay."

Olivia groaned. "Of course you did."

Marlene thought she had gotten past the resentment, but it ripped her in half to know that Olivia wanted Joe to stay at Chameleon. She shook her head, ashamed of herself. The restaurant was the important thing. "I'm sorry. Of course Joe should stay," she said thickly. "I wasn't thinking about Chameleon. You need a chef. Joe is perfect." Marlene swallowed hard. "It's just…" She shook her head. "Tell Nonna I'll see her soon. I'm going home."

Chameleon was safe. Keith was under control, probably for the rest of his life, from the proprietary look on Nikki's face, and Olivia and Sean were standing side by side. They looked good together. Anthony stood near them, dazed, but cheerful for the first time since Marlene had met him. Even Nonna Lucia glowed, luminous under Big Daddy's dark gaze.

Everything was good.

Hot tears burned Marlene's eyes, and she squeezed them shut, stunned by her overwhelming misery. She moved toward the door.

A soft hand gripped her arm, pulling her back. Olivia was behind her, shaking her gently by the shoulders. "Jesus, Olivia, let me go." She did not want to cry in public.

"You think I'm going to hire Joe?" her friend demanded.

"Well, yeah, like I said, he's perfect."

Olivia shook her head. "I'm not hiring anybody."

"Not this again. You have got to get some bodies in that kitchen! You can't run with a skeleton crew anymore. If you don't want to hire Joe, pick a name off of a résumé. Hire somebody!"

"I'm not hiring anyone," Olivia insisted. "You are."

Olivia's words didn't make sense. Too many hours staring at the cards. She had missed something important here.

"I want you to do the hiring. And the firing," Olivia announced.

"Olivia, use smaller words, please. My brain is fried."

"Wouldn't you be mad if I hired Joe?"

"Olivia, Chameleon needs a good chef. Joe is better than good. Hire him."

"What about you? If I hire Joe, will you stay at Chameleon?" Olivia asked.

Marlene didn't have to answer the question. The truth

was in her eyes, and she knew that Olivia could see it.
"It's for the best," she said. "I should have left when you
brought Keith home."

Olivia flinched. "I'm sorry, Marly. I was an idiot not
to realize you left the line because you didn't want to
work with Keith. I understand why you're so angry. Join
the club. Joe's pissed. Nonna's pissed." Olivia grimaced.
"She gave me an earful on the way from the airport, by
the way. I deserved it. And more. It would serve me
right if you turned me down, but it would also break my
heart. Marlene, please, I'm begging you. Don't leave
me. I can't do this without you. Please, please be my
chef—accept the job you have been training to do for
fifteen years. Chameleon needs you. I need you. Don't
quit on me now."

Tears clogged Marlene's throat and made it impossible to speak. Olivia didn't want Joe to be her chef. She
wanted Marlene.

Finally.

Olivia mistook Marlene's silence for refusal and
scrambled for words. "I don't blame you for wanting to
say no, Marly. I pushed you too far. I've had my head
up my ass—" She burst into tears.

"Yeah, well, I'm used to that."

Olivia sobbed harder.

"I'm not going to lie," Marlene cleared her throat.
"I've had my moments. I did call your grandmother."

"Yeah, but you also stuck by me. You fixed everything. You called Pymco and pushed our order through,
even with no credit. You organized the staff to pull off
a wedding in twenty-four hours. You made a beautiful
wedding cake. You fixed Joe's sauce and you figured

out who was sabotaging Chameleon." The list embarrassed and thrilled Marlene.

"Joe did that."

"Yeah, well, you won my restaurant in a poker game. Holy cow, does that mean it's yours now?"

"Nonna had it covered."

"Would you shut up? I'm trying to apologize."

She shut up.

Olivia's eyes still held tears. "Marlene, you are the heart and soul of Chameleon. I am so sorry I've been such an idiot. It was bad enough that I married Keith, but I never should have given him your job. I'll probably apologize every day for the rest of our lives for doing that. Will you ever forgive me?"

Marlene was crying now too, and didn't care who saw her. "I thought I'd never see the day when Olivia Marconi would realize that running a restaurant isn't a one-woman show. Does this mean I can actually call a couple numbers on those résumés you've been hoarding in the office?"

Olivia nodded.

"Then I want another garde-manger cook. And Anthony stays." Marlene held Anthony's eyes. He wouldn't let her down again. "We traded Keith for him."

Olivia glared at Keith, now dead center in the middle of the Capozzi clan with Nikki reading him his rights and Rocky supervising. He looked wretched. Olivia grinned.

"We also need a pastry chef. I can't do everything."

Olivia nodded again.

"And another grill cook."

A slower nod. "Anything else?"

"Nope, I'm all yours." Marlene held Olivia's eyes. "I

always was. I don't think I could have left Chameleon, even if I wanted to. It's home," she said simply.

A home she hadn't been willing to share, and because of that, Joe was gone.

"I do have one small favor to ask," Marlene said to Olivia.

"Name your price, chef."

She winced.

"Better get used to it," Olivia said with a giggle. "How much do you want?"

"No, it's not money. I, uh, just…well." The words broke free in an awesome rush. "I promised God I'd go to my father's wedding if He gave me a break on the last river card, so I need a day off."

Olivia burst out laughing. "You got it."

Marlene walked back to the poker table and picked up the deed to Chameleon. She put it in Olivia's hand.

"Try to keep an eye on that," Marlene admonished.

Olivia turned. "Nonna? Are you coming?"

Both girls stared, wide-eyed, as Nonna Lucia slowly shook her head. "You go. Benito will take care of me."

Marly grabbed Olivia's hand and pulled her away from the bizarre spectacle of Olivia's seventy-year-old grandmother sitting on the lap of Big Daddy Capozzi while a naked woman gyrated overhead. Nonna Lucia was old enough to play her own games.

Marlene was ready to cash it in for the night. She didn't want to push her luck.

Chapter 29

"PATHETIC," OLIVIA SAID.

"Oh, shut up." Marlene shot back. So what if the steaks falling away from her blade were a little over or a little under? They were close enough.

"Maybe if you hired a grill cook, you'd have time to use the scale."

"It's harder to find a good cook than I thought." In fact, it had been downright impossible. Four cooks had tried out on the line this week. Nobody had stuck.

Even Anthony was getting irritated. Next to Marlene, Joe's absence had hit him the hardest and not only because some of the extra work was falling into his station. Marlene hadn't realized how much Anthony had idolized Joe. Now she felt guilty for his sake too.

In fact, everybody seemed to miss Joe. Jacques was grumpy without his sweet-toothed ally. Even the freaking health inspector, as good as his word, had given her crap for losing such a clean cook when he stopped in for Sunday brunch.

Olivia cleared her throat. "Yes, it's tough to find someone willing to work with a chef who criticizes every move they make. Ease up, Marly. You aren't going to find anybody who can cook like Joe."

Marlene kept her eyes on the meat. She didn't want to see pity in Olivia's eyes. She carefully layered the steaks in a pan, being careful not to splash blood on her sundress.

Olivia sighed. "When are you leaving for the wedding?"

"Right now." Marlene untied her apron and carefully pulled it over her head. "Mom's picking me up. You're all set for service. Thanks for covering my shift."

Olivia nodded.

Marlene had been shocked when her mother offered to accompany her to her father's wedding. Her heart flew into her throat every time she thought about seeing her father again. She couldn't imagine how her mother felt.

Olivia touched her arm. "Joe didn't go to California, Marlene."

"He didn't?" Surprise stopped her in her tracks.

"He went to Kentucky. To see his dad."

"You're kidding me."

Olivia shook her head.

"Well…that's nice," Marlene finally managed. She washed her hands and escaped through the swinging door into the dining room.

Her mother was already waiting for her, looking beautiful and calm, not in the least bit rattled that she was about to attend the wedding of the first man to break her compound-fractured heart. Marlene ran her hands over her hair, trying to equal the casual perfection of her mother's elegant twist.

"You look beautiful, baby. Are you ready to go?" she asked, tucking Marlene's wayward curls into place with deft fingers.

"As ready as I'll ever be," she mumbled, not that she was looking to her mom for moral support. Marlene led the way out the front door of the restaurant where her mother had parked squarely in front of a fire hydrant.

Typical.

There was no ticket on her mother's windshield. Also typical.

She sank into the passenger seat.

Awkward silence settled between them as they pulled away from the curb. "So, how's life?" her mother asked. By life, she meant love life, of course.

"Fine," Marlene said.

"Anyone new?"

"No." Nobody new. Just somebody old Marlene couldn't forget. And she'd tried to forget Joe. With a vengeance. She had spent every night this week sitting at Johnny's bar, looking for someone new to take home with her.

Nobody caught her eye. Worse than that, every time she walked into the bar, she scanned the room for a certain set of broad shoulders, a perfect pair of cool, blue eyes. Every time the bar's door opened, she looked up to see if it was Joe. Olivia was right. She was pathetic.

"Want to talk about it?"

"Definitely not."

"It's been hard for me too, you know," her mother admitted.

Thank God she thought Marly was upset about the wedding. "Watching you grow up without your father, knowing that if I just could have been a bigger person back then, when he left, you could have him in your life right now. If I had been less selfish, maybe you wouldn't be so alone," she said, looking at the road. "I know all about your men, you know."

Okaaaaaaay.

Marlene eyed her mother. She was driving, negotiating

traffic easily, as if she wasn't wielding an AK-47 on her daughter in the passenger seat. "What men?" she asked cagily, inner teenager on full alert.

"Oh, please, I'm your mother. You haven't pulled a stunt in twenty-nine years that I haven't been aware of, including all the smoking." Marlene looked at her mother with dawning horror. "You've got a good head on your shoulders, baby. You're more sensible than I am most of the time. I realize that. That's why I don't like to interfere in your business."

"Thank you," she said. Inner teenager slammed the door. End of conversation.

Her mother laughed. "Not so fast, babe. I know I've been tied up in my own romantic trauma for most of your life. I was a mess. Every man who walked out that door was your father, over and over again. I got stuck in my own repeating pattern: falling in love with a man and then driving him away, all the while hating him for leaving me. I was attracted to worthless men because they reinforced my belief that I was worthless too." She paused.

Whoa, what self-help book had her mother been reading this month?

"I'm afraid some of my bad habits have rubbed off on you," she finished.

Ordinarily, Marlene would have laughed at her mother's psycho-babble, but, holy hell, she had a point.

Unworthy men. Huh. Marlene tried it on for size. It fit. Until Joe, that certainly described the men in Marlene's life. Temporary. Easily forgotten. Unimportant. Marlene had wanted it that way because marriage brings misery. Men leave. She'd said as much to her father the other night, only without the ache of self-awareness. She had circumvented that little problem by kicking her guys out the door before they decided to go. Low expectations were a sure cure for disappointment, right? Would any of those men have stayed with her? Danny would have, Marlene imagined. The thought made her heart hiccup. Danny wasn't the one for her.

"What about, uh, Richard?" Marlene remembered the name of her mother's new fiancé.

"Richard has been helping me understand myself. He's a wonderful man," she said, serenely, pulling into the church parking lot.

Now that Marlene was paying attention, she realized her mother had been different lately.

The other night, her mom hadn't had more than a glass of wine, and she had let Marlene do most of the talking while she was working on Marlene's hair. Not to mention, it had been almost a year since she had called Marlene in the middle of a meltdown. Maybe her mother was finally growing up.

The question was: where did that leave Marlene?

More to the point, where did she want to be?

Not here, she discovered. Not stuck in her own re-peating pattern. Not hating her father. Not alone.

"Mom?"

Her mother turned off the engine.

"What do you do when a man wants to stay?" she asked.

"What did I always tell you, baby? Life is like poker. You gotta play big to win big. You can play smart. You can play safe, but sooner or later, you have to pick a hand or you're gonna lose all your money anyway. Of course, the tricky part is picking the right hand."

A car pulled into the parking lot next to them. Richard waved to her mother.

"Richard is the right hand?"

Her mother took her hand and squeezed it. "For me, he is. That's why I wanted to introduce him to your father. Now, are you ready to do this, baby?"

"Yeah," Marlene said, as peaceful resolve temporarily gagged inner teenager. "I really am."

After the drama in the car, the actual wedding ceremony wasn't as painful as she had though it would be. She was honestly happy for her father. And her mother. The hard part was sitting still in the church pew while piercing realizations jabbed her heart. By the time the I do's were said, she felt like a pincushion.

Marlene caught her father's eye as he walked up the aisle, hand in hand with Margaret. She wanted him to know she was there because she was going to skip the receiving line. When he saw her, a broad smile creased his face. Margaret's damp eyes asked for understanding, which Marlene was happy to supply.

"Mom, can I borrow your car?" she asked. "I'll leave it in the Chameleon parking lot. Can Richard drive you back?"

"Sure, baby. You okay?"

Marlene nodded. "Never better. Gotta go see if I'm still in the game."

Her mom winked at her. "You've got a full house now, baby."

Chapter 30

JOE SAT ON THE BACK PORCH OF HIS FATHER'S CABIN AND stared into the trees. He had spent an entire week at the log house, the de facto haven of heartbreak for Rafferty men. It was a new record for time spent in his father's company since Joe had gotten his driver's license. A few minutes ago, he had broken his silence and told his father about what had happened at the casino.

"Sounds like you really screwed the pooch this time, boy. It's not easy to go back when you've made a mistake, is it?" he sympathized. "You really thought your money was all you needed to get Marlene to let you stick around?"

Joe didn't bother to nod. He'd already copped to the details. His dad was just rubbing it in now.

"Yeah, boy, it's always worse when they tell you to go, especially when you're afraid they mean it. When your mama kicked me out of the house, she told me if I ever came back, she'd shoot me."

That was new information. "Mom told you to go?" he asked.

"You bet your ass, she told me to go. Swore she meant it too. What with the screaming and the cursing, it took balls I didn't have to go back to the house. Had my tail so far between my legs, it was wrapped around my cock. Couldn't even look her in the eyes."

Joe could well imagine. Helen Rafferty in a rage had

been a truly terrifying vision. He kept his eyes on his dad, waiting for the end of the story.

"It was the most humbling moment of my life when your mama forgave me. I never strayed from her side again."

Just the once. A mistake then, not a curse.

"Go back to Marlene, son. Learn something from your old man. Apologize. Stick around until she knows you mean it."

"She doesn't want me to stay, Dad."

"Women are complicated. They say things they don't mean. They mean things they don't say. And sometimes they don't know what the heck they want in the first place until they try it on for a while. Your mama drove me flat-out crazy, but I didn't care. She was worth it. The good ones are worth it. You'll see."

Joe hung his head. "She heard me call her a piece of ass."

His dad chortled. "Well, then you better get your tail between your legs. Unless I miss my guess, she'll want you to come back, just so she can torture you some more. Just like your mama liked to torture me." He glanced at the table where his drink wasn't. "My girl is gone—yours is still waiting. Go get her, son."

"She's not waiting for me." Joe's voice was dead certain. "Marlene's either running Chameleon right now or she's quit and has moved on to another restaurant entirely."

"So go find her. No boy of mine wimps out and hides in the woods when he still has a chance. You've got too much of me in you to give up a good fight." Joe was shocked to hear pride in his father's voice.

His dad fished around in the front pocket of his bib

overalls. He pulled out something shiny and examined the small object. Then he flipped it through the air.

Joe caught it.

His mother's engagement ring.

Damn.

His dad had made a mistake, a huge one, but in the end, his father had made amends and Helen Rafferty, with her clear eyes and fresh lipstick, had loved him to the very end of her life. His father, for all his sins, had whispered a kiss into his wife's last breath. Joe would bet on it.

"Go get your girl, son. Your mama would approve."

Before Joe had a chance to respond, he heard gravel crunching under slow tires. A car was making its way over the ridge.

"Expecting company?" he asked his father.

"Nope."

Both men grinned when a car with a New York plate crested the ridge. "Told you she was a keeper."

Chapter 31

MARLENE PARKED IN FRONT OF THE WIDE BARN. No sign of life out front. She slid out of her car and eyed the cabin nervously. She didn't want to be met at the door with a double-barreled shotgun.

Squaring the time off from work had been easy. Of course, she had been screwing up orders right and left for the past week, so Olivia might have been glad to see her go. Marlene's indifference to the size of the steaks was becoming a problem. So was her inability to hire a grill cook. The hangovers weren't helping either.

From the minute she'd found out Joe had left town, Marlene had begun to unravel. She'd fallen out of sync, and she couldn't quite wrap her head around what was happening until her mother's pointed revelations before the wedding. The final shoe had dropped during the ceremony.

She had gone to her father's wedding because she'd caught a card on the river, but sitting in the church pew, she'd had a revelation. A terrifying, surprising, divine revelation.

She wasn't angry with her father anymore.

Holding a lifelong grudge against him had given Marlene the perfect excuse to never fall in love. Without her resentment, she couldn't remember what was so much fun about being alone. In the face of her mother's calm joy in Richard and her father's wedded bliss with

Margaret, she couldn't quite cleave to the belief that marriage caused misery anymore, damn it.

She was out of excuses.

Her parents had found love. Just not with each other. Maybe her father's departure had only been a tragedy for Marlene. Maybe it had been the right thing for her mother and father. Had she actually believed that the best cure for the last guy was the next guy? She recognized it now as the hardcore bad girl enabling behavior that it was.

Her mother had evolved. Joe, holdout playboy and career lady-killer, had changed his tune. Unless Marlene wanted to be left behind, she needed to grow up too. It was time to let go of her bad girl persona and learn to love someone.

Like Joe.

Of course, there was every chance he was perfectly happy to leave her far behind him. He and his dad might be holed up down here throwing parties every night. Even as her brain spun out that thought, she knew it was another excuse. Joe had gone to his father. His *father*.

Marlene stepped away from the car. She hoped Joe and Frank had forged some peace. She also hoped Joe was waiting for her to catch up with him, and that he'd meant it when he said, "I'd never let a woman think I was going to stay unless it was true." Marlene had played that memory over and over in her head on the long drive to Kentucky. Joseph Rafferty had said he wanted to stay. The thought had kept her from turning the car back around and heading north. It had to mean something. Pulling into the gravel driveway of the log cabin was the first thing that had felt right to her since she'd caught that card on the river. That had to mean something too.

GPS had gotten her to Kentucky, and now that she was standing on the front porch, she hoped love could take her the rest of the way home.

She peered into the kitchen through the top half of the open Dutch door and saw Joe, coming through the great room door. Were his eyes hot or cold? Blue or gray? The kitchen was dim and Marlene was afraid to look too closely. She was afraid she'd jump into his arms and take him straight down to the floor, and she had some things she wanted to say to him first. She hoped he would want to hear them. She opened her mouth to begin the speech she had prepared on the drive, but Joe held up his hand and said, "Shhh."

Confused, she stepped back as he opened the lower door and stepped onto the front porch beside her. He took her hand and led her into the barn and up the stairs into the hayloft.

"I was just about to head back to Norton," he said casually, pulling her down next to him on a bale of hay.

"You were?" she asked.

"Yup."

She risked a sideways glance at him.

"It was time to do that apology thing again. Dad and I were discussing strategy."

"Really?" She was amazed that he had covered that much ground with his father in a week.

"Dad is all for groveling and abasement. That's what worked with my mother." She raised her eyebrows. Whoa. Male bonding to the maximum. "And I figured the last time I apologized to you, you took it pretty easy on me. And then I got laid. That's why I brought you up to the hayloft. Since you drove all the way to Kentucky, I'm feeling optimistic about my chances this time too."

"Wait just a minute, cheffie boy—"

"Oh, say it again," he whispered, leaning closer to her mouth.

Marlene braced both hands on his shoulders and held him off. "You are not apologizing first."

"Talk fast."

Marlene took a breath. Of sweet hay and warm Joe. She lost her train of thought.

"Too slow."

Joe's lips told her everything she wanted to know. It was so obvious to her now. She didn't know how she had missed it. Joe gave her everything, held nothing back. He put it all in his kiss. Marlene felt humbled. But not that humbled. "I changed my mind," she mumbled against his lips.

"What?" he asked, not pulling away but definitely startled. Marlene enjoyed his discomfiture.

"You can apologize first," she said.

Joe clutched her so tightly to his chest that all she could breathe was him. He pinned her in the hay, but there was no need. She wasn't going anywhere.

Joe looked deeply into her eyes. "I'm sorry I pulled a power play at the casino. I wanted to stay with you so much, I think I would have tried anything. But I'm even more sorry that I left when you told me to go. I thought you meant it."

"And now?"

"Now? I don't care." She jerked underneath him, horrified, and Joe laughed. "Not that way, sugar. I don't care if you mean it or not. I'm not leaving. I'm going to stick around as long as it takes to convince you that you love me too."

Marlene gazed into Joe's clear, blue eyes and discovered they weren't hot or cold. They were warm. With love. For her.

The way her heart swelled with joy was even more satisfying than the way Joe's body swelled against hers as he pressed her into the hay. She now had a new basis for comparison. Love was more satisfying than sex? Who knew? That opened up a world of possibilities.

Marlene reached up to pull Joe back down to her mouth. It was still there, the heat, the crazy communion, but it wasn't enough. She wanted more. She wanted to be sure Joe was really going to stay.

"Hey, uh, there's been some reorganization going on at Chameleon," she said. "There's a new…chef…in charge of the kitchen."

"Oh, yeah? Who?"

"Me," she said, supremely satisfied by Joe's lack of surprise.

"About time." He bent his head.

Marlene wasn't getting anything accomplished on the bottom, so she wrapped her arms around Joe, threw one leg over his hip, and flipped him. He looked up at her, one eyebrow flying, wicked grin in place.

"You looking to take care of my meat again, sugar?" he asked, crossing his arms behind his head and getting comfortable underneath her in the hay. "I'm all yours."

"Not exactly. I'm looking for a decent grill cook. Or a sauté cowboy. Interested?"

"You've got a job for me?" He was all business as he rolled to his knees.

Marlene was well aware that Joe was too good a cook to work the grill forever. He'd want something more. Maybe he wanted to start his own business. Hell, maybe he wanted to go to California after all. Whatever was on his mind, he looked awfully serious.

"I have a job offer for you too." He reached into his jeans pocket. Held out something shiny. Very shiny. "Wife."

Marlene had never seen this particular smile on Joe's face. It was a variation of his wicked grin, but it was tender too. And fearless. He looked like a man who was ready to make a commitment. *Or be committed*, inner teenager muttered. Marlene banished her to her room. Forever.

"Marlene, will you marry me?" Joe asked.

"Are you kidding?"

"Hell no. Let's do this right. Two objects in motion, colliding. We can work together, live together. Love together." His eyes were solemn. "What do you say, cheffie girl? You in or out?"

Marlene looked at the sparkling diamond ring clasped in Joe's fingers. The setting was smooth and flat. It wouldn't catch on anything in the kitchen, she thought randomly. She held up her left hand, and he slid the diamond onto her finger.

"This was my mother's ring. If you don't like it, I'll get you anything you want."

"Mine." She closed her fist.

"Mine," Joe echoed, pressing her down into the hay.

Distantly, Marlene heard the front door of the log cabin shut with a resounding bang. She was glad Frank approved.

Marlene smiled into the eyes of the next guy, her

last guy. When the right man wanted to stay, you didn't send him packing. *You let him stay.* Joe might have been ahead of her with this commitment stuff, but she was definitely catching up with him. She was right there with him now, that was for sure, kicking off her shoes, shucking her jeans.

Marlene pulled him back down into the hay and kissed him. Boy, was she ever with him on that.

Acknowledgments

I will always be grateful to chefs Corey Griffith and Alisa Huntsman of Nashville, Tennessee, for instilling in me a lifelong passion for food and inspiring me to go to culinary school. Without them, I might never have met my husband in class at the Culinary Institute of America. I also owe a debt of gratitude to the other chefs I've worked with over the years who continued my education. Y'all know who you are, and I thank you.

More heartfelt thanks to the members of the Western New York Romance Writers for their support, knowledge, encouragement, and enthusiasm—and for helping me brainstorm a reason a man might possibly say no!

Hugs to my parents and in-laws for their unwavering support. Kisses to my kiddies for bringing me flowers, drawings, and sculptures to perk up the long hours spent at my desk—and for being proud of me. Big love to Erin Kelly-Park, lifelong wingwoman, first reader, and go-to girl for nearly everything. Smooches to my foodie friend Melissa Cook for all the shared lunches and family happy hours. Love pats to my critique partners Natasha Moore and Alison Stone for being generous with their time and brilliant advice. A huge squeeze to my agent, Nalini Akolekar of Spencerhill Associates, for saying yes.

Every writer hopes for the Call. Thank you to the staff at Sourcebooks, particularly my editor, Leah Hultenschmidt, for loving my book as much as I do.

About the Author

Amanda Usen knows two things for certain: chocolate cheesecake is good for breakfast and a hot chef can steal your heart. Her husband stole hers the first day of class at the Culinary Institute of America, so she married him after graduation in a lovely French Quarter restaurant in New Orleans. They spent a few years enjoying the food and the fun in the Big Easy before they returned to Western New York to raise a family. Amanda spends her days teaching pastry arts classes and her nights writing romance. If she isn't baking or writing, she can usually be found chasing the kids around the yard with her very own scrumptious husband. Visit her at amandausen.wordpress.com if you'd like to chat about romance, writing, or recipes.